TEETH

WHERE THEY SHOULDN'T BE

A SHORT STORY COLLECTION BY

CHAD STROUP

TEETH WHERE THEY SHOULDN'T BE
FIRST EDITION JULY 2023
ODDNESS

To request permission, contact the publisher at:
info@forbiddenfuturesmagazine.com

Softback isbn: 978-1-960213-16-7
Hardback isbn: 978-1-960213-17-4
Electronic isbn: 978-1-960213-18-1

Edited by Oddness
Cover art by Mike Dubisch
Layout by Oddness
Illustrations by Mike Dubisch

Ordering information:
info@forbiddenfuturesmagazine.com

www.forbiddenfutures.com

TEETH

WHERE THEY SHOULDN'T BE

A SHORT STORY COLLECTION BY

CHAD STROUP

ALL ARTWORK BY
MIKE DUBISCH

CONTENTS

FOREWORD

Chad Stroup is a weird guy, and I mean that in the best way possible.

I first met Chad through my local HWA chapter. His debut novel was about to come out, *Secrets of the Weird,* and he invited me out to a reading he was doing at a local coffee shop. There was a Misfits cover band playing, so I knew it wasn't going to be your typical reading, but I had no idea how crazy things were about to get. See, one of the chapters in *Secrets* is written from the perspective of a drag queen, Ms. Jessica, and Chad—who, for point of reference, is a tall, beefy punk rocker with slicked-back hair and several tattoos—read the entire thing in the most flamboyant fashion you can imagine. It was incredible (and little did I know, but Chad would eventually create his own drag persona—Jenn X).

Obviously I bought the book.

That was my first introduction to Chad's work. Blazed through the novel, which was quite the singular experience—the book is peppered with ads and comics, including a parody Chick tract, and features a cast of incredibly bizarre and memorable characters. The novel is unorthodox in every way, in form, plot, everything, and yet it works, unbelievably well.

Over the years, I've been lucky enough to share a table of contents with Chad a few times, and some of those stories can be found in this volume: "The Perfect Playground," which first appeared in *California Screamin'*, and "The Fabulous and Tormented Life of a Serial Extra" from *Lost Films*. I've become pretty familiar with his work, and I can tell you there's a few things that make a Chad Stroup story what it is.

Chad describes his work as "for left-of-center thinkers," and that's unquestionably true. His characters are true outsiders—the husband in "Sex With Dolphins" even thinks JAWS 3D is scarier than the original! These people don't march to the beat of their own drummer, they're dancing jigs to an electric accordion. On their hands. One of the things I crave the most with fiction in general and horror in particular is to see the world through new eyes. To view perspectives so different from my own they feel alien, dream-like, like Victor Keirion's desires in Thomas Ligotti's "Vastarien." That sort of thing is what's on offer here. You'll find post-apocalyptic serial killers, self-mutilating trophy wives, demented taxidermists, dementia sufferers, neurodivergent party hosts, repentant monsters, troublemaking teens, tweakers, punk rockers, and more.

Every last one coping with their own forms of *red thoughts*.

There are few things less punk than arguing what *is* punk, but the people you're about to meet? Each in their own way embodies the punk ethos, if not aesthetic. There's a moment in punk horror classic *Return of the Living Dead* where the character Suicide says, "You think this is a fuckin' costume? This is a way of life." A Chad Stroup character embodies this sentiment. These are people who are at odds with society, at their core. You can't pull out their nose piercings, wash the Manic Panic out of their hair, trade their Docs for wingtips, and set them loose in an office. Their fashion sense doesn't make them who they are. Their damage, their skewed perspectives, their unwillingness to submit to the ordinary, the banal, to live inauthentic lives, whatever that might mean?

That sure as fuck does.

The other thing that strikes me about Chad's work is the body horror (his second novel is called *Sexy Leper,* for Pete's sake), and there's plenty of that here. I'm not the first person to compare his stuff to Clive Barker, but when you meet the Forever People, or the socialite Madeleine, or dozens of other characters, you'll be shocked and awed by all the fucked up things that can happen to bodies. Willingly or not. And like the great Barker's *Cabal,* a formative influence of Chad's, the worst monsters are not those with a monstrous aspect, like the denizens of Midian, but those with normal appearances and monstrous natures, like the manipulative, serial-killing psychiatrist Dr. Decker.

But also, the thing is? Chad is *funny.* There are quite a few moments in this collection where I laughed out loud, in addition to squirming in my seat, checking my pulse, and doing a few breathing exercises before turning the page. I won't spoil any of these moments here, but reading the stories—which are not horror comedy, but have a little pinch of bizarro and are told with a certain zest—well, sometimes you'll come across a line that'll make you snort. Horror and humor are kissing cousins, the structure of a joke is similar to the structure of a horror story, and they sure go together like peanut butter and chocolate. Chad knows just how to combine them for maximum effect. You get real tense, and then this killer line presses your release valve, and then bam—you're ready for the horror once again.

That said, I'll make way for the main event. But one last word of advice: have a care when you read the fifteen stories in this volume, and remember, you don't have to worry about the guy whose brains are showing, or the woman with the sewn-up mouth, or the mutant dolphin who's checking you out from the other side of the cove.

It's the normal ones who are trouble.

–Brian Asman, author of *Man, Fuck This House*

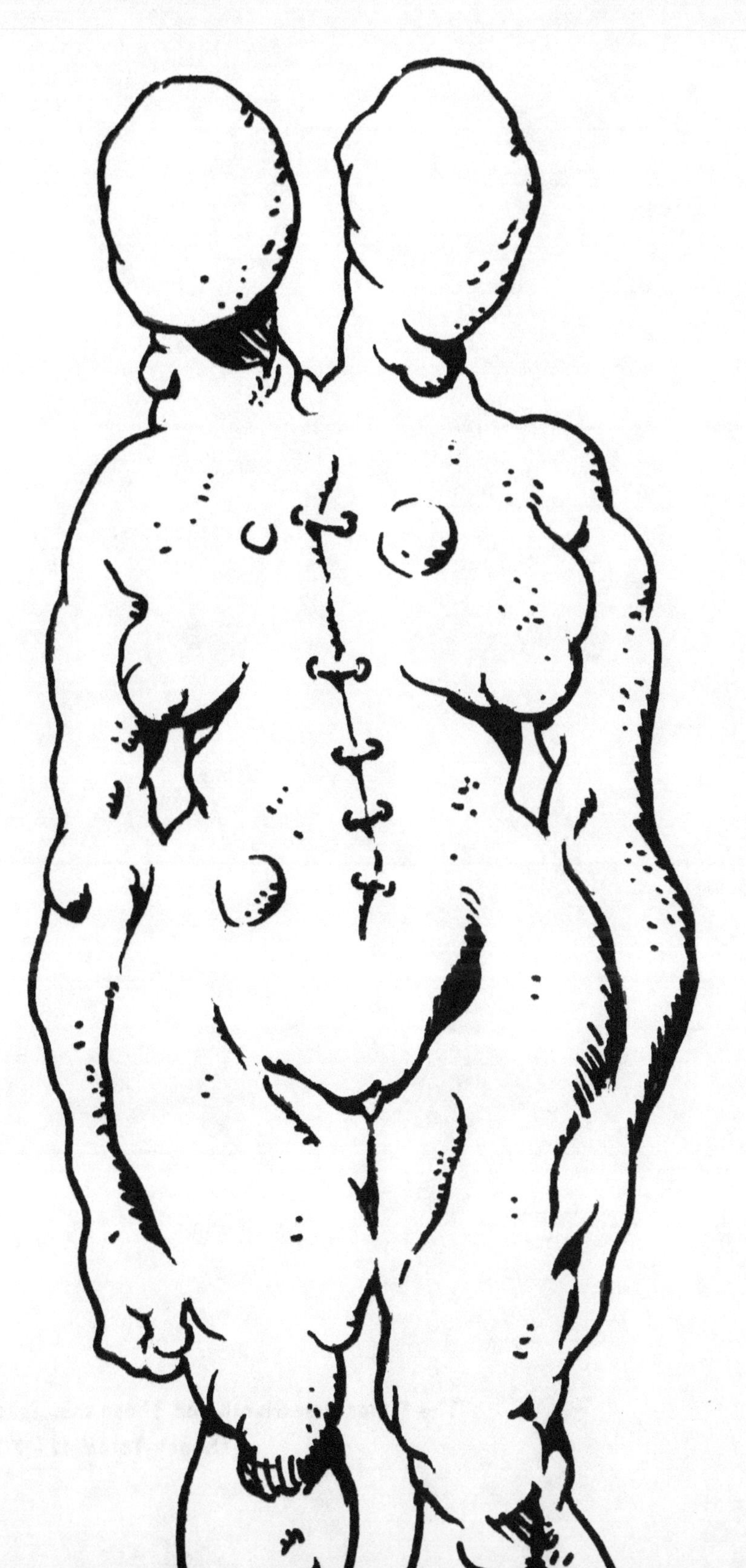

"The Fluids that Giveth and Those that Taketh"

(Shock Totem 11 - 2019)

the fluids that giveth and those that taketh

The Leather Man crossed the city limits into the sixth settlement. He'd been dragging his feet for days, been parched for hours. No dead vehicles along the highway worth resurrecting, every abandoned tavern he'd encountered just a succession of dry, empty taps. The unforgiving desert had claimed anything worth fighting for.

Still, there'd been a few souls to meet along the way. None of them kind. Bribery, blowjobs, whatever it took for him to secure a solid lead on the location he was searching for. And some leads had been lies.

A handmade street sign hid within the brush. The Leather Man removed his dirt-caked goggles, rubbed his eyelids. He wiped the sign, scraped off dust thick enough to fry and serve. Scrawled in charcoal were the only words he needed to see:

WELCOME TO SIXTHTOWN: POPULATION 67

He'd finally arrived. And he had a duty to fulfill.

Too late in the day to make a move. The Leather Man crept the outskirts of town, chanced on a cave. Big enough to squeeze into, but small enough he had to crawl. Once he found the most comfortable rock to rest his head on, the world ceased to exist.

He slept two days straight in the near-tangible darkness. Maybe three. Time didn't matter here. Not where the forever folk lived.

His mind now awake, he willed his body to join it, but it wasn't ready. He wished he could just lay here and sleep forever, let the darkness consume him. A nice alternative. The world might find a way to right itself without him.

Fools might sooner become wise.

Something crawled across his face, snapping him to life. His reflexes took over, and he trapped it in a fist. The thing squirmed and tried to slip through his fingers. Multiple legs tickled his palm. A sand cockroach. The Leather Man tossed the bug in his mouth and crunched down until it exploded. The pungent innards slid down his throat, shaking loose a memory from the old world. Way down in Rosarito. His body soaked in saltwater. Riding the waves on a catamaran. Trying raw oysters for the first time with his…

Wife. Yes. He'd had one. Once. She had a name. Once. But The Leather Man couldn't recall it. And her face, just a blank ball of clay he couldn't mold.

He stretched, popped his knuckles. Rest had done him well. Now he could get to work. He followed the faint beams seeping through the cave's cracks until the light grew and he found his way outside. He hung close to the outskirts of town again. So quiet, such a sense of slumber hovering in the air. The forever folk didn't need to sleep. Old habits.

Or perhaps they'd moved on to a new location. Always migrating, never stagnant long enough to put down roots. The Leather Man wasn't sure he'd be able to cope if that happened again. He'd been tracking them since Thirdtown. If they'd vanished this time, he'd just cut his losses, find the least damaged home in this hellhole and see what age the gods allowed him to reach before his body failed him.

The sun raked his skin. Sweat stung his eyes. He snapped his goggles back on, then ran his fingers through his long hair, pushing it forward into a curtain of bangs, dulling the blinding light.

A house in the distance. Slight movement in the front yard, if a hill of dirt could be referred to as such. Too much sand whirling in the air. Difficult to tell. Could have been a trick of the light, or it could have been the first signs of what he sought. He steeled himself, then approached.

As he neared the house the sandstorm died down. A little girl danced barefoot, holding hands with a tattered dolly. All by herself, kicking up dust. And the house wasn't a house at all. The roof had been ripped away and taken to heaven, and with it the top half of a gold-coated Christ, complete with cross. Only the stained glass windows in the front remained, and even those were riddled with cracks and grime.

The Leather Man moved closer, eyeing the perimeter for fear of a trap. The little girl caught wind of him. She turned and stopped dancing. The Leather Man stopped as well. The girl waved, and he took a few more steps, paused again when he was two arm's length away from her. Most of her hair had fallen out, save for a few greasy blonde strands plastered to her scalp. Dark red welts decorated the bald patches, the leopard-like pattern continuing down her arms and legs.

His tongue was freshly picked cotton. As if the girl could read The Leather Man's mind, she passed him a jar of water. He unscrewed the top and gulped the drink down in one shot. Warm but wet. The first liquid he'd had in forever that lacked grit. He wiped his mouth with his sleeve and nodded.

The girl took the jar back, screwed the top down tight, and set it on the ground. She smiled at him, only three brown teeth to share. He tried to guess how old she'd been when she'd received the initial transfusion, and how long it would take her to reach his age. If she ever would. Enough of the fluid in her system and she'd never be cursed with maturity.

She gazed up at him, cloudy eyes the size of fried eggs. She tugged at the hem of her flowery dress. In another life it might have been white. "What's wrong with your face?" she asked, no sign of fear tainting her voice.

The Leather Man didn't answer her. His eyes fell to the dolly. Its head had been removed and crudely stitched back on. Clownish paint tarted up its face.

"Mister, are you okay?"

He turned his gaze back to the girl. Some long-forgotten instinct forced his hand toward her head to tousle her hair, but he quelled the urge before it bested him. She looked a little like a daughter he might have once had. A precious beauty. A name that had left his memories long ago.

The girl took no offense to being ignored, went back to playing with her dolly. The Leather Man kneeled next to her, told her everything would be just fine. After all this time, he almost believed his own words.

The water had already run through his system. He swallowed dry. He knew what he had to do, and it sickened him deeply. Nothing destroyed him as much as the young ones.

The church turned out to be empty. The Leather Man discovered a few decrepit houses lining the street. Same story there. The true heart of Sixthtown was set further down in the valley, buzzing with the sounds of treacherous life. And now night had fallen. In the center of the valley a tall blue fire burned, highlighting a few rows of makeshift shacks and the silhouettes of movement. The Leather Man began his slow descent down the hill, toward the town.

Within thirty feet of the fire, the forms of faces became visible. Two, three dozen, maybe more deeper among the trees. He paused, called out early to make his presence known. Better they hear him before seeing him. When someone saw him first it rarely ended well.

He hadn't heard himself speak in weeks, and he didn't recognize his own voice.

"If you're a friend, you're welcome to join us," one of the forever folk called back. "If you mean us harm, there's a clear path up the hill toward the west. I suggest you take it. A day's walk and you'll reach the coast."

The Leather Man stepped into the light of the flames. He received no reaction beyond curious stares. Among this group, he could be considered an Adonis. The man who'd spoken beckoned with a nod of his head, for he had no arms with which to welcome. Only stitched-up stubs. He scooted over to make room for another seat on the sand. The Leather Man obliged.

"You must surely be hungry," the armless man said. "We have roast."

Despite the charred carcass smelling like kelp left to rot, The Leather Man's stomach grumbled. Whatever endangered creature they'd impaled on the end of several sticks would have to be better than what he'd been subsisting on for most of his journey.

A woman with a patch covering one eye passed The Leather Man a plate with a single crusted sliver of meat. He nodded his thanks and bit into the offering. Gristly, gamy, but edible.

In the old days The Leather Man might have believed he'd stumbled upon a lost leper colony. Nearly everyone circled around the fire displayed some blasphemous grotesquerie. A young man with a hole blown through his chest, allowing a perfect view of the trees behind. A woman with shattered bones protruding through her skin like miniature branches. An older man with a third of his skull removed, his grey matter exposed to the elements. Most of their wounds had been self-inflicted or assisted, if the details provided to him on the road were to be believed.

"You know who we are," the armless man said. A statement, not a question. The Leather Man nodded. "What are you called?"

The Leather Man mumbled his answer.

The armless man eyed The Leather Man up and down. "Not a man of many words, are you?"

The Leather Man took another bite of his meat. On the other side of the bonfire, the man with the missing skull approached a woman who, unlike the others, appeared unscathed. Somewhere beneath the collected dirt caking her face hid something alluring. The man affixed a plastic tube to the back of the woman's neck, snapped it into something The Leather Man couldn't see. But he knew what it was. Emerald green fluid traveled through the tube. The woman shut her eyes. Within a few seconds it was absorbed into her body.

The armless man turned to The Leather Man. "You're welcome to stay with us until we move on. We do not require you to be…like us. Unless you plan a permanent stay." The eye-patched woman fed the armless man a sliver of meat.

The Leather Man muttered a thank you, finished his meal.

Rustling in the brush, panicked movements. A woman hobbled down the hill, supporting her missing foot with a shoddy cane. "Has anyone seen my baby? She left this morning to play and never returned." She only seemed half-worried.

"Told you to keep an eye on that one," the armless man said. "She doesn't yet understand what she is."

"She'll come back," the man with the missing skull said, tossing his plate into the fire. "They always do."

That night The Leather Man slept beneath a Sweet Acacia. He dreamed of the past, as he did every night, unpleasant memories invading his space.

Through the foggy scene he recognized a few clear signs of the old days. Back when he went under a different name. The name his mother and father had given him, not the name he came to be known by. The name the rest of the world had christened him with.

Locked away in the basement. Wanting to be alone. Folk guitar traveling from vinyl to needle, the scuffs and scratches audible through the cheap speakers. Rows of newspaper clippings wheat-pasted to the wall. Screaming headlines. Sex and violence. Lock your doors. Hide your children. Hide *everyone*. Skin severed and sewn. A human quilt. No one safe, least of all himself. Fingers pointed, shots fired.

A dream. Only a dream.

The Leather Man waited two weeks before claiming his next quarry. Blending in, building trust, keeping to himself until almost becoming invisible. For so long these people had allowed themselves to become comfortable, thinking nothing could get in the way of forever. After staying with a much smaller group out east and ending them all before they'd had a chance to blink, he'd broken a bottle and carved a tally into his bicep. He looked forward to adding to that tally, letting it run down his forearm. His plan had worked the last time, and it would work again here in Sixthtown.

Word traveled slowly now, if at all. And this group had never met his kind before. A bringer of death to those who believed they could never meet such a fate.

He chose a man. He loathed doing the males. Not as much as children. Not as much as the little girl with the dolly. She'd somehow been the worst. He'd suffered nightmare clips in his sleep since his first day in Sixthtown and feared they'd never let him rest.

Penetration was the only way to bring the end. And they all had to go.

The Leather Man knocked at the man's door just after twilight, while the rest of the town still hid within their homes, preparing for the night's fire. His eyes went right to the man's neck, the healed indentations of a tightened rope acting as flesh-bound ornamentation. The man caught him staring but only smiled. He moved to the side and allowed The Leather Man to enter. Everyone so trusting and hospitable in Sixthtown. Fools, all of them. Immortality removed cynicism from the equation, even when a monstrous spectacle came to town, his dangerous hands stuffed firmly in pockets.

"A drink?" the man asked, his voice a shredded rasp. The Leather Man nodded. When his host turned around and moved toward the kitchen, The Leather Man did not hesitate. He lunged. One hand almost eclipsing the man's throat, the other wielding a syringe. He plunged the needle into the man's upper spine, perfectly between the atlas and the axis, puncturing the dura mater. The man moaned briefly, then fell silent. His limp body collapsed.

So much easier this way. They felt no violation. They only slept forever. A blessing. He only wished a syringe were capable of transferring the most vital fluids and bringing the end. All past attempts had proven unfruitful.

The Leather Man trudged to the door, locked it, checked it again. He removed his boots, unbuckled his belt. He hesitated, then did the same to the man sprawled on the floor.

He closed his eyes, crouched down. The man's potent musk smacked him. He could taste it. His weight atop the still man, The Leather Man let his mind wander.

The climax was mercifully short.

Daylight almost gone, and soon others would be stirring. He covered the body with a ratty blanket. It would have to be dealt with later.

He was not the first to arrive at the bonfire, nor was he the last. More had decided to come tonight than any other night since The Leather Man had joined their group, perhaps close to the entire population of the town. The undamaged woman he'd seen the night he arrived approached him and sat in the empty space next to him. He almost spoke to her, uttered his first words in days. He wanted to ask her name, but the denizens of Sixthtown no longer had names, their scars their only identity. The flames flickered near the woman's face, highlighted her black ropes of hair, burned her eyes blue, and The Leather Man reached for feelings he'd long forgotten. Lust. Adoration. Some vague combination of the two. He wasn't convinced such desires existed in this world anymore. And if they did, the rules had changed.

But the woman had other ideas. She slinked her fingers across his knee, dug into it with her jagged nails. Claimed him without so much as a word. He allowed it.

The man with the missing skull moved around the bonfire, feeding tubes of fluid to those who begged him for it. Nearly all of them had their fill. Then the man with the missing skull switched places with someone who'd been burned so badly The Leather Man could not determine the gender. The burn victim inserted the tube into the back of the man with the missing skull's neck, doing for him as he had done for his neighbors.

After the fire died and the crowd dispersed, The Leather Man followed the woman uphill to her home, an unspoken request. She allowed him to enter the shack first, then shut the door behind them.

"You're staying here with me tonight." A smoker's croak. The Leather Man recognized his kind.

The woman lit a candle. Flames were the only light allowed at night. She pulled her hair back into a temporary ponytail, revealing her neckpiece. Though it was far from the first time The Leather Man had seen one, the spectacle never ceased to startle him. A hole dug deep into the flesh just above the spine, surgical staples attaching a narrow funnel to the hole, the surrounding layers of skin peeled back then stretched outward to blend metal with man. An abomination to be admired.

As if she'd been commanded, the unscathed woman removed her rags. The Leather Man's gut tightened, but he did not move. He'd been wrong about her. She'd lived just as damaged a life as the rest before accepting their juice. Worse than some.

A double mastectomy. A relief map of growths traveled across her chest, trailing down the front of her torso and stopping just before her groin. Cancers frozen in time, festering killers rendered useless by magic. Or by science. The truth depended on who you asked, who it benefited most.

"Come to me," she said. He did. She held the candle up to his face, observing him in awe. With her free hand she brushed her fingers across his cheek. She recoiled, then went back again for another touch. "I've never seen a soul so scarred and ugly."

The Leather Man grunted.

The woman leaned up and kissed him. His raw razor lips chafed against hers. Their combined fetid breath merged, became corporeal.

"Share my bed with me," she said, leaning back onto the mattress, her legs slightly spread. "I haven't been loved in so, so long."

The Leather Man took two steps back. Deep down he wanted to take her, do what he'd done with the wife he struggled to remember. To prove once again the cheaters of death could also be cheated. But he couldn't chance it. Couldn't erase two souls from existence in the same night.

The Leather Man held his finger up. He lay down next to her, still clothed, opened his monstrous arms, and enveloped her in them. At first she resisted, but then she relented.

They both remained warm through the night.

After the third disappearance—the mother of the little girl, the forever folk could no longer mask their misgivings. Despite dwelling in Sixthtown for just shy of two months, The Leather Man was still an outsider. Suspicion flickered in their eyes. The doubt. The fear. The planning. He needed to leave soon. With proof of his accomplishments. Trudge back cross-country, then return with numbers. Let the others of his breed do what he was no longer sure he could manage.

Six months of walking each way. Unless reliable transportation could be located, which was unlikely. The forever folk would surely have moved on by then. But The Leather's Man's people would sniff them out eventually. And he couldn't do this alone.

He'd been staying with the cancerous woman since the night she'd first brought him home. He could only hold out so long. She'd be his next. And his last. For now. Forever, he hoped.

Tonight her advances would be rewarded in a way she'd never be able to appreciate. Willing yet unwitting. His first victim ended while conscious. A landmark decision. Something for the history books. An experience he would quietly enjoy as he slipped out of Sixthtown and began his long trek home.

He woke her in the middle of the night, his sun-ravaged body naked and exposed. Her eyes widened, curious bloodshot orbs. She scanned the tattoos on his chest and biceps, all faded like chalk drawings on the sidewalk after a light rain.

The woman scraped her nails across his chest. "Yes. You are so very ugly." She stroked The Leather Man's body, a lioness petting its post-mortem prey. "How did you ever come to be this way?"

The Leather Man asked her the same.

She laughed. "Don't be so callow."

They caressed, their sweat and filth mingled. She squeezed his cock with her callused hand, and he winced.

"Take me."

He pinned her, entered her. And wept while doing so.

The love lasted much longer than he'd anticipated.

While The Leather Man slept, the past came surging back. A dream, a memory, an amalgam—it didn't matter. It was his only current truth.

There'd been a time when he'd been handsome. Not the type of dashing good looks that made him the constant object of desire, but rather the sort a mate's mother would approve of. On some level it had won him his wife. And for a while they'd been happy. Normal. He couldn't recall when that had changed. Why he had changed. Couldn't pinpoint what had broken inside him.

And no matter how hard he tried, he still could not remember the wife's name.

But her face came rushing back. A work of art he'd redesigned with his brutality. Bruised cheeks, swollen eyes, a Chelsea smile carved by his own immense hands. Her body a limp, gutted fish.

She'd found what he'd been hiding in the basement. All of it.

And his daughter, cowering in the corner, covering her face. The next one in his disassembly line. He tried to black out the horrors, but his dream eyes remained open, showed him everything.

He couldn't remember the what, the why. The trigger. Something had fallen apart inside him, no thread linking A to B. One day a devoted husband, a proud father. The next day a ruthless killer. Of men, of women, of children. Of everyone. A slave to indiscriminate rage.

For years all he saw was three sides brick, the fourth side bars of solid steel.

And one day, when the rest of the world ended, he rejoiced.

Someone knocked at the door the next morning. The forever folk. One of them, all of them. An everlasting wall of moribund meat.

The room still smelled of ammonia and the sea. The Leather Man's throat burned with bile. He cradled the woman's limp body, his pants still wadded in a pile on the floor, his weapon still wielded yet flaccid. Nowhere to run. No windows. No alternate exit. Remorse had finally caught up with him. He had to face the people, own up to the truth. And he was so tired.

Still naked, he opened the door. The man with the missing skull shoved past him and kneeled by the woman's body.

"How is this possible?" he asked no one in particular. His eyes looked like they wanted to form tears, but none came.

The armless man entered the room. The others remained outside.

"You did this," the armless man said, looking down at The Leather Man's crotch.

The Leather Man nodded. "I'm the cure."

"We cannot allow you to leave." The armless man nodded to the man with the missing skull. "Take care of this."

The man with the missing skull snapped his fingers, and two more men entered. One whose arms were peppered with track marks, the other so obese that gravity threatened to tear his flesh from his bones. The Leather Man did not resist.

"You have two choices," the man with the missing skull said. "Death or perpetuity. Do you understand?"

The Leather Man answered with a shit-eating grin, motioned to the bottle of fluid one of the mob carried. He'd take his penance, join them in their endlessness. An eternity to consider what he'd become, the impulses he'd acted upon. A fair punishment. No easy ways out like in the old days. No slit wrists. No bottle full of pills. No sheets tied tight and hung from the ceiling. No leaping from tall buildings. Like the rest of them, he'd rot from the inside and continue to thrive on the outside.

He'd suckle their sweet punch and love it for all time.

sex
with
dolphins

Not many marriages dissolve after three days.

The newly christened Kristy Gonzales, however, knows that exceptions are often prone to shoving majorities out of the way. Intoxicated vows mistakenly spoken in the presence of a Vegas Elvis, ending in annulment. The groom who cheats with one of the bridesmaids. At the reception. Or the bride who catches one of the groomsmen going down on her brand-new husband.

But it's different when a marriage ends involuntarily. There's a voracious hollowness that can never be sated, no matter how hard you try to stuff it with empty calories.

And in those rare instances when your spouse leaves you and tries to come back? Forget about it. They've become something new altogether. A unique beast.

Daniel didn't leave Kristy on purpose, though. No, that never would have happened. She knew that at the time, and she still knows it now. He was one of those mate-for-life types, like penguins or seahorses. Most people roll their eyes at such statements. They presume there's always one side pulling less weight in a long-term relationship, that there's darkness lurking behind the constant smiles shown to the public. And, in certain cases, they'd be right.

But something needs to be clarified.

"Leaving" is an inaccurate term in this instance. It implies an act performed of one's own volition. Daniel didn't leave Kristy at all. He was taken from her. Vanished in the heart of their Hawaiian honeymoon. The sea claimed him, made him one with the barnacles and the coral, nourishment for the long-forgotten creatures of the deep.

Their love, swallowed by saltwater. Perished in paradise.

Speeding down a winding two-lane road somewhere between Diamond Head and Hanauma Bay, steering a Jeep Wrangler, allowing wind to scream through her hair.

Kristy and Daniel are running away from the rest of the universe. After this honeymoon ends, Kristy has vowed to never run from anything ever again. It's the last thing she wants to do. Too many years of escaping responsibility, sidestepping reality. She's found her perfect rock and wants nothing more than to cling to it, to bring it with her everywhere she goes.

On this stretch, it's too early in the morning for the locals, too late for the less adventurous tourists who have no desire to leave the safe confines of Waikiki. But Kristy's got herself a hell of a husband, and he's scanning the coast, looking for the perfect place to stop and soak in some life. Kristy loves him so much she just might puke.

"Babe…pull over, pull over!" Daniel's tone seems culled from childhood. Kristy slows down, finds a safe enough spot on the side of the road to stow the Wrangler. She leaves it unlocked. It's a rental. Hands latched, they cross the road after looking both ways because life is somehow more precious when there's someone to spend it with forever.

"Why here?" Kristy asks, knowing full well Daniel's going to answer with one of his typical pseudo-profound non-answers. *Why not here?*

"Don't know," he says. Quiet enough to avoid disturbing the blissful sounds surrounding them. The wind singing. The sea dancing. "Just feels like it was calling to me, I guess."

Daniel releases his grip and darts ahead. He hops over a dented guardrail, reaches the cliff first, slips, and teeters toward the edge. Kristy shrieks, then mentally slaps herself for falling for yet another of her man's infamous pranks. His laughs are good-natured, and he keeps them going until she joins in. Then she swats him in the chest, calls him an asshole, and he grunts.

Kristy peers over the cliff's edge. The view is idyllic, a movie moment forever burned in her brain. And now she agrees with Daniel's last statement. They had no choice in the matter. This spot has chosen them.

A near-vertical drop. No stairs for convenience, but a clearly carved dirt path down the side makes for a somewhat easier trek down to the beach. The daring lovers of the past have put in the work to make it possible. Because Kristy and Daniel are young and subsisting on spontaneity and passion, they aren't yet concerned about how to climb back up. They'll find a way. They always manage.

It isn't completely private down here—a few other couples have claimed the space as well—but it's close enough. No screaming children. No sunbathing crowds. The water is such a shock of blue it's almost impossible to tell where the ocean ends and the sky begins. Within moments of their bare toes wiggling through the virgin sand, Daniel swears on his life this is the same beach featured in the famous love scene in *From Here to Eternity*. His conviction is convincing. Kristy doesn't buy it, though, and hasn't even heard of the film, but she pretends to go along with it.

The cove is a liquefied runway. Jutting from the shore is what can best be described as a hot tub formed by erosion, perfect for the two of them to intimately share. As the tide goes out, it leaves them with barely a splash of water to sit in. When the tide returns, it is magic. The water floods the roughly formed circle and rises to their chests, bringing with it all manner of aquatic life, fish with colors so east and west of the spectrum they might as well be extraterrestrial. Daniel knows the scientific names of nearly all of them. Every class, order, family, and genus. Kristy expects nothing less from a freshly graduated oceanography major, nicknamed Aquaman by his closest colleagues. A man who has spent more hours of his young adult life navigating the sea than keeping his legs secure on land.

Daniel loves the ocean and everything in it. No—"loves" is an understatement. He respects it. Believes he should have been born of its wet embrace, conceived within its depths. He'd choose to live in the salty water if his body were capable of adapting.

Her husband's affair with the sea was evident as early as their first date. And she'll never forget the bizarre conversation he instigated that evening.

"You know, dolphins are sexually confident creatures," Daniel had said mid-meal, his cheeks chipmunked with onion rings. "And here's the really weird part. There's actually people who've come clean about their attraction toward dolphins and how they've…uh… mated with them."

Kristy had gagged so hard she'd almost spat out her quinoa burger.

"I find it fascinating," Daniel continued. "Scientifically, I mean."

She tried to hold back a wicked grin. "So what you're saying, is that if tonight turns into a second date and a third, and so on, I shouldn't be shocked if you suddenly attempt to bring some sort of Flipper fetish fantasy to the bedroom?"

Daniel kept a straight face, eyes darted off to the side, and Kristy's stomach dropped. Then he broke character, releasing his signature caw that she's since grown to adore.

"Surprised I haven't seen a viral video of one of these dolphin-lovers proposing or something," Kristy said.

"Well, dolphins aren't known to be monogamous."

"Oh, so they're like the sluts of the sea, then, huh?"

A pause. They both tried but failed to withhold their laughter.

Their fingers touched.

"I'm sure there's exceptions," Daniel said, smiling with his mysterious eyes. "Always are."

At first she'd thought herself ill for falling for a man who beamed with childlike glee when speaking about people who yearned to have sex with dolphins, but Daniel possessed many odd little quirks such as these. Never drinking soda on Sundays. Speaking openly about his personal experience with delayed puberty. Getting up to watch the sunrise to help him sleep in better. Believing *Jaws 3-D* was scarier than the first film because of how often he'd gone to SeaWorld as a child. It was these quirks (as well as her own) that had brought them closer and eventually led them here.

To Hawaii.

To this beautiful cove.

To this very moment.

They hog the hot tub-shaped rock until wrinkles form on their fingertips. The other couples give up on their turns and move on to enjoy the rest of their day elsewhere on Oahu. More heaven for Kristy and Daniel to steal for themselves. No one is willing to go to war for romance as much as newlyweds.

Daniel motions across the water to a tiny cliff. Behind it, there's an intimidating wall of rock. The cliff houses what appears to be an underwater cave, barely forty feet from where they sit and splash. Daniel grins and Kristy sees the devious child that still resides within him. Kristy grimaces and shakes her head, but the next thing she knows they are heading toward it. She wades, her feet barely touching the bottom. Daniel chooses to swim, revealing a grace he'd be hard pressed to replicate on land. A malcontent mammal who wished he were a fish, a being who yearned to split his time between both worlds.

A clawed hand here, a clutching foot there, and Daniel is atop the ledge, five feet above the surface, six at best. He flexes his arm with faux machismo, shows off the nautical star tattoo on his bicep, and Kristy rolls her eyes. She's never been so happy.

Daniel hollers, "It's away!" and cannonballs into the sea. He bounces to the surface almost as quickly as he breaks it, his face beaming. "Babe, you gotta try this!" He immediately goes back for more.

Kristy shakes her head, but eventually gives in after Daniel's third jump. She wants to accompany Daniel wherever he goes, no matter how scary it gets. He extends a hand and helps her up. The surface of the rock is slick with fluorescent moss. She creeps across it with her toes curled for traction, and balances herself with one hand behind her, flat against the rock wall that seems to stretch all the way to heaven. Daniel offers her a few tips on how to jump and land. She follows his advice to the exact note. Trust is everything.

Kristy flings herself off the cliff, into the water. One second she's splashing, the next her tailbone collides with solid ground. It almost knocks the wind out of her. Water rockets up her nose, and it's enough to make this a one and done experience. Her back burns. Later, when they're in the comfort of their hotel room, she plans to make puppy dog eyes at Daniel until he gives her a massage. And she'll make it worth his while, too.

Daniel goes back for more. Kristy wades back to nature's hot tub to watch. Her husband never seems to tire of jumping, and her stress is never-ending, her stomach using climbing spurs to scale her throat. Ever curious, Daniel treads water and maneuvers himself closer to the underwater cave, clinging to the slick rock at its opening.

"Hey, you're getting too close," Kristy calls out. "Be careful. There might be a current."

"Eh, it's fine." Daniel peeks into the cave as best he can, only a few inches of it visible above water. He leans in deeper and calls out a hello. A slight echo bounces back. He turns back to Kristy. "Honestly it doesn't look like it even goes anywhere."

He edges away from the cave, and Kristy releases a hesitant breath.

"Just one more jump and let's go, yeah?" she says. "I still wanna go check out the Dole Plantation today."

"Mmm," Daniel says, pretending to drool. "Dole Whips." He shoots her a thumbs up, climbs the side of the cliff, and leaps. The water explodes.

He doesn't come up immediately, which seems impossible. The sheer force of hitting the bottom should have pushed him right back up.

Barely a ripple on the water's surface. Kristy counts the seconds. At twenty she starts to panic.

"Hey, don't be a jerk," Kristy says, knowing he won't hear more than a muffled voice down below. The sun hits the water, blinding her with its glare. A few more seconds pass, and still no Daniel.

Kristy squints, shields her eyes with her hand. Motion in the water. Maybe.

Then his head surfaces.

"Dammit, Daniel. You had me—"

"Get out of the water!"

Without thinking, Kristy does the opposite. She leapfrogs over the edge of the hot tub and into the ocean. Frantic, splashing, Daniel goes under. She's already cursing herself, knowing she's falling for one of his lame pranks.

Daniel surfaces again, spits out saltwater. His eyes have seen the devil. "Go!" he yells. "Please! Something's got—there's something in—" And he's dragged under yet again.

She's caught Daniel in more than one innocent fib during their three years together, and she's certain his lips are telling the truth this time. She's never seen him afraid before, never knew he was even capable of such raw fear. She tries to reach toward him, but the water slows her down.

A shape moves next to Daniel, just below the surface. Something dark. More than a shadow. Something large. Long.

Daniel's body lunges backward, as if being pulled toward the cave.

Kristy screams. There's no one left on the beach to help. She dives into the shallow water. Despite it being clear enough to be bottled and sold, she sees nothing. Neither her husband, nor the ominous shape she's positive she saw.

Only the blackness of the cave. A deep, endless hole leading down, down, down.

Nearly nine months later, and time couldn't have gone any slower. Isolation makes the days drag into double.

Kristy's back in Oahu. Her bank account is drained, her belly ready to burst. Maybe she hates herself more than she previously thought. Hawaii has become her personal hell, sending out a siren's call so she can kneel in front of its merciless gods and beg for... what, exactly? She's not getting Daniel back, so any other wish granted would bring no consolation.

She has plenty to atone for, though. *That* the gods will surely gobble up. She never knew how much sin in the guise of suffering could be squeezed into such a short period of time.

To be fair, Kristy had no clue she was carrying Daniel's child until six weeks after her husband was taken from her. Not that it mattered. She still ultimately chose moaning over mourning.

She'd planned to take care of it, thought she couldn't live with a breathing, crying reminder of everything she'd lost. At least only one of them would have to endure the resulting pain. But Kristy has lost more than she can quantify and doesn't know how much more she can bear. Too many protest lines to cross to get the outcome she thinks she wants. She deserves a medal for every day she doesn't drink herself to death.

Or she could always bathe the forthcoming child in enough secondhand alcohol to burn it, the umbilical cord an eager fuse.

She was never much of a drinker before. Practically a teetotaler. Wine at a wedding. Half a beer at a party. But she became an enemy of moderation almost the moment she stepped off the plane and set foot back in San Diego, where the sun shines three-hundred and sixty-five days a year, but only for those who have something special to live for. Otherwise the forecast is permanently dismal.

No way she'd be a fit mother. The resentment started forming in the womb immediately and only grew uglier with each passing day.

Somehow fate had allowed the fetus to thrive despite her best efforts.

And now it's almost ready to come out and play.

She's swaying on the sand in the same private cove that robbed her of her entire universe. Where countless others have no doubt enjoyed the stuff romantic dreams are made of and gone on to live the fruitful lives they expected. But, to Kristy, this place is nothing more than a gorgeous graveyard.

At least the rest of the living world has left her alone today. Being in the presence of others might force her to feel. And that racks her with dread more than anything, sends roach leg shivers down her neck. If she allows emotion into the equation, everything that's occurred becomes impossible to ignore.

Lost her cushy copywriter job. Sold nearly anything she owned that was worth a penny. All so she could return to the place where she could relive her nightmare. She tries to convince herself she came here for closure, but that's a pitiful pipe dream. The gods will never grant her closure.

They never found Daniel's body.

The Coast Guard checked the area, had her holding out hope that maybe he was just sucked under for a second and spat out the other side. Like he'd taken a ride on some crazy new waterslide and was having the time of his life. He'd surely ask Kristy to try it, tell her she'd love it, just be careful, that last dip's a doozy. But the search was just a formality.

That night, one of the officers had tried to talk to her at the station. She tuned him out. Mostly. Only bits and pieces made it past the invisible partition in her ears and into her brain, and over time she'd twisted them into painful prose that became her silent mantra.

Plenty of unexplored underwater caves on the island. Currents make them dangerous. So many tight spaces a full-grown man could get wedged into and count down his last few seconds until he takes a deep drink of the sea.

Kristy tried to explain to the officer that something had been in the water with Daniel. Attacking him. Might have been a tiger shark. But the officer crushed the idea. There hadn't been any sightings in the area recently. Plus, no blood in the water. She'd confirmed it herself. Not a drop of red staining the beautiful blue.

Back home, none of Daniel's friends could figure out how the finest swimmer any of them had ever known had suffered such a fate. Aquaman had drowned, and it shattered everything they believed in, made them atheists of logic. They attended the funeral, paid their respects, and Kristy had yet to see any of them since. For this, she was thankful.

She cried for months. Maybe the tears weren't always presented to the public—she couldn't allow herself to become a complete mess—but they poured inside with no reprieve.

Now, here, her bare feet digging into the warm sand, she only feels numbness. Better that way. The numbness keeps her alive. Keeps her living out of sheer spite.

She regrets what she's been trying to do, the monster she's become. But regret isn't enough to stop her. All she has left of Daniel are a few blurry pictures on her phone and images burned into her memory. The memories get just a little hazier with each drink she takes, each attempt at expelling the unborn.

Plenty of wine to comfort her today. A bitch to get the bottle down here, and it's far from vintage, but it'll forgive her choices the way a friend made of flesh never could. Temporarily, at least. Fitting. Forgiveness is always temporary anyway.

Kristy sits because standing is so unbearable. So is living, but she has to go on because someone needs to remember Daniel at his best and his worst, as the wonderfully flawed man he was. His horrible taste in cinematic comedies. His secret cooking prowess. His ability to make her melt with a single cock of his head. Now he's nothing more than a name etched on a grave with no inhabitant, a name no one dares whisper anymore.

Hours pass. The wine drains. Night comes. She's done wallowing and is about to leave, but then something stirs in the water. She's been transfixed on the soothing low waves for so long that any transgression is amplified. The ripple occurs a few feet from the cave that took Daniel. Something breaks the surface. Something long and sly.

It swims toward the shore.

From the shock, from the wine, from the exhaustion of life— Kristy passes out.

Kristy always dreams of darkness.

It's been this way ever since she was a girl. No matter the scenario. Whether the dream consisted of the end of the world or the mundaneness of a day at the office, no visuals have ever come along for the ride. Only sounds. Feelings. Possibilities. A story being dictated to her.

A nagging loneliness, smothered in blackness.

Oftentimes, her dreams blur with reality. Like the time she woke up late for a test she hadn't studied for, only to realize it was

Saturday and that the test was still looming in the distant Monday. This dream is no different. She's at the cove, the night after Daniel disappeared. Swapping spit with a fermented friend, not unlike tonight. The slight sound of the waves soothing her. The damp sand chafing her back, creeping into her underwear. But she shouldn't be able to feel. Not this way. Not in a dream.

Something has slithered out of the sea. A clumsy splashing, then a soggy crawl the rest of the way. Something that once walked on two legs but has spent so much time below it has forgotten how to pose as a man. But it can relearn.

A scent wafts up Kristy's nostrils. Sour brine. Overwhelming nitrogen. Her dream self wonders if the sense of smell can exist in this dimension, or perhaps if there is a sensation only present during dreaming that makes one believe they are experiencing a smell.

The deep urge, the wetness she feels down below, however, is an intimate, if not altogether welcome, friend.

She still can't see it but she can hear it—the writhing thing from the sea. Inching toward her like a pathetic worm, chittering with glee. It pauses just before reaching her, as if awaiting consent, but nature does not wait for the world. It exists to create.

The creature slides on top of her, an oppressive weight. It whispers in her ear, in words that take time to make sense.

And then they do. Words so sweet. So familiar.

And she remembers that some dreams aren't dreams at all.

They are memories.

She should have known all those months ago when she'd awoken on the beach, dawn tearing away night's heavy curtain. Waiting for Daniel to quit it with his joke. Her mouth filled with sand. Drenched in slime and the stench of day-old seafood. So stupid. She'd fooled herself into thinking she'd vomited all over herself. A typical night for the lonely lush.

But she didn't notice something was off until she was a week late. Could have been a fluke. Wouldn't be the first time she'd had a scare. But then a couple of weeks later she got sick. The kind of sick where you just know.

She'd lived through a few regrettable nights since Daniel's disappearance. So much liquid courage and so little pride that she couldn't recall the names of the men she allowed to use her, much less their faces or the circumference of their pathetic cocks. She remembered Daniel mentioning something about dolphins, that the females would often mate with multiple partners during estrus. Maybe this was just her fucked up way of honoring his interests.

A close call or two, but not enough to teach her a lesson. At first she was certain the child inside her had to be the result of one of those encounters taken to its extreme. To its most likely outcome.

Except once she felt the growing being stir within, she understood what it really was.

A gift.

And who had given it to her.

And when.

Now—it's the second night of her return trip to Oahu. Perhaps the third. She's lost track. Once she arrives at the cove again, she doesn't have to wait long. Because she knew to come at dusk. Just as the cove once called to Daniel, now it beckons her.

Redemption's a real thing, almost tangible.

Maybe she'll make a decent mother after all. Hard to say, since the rules are about to change significantly.

The moonlight shines a pathway on the water. Moments later, it emerges.

He emerges.

An evolution of the man he once was. The man he no longer is. Her Daniel.

Always here, waiting for her.

Even after the night Kristy felt him inside her and—deep down, despite such drastic changes—recognized him, she still didn't believe it was him. Dreams can be tricky that way. Especially when they're not dreams at all.

Except tonight the details are crystal. The nautical star on the area that had once been his arm, now faded and blending into the smooth, rubbery, grey flesh. His face elongated and smoothed to a point, his head bald and domed, his smiling teeth tiny and plentiful and perfectly sharp, his body a shimmering wet wonder.

And—even though they've shifted to the sides of his head—it's the eyes that sell it.

Those mysterious, laughing eyes.

She wades into the water. Once her belly feels the shock of cold, the baby kicks inside her. It's ready.

But she's not sure if *she's* ready.

She takes Daniel's hand. Fin. Flipper. Something new altogether that nature has failed to share with the rest of the world.

There are others like him waiting in the water, a protective semi-circle, their faces barely breaking the surface. The ones who changed him. Who gave him his true purpose. Kristy forgives them. Sympathizes. They made choices, however long ago, and now she must make hers.

They've come to congratulate her. To welcome her to the family. And she knows it's time for a change.

The new Daniel guides her toward the cave. They're going where she should have followed so long ago. To finish their honeymoon.

Gently, he tries to push her under, but she hesitates. She's shivering. Fear, anticipation, ecstasy, what's the difference? He whispers in her ear, the echolocation making perfect sense. She understands his intent. Everything will be just fine. She'll be safe down below. He won't let her drown. He'll teach her to breathe.

His fin nudges her again. She sucks in a deep breath, and then she allows it.

Trust is everything.

"Voices Carry"
(original to this collection)

voices carry

Maddy had no mouth, though she had teeth.

Sweet, sweet teeth with even sweeter secrets. She could never let Richard know the truth that hid behind her reticence. Not that he'd bother to notice. No, it was safer to euthanize her freedom. Keep the lie on life support. Indefinitely.

The bathroom's floor chilled her feet and her almost bare ass, a thin layer of silk the only thing separating meat from marble. She huddled in her happy spot, the corner nearest the claw foot tub, opposite the "his and hers" glass faucet sinks. Unopened toiletries adhering to a blueprint. Not a single item out of place. Not a speck of dirt in sight. More a museum than anything resembling a room where one rids themselves of impurities.

Maddy despised nothing more than a pathetic cliché, yet here she was caught in the midst of one, clutching the handle of an antique mirror, staring deep into its blinding pool. She caressed the sterling silver casing, the patterns of angels and flowers acting as substitute braille, unsure of what it wished to express. Messages from heaven, perhaps. Or, more likely, heaven's wicked stepsister who lived in the wine cellar.

Not long ago, a crack had formed in the mirror, dead center. No indication how it had happened. Another precious heirloom irreparable. She'd removed a rhombus-shaped shard, accidentally slicing a perfect line down the outside of her thumb in the process. Then she'd doctored it carefully. Heaven forbid Richard's trophy suffer such damage. The shard was promptly lost or tossed. Cleaned up by the maid she'd never met.

Now, however, the mirror was far more meaningful with this key piece missing. The reflection told the ultimate truth. Of her pulchritude. Her potential. Not her current beauty that came courtesy of a sharp blade, a steady hand, and some time to heal. Not her charmingly chiseled cheeks, her enormous unblinking eyes, her flawless ski-jump nose. All meaningless, stagnant. The work of a skilled doctor rather than the fruits of her will. Barely turning thirty yet somehow carved into something ageless. A mannequin with benefits.

Plastic perfection, like an obsession.

No. That wasn't it at all. What she'd become and would forever be was strictly the result of what *he* craved.

Unless she had a say in it. Unless what had begun to develop behind her jaw, deep down inside her throat was real. If so, her obsession would soon prove to be far more impressive than anything Richard could concoct.

But Richard hadn't always been this way. He'd been kind. Once. Or, perhaps more likely, he'd been a phenomenal actor, she the fantastic fool. When they'd first met in college, he feigned gentleness, selflessness, chivalry even. A coat wrapped tight around her bare shoulders when the frosty evening became too much to bear. Deep, passionate phone calls from the other side of town that lasted from dusk until dawn. Listening intently to her treasured goals. Goals she now couldn't even recall. Then—showered with more gifts than she could have ever desired. Crystal earrings sparkling from her lobes. A pearl necklace hugging her throat.

A ring. A diamond ring the size of Saturn.

The night of their honeymoon had come without warning. Her handcrafted Enzoani hiked up to her hips. Her open, willing legs. Exposed cleavage that teased a view of the auburn areola. She felt something. They shared something. She was sure of it. The first taste of something legendary. Of being Mrs. Holland.

But mere months into their marriage that intangible something changed, ended its brief hibernation. The first time Richard had hit her she'd brushed it out of her mind as a fluke, a dark cloud that occasionally hovered over all couples at some point. Except the storm raged on. Versace sunglasses and Chanel powder worked wonders against such weather.

And the bedroom had ceased to be a place of passion. Instead it had become a vessel for Richard's demands, for his deviancy. During their courtship he'd often joked about the acts he'd wished she'd perform when the lights went out. She soon came to realize that behind every laugh hid a law. Richard brought in another man, one she'd never met before. And Richard's eyes had told her everything she needed to know. Comply, or accept the consequences. He'd slithered back into the shadows, watching through the black. Breathing. Erupting.

Repeat, ad nauseum.

The other man had never spoken a word to Maddy. She'd never known his name. The same could be said for the endless others. They may as well all have been the same.

Maddy held the mirror inches from her face, willing herself to forget but never forgive. Tonight's more pressing matters took precedence. Where the missing shard had once dwelled, blackness now prevailed. An opaque void. She shifted it ever so slightly so it obscured her mouth.

I have a voice. I exist. I have a voice. I exist. A whispered mantra built into a crescendo. Without being able to see her lips move, she couldn't be completely sure the voice belonged to her.

The door flew open, sending a jolt through Maddy's body. Richard strode into the bathroom, his silver hair shimmering beneath the chandelier. His eyes calm, his demeanor controlled, his unmatched charm circling her like a quiver of cobras.

Maddy stood, set the mirror face down on the counter.

"Madeleine, who are you speaking to?" His face twisted into an endless succession of wrinkles. "And why on earth are you in the guest bathroom?" The last two words of the second question left Richard's mouth as if a small piece of meat wedged in his throat had finally come loose.

"Oh. No one. No reason. I was just closer to—"

Beads of sweat trickled from Richard's temple, accentuating his prominent brow, a widow's peak worthy of Lugosi's legacy. "How many times have I stressed how much I loathe your lies?"

Maddy was an ice sculpture, Richard's dead stare straight through her confirming it. "But I'm not—"

Richard raised his hand. Maddy flinched, instantly regretting it.

Before Maddy could defend herself further, Richard stroked her unraveled hair. He chuckled. "Really, Madeleine…why don't you smile more? On those rare occasions when you take the time to shut your mouth, you have such a lovely smile."

Her vow of silence began later that night.

After Richard had his expelled his seed inside her, left her damp and dead-eyed, she'd returned to the guest bathroom, carrying a sewing kit she hadn't used since high school. This time she remembered to lock the door behind her. Richard's snoring seeped through the walls, soothing her.

Once she located the essential tools in her kit, she took a deep breath. Hesitated. The time had come. With needle and thread she zigzagged between her creamy collagen lips. The first fresh hole full of unbearable pain, each new puncture a faint pleasure. The more she stitched, the less she was tempted to scream. After an hour or so of agony, her lips were sealed tight.

By first light the next morning, healing had already begun, and in the depths of her sleep she'd forgotten about what had transpired. Richard wasn't in bed when she awoke, and she attempted to call for him, soon regretting her error. The early stages of ravaged tissue resulted from the quietest peep. But Maddy remembered. Keep it down. Remain silent and prosper.

And her resolve did not waver.

She fished through her nightstand drawer until she found what she was hunting for. A magnifying glass, which she took with her to the bathroom mirror, then placed in front of her lips to examine the insignificant rips. Swelling building, the wounds clotting in all the right places. Crispy scabs had formed, punishment for the chittery canary.

What a wonderful, wonderful start.

The foyer, a gaping maw. The stairs its perfect teeth.

Maddy hobbled down the hallway, her ball gown painted on, forcing a geisha gait. Her long, blonde hair pulled into a tight cone, hermetically sealed. A wonder she had proper access to oxygen.

"We're going to be late, Madeleine. Are you almost ready?"

Maddy did not, could not respond. The threads hugged her mouth like tiny black larvae. Full healing would take time, but in patient time there would be no trace of the former flesh.

She reached the top of the stairs, looked down at her handsome husband, so tall and strong when in her face. But from up here—so small, so pathetic. Dressed in an Armani tuxedo she'd not seen him wear before. Of course not. Richard would never be caught dead wearing the same outfit in public twice. And she'd honor his wishes soon enough, once he was prepped and ready.

Maddy took her time descending the stairs, Richard busy adjusting his cufflinks. When she reached the bottom, he leered below her neckline.

"You know," he said, "you could use a trip to the tanning salon. You're looking a bit peaked these days. I'll call Alfonso tomorrow and schedule you in."

Maddy decided she would not attend the appointment. She'd become such an expert at impersonating a pale phantom that it would be a shame to ruin the effect.

Richard gazed into a mirror near the front door, slicked down his unruly eyebrows. So many mirrors occupying their enormous home. So many reflections, yet Maddy had never truly been seen. Richard squeezed her side lightly, his fingers struggling to find an ounce of fat to ridicule. Somehow he succeeded.

"And I'd appreciate it if you kept the hors d'oeuvres to a minimum tonight."

Maddy set her hand on Richard's shoulder, stepped on her tippy toes, her sling back heels hovering behind her. She brushed her sutured, deformed mouth against his cheek, doing her best impression of a kiss. His freshly shaved whiskers already magically growing back. He was not particularly interested in the affection, which came as no surprise. Kisses had always been far too intimate for Richard's liking. In her husband's perfect world, a man got right down to business and didn't mess about with unnecessary sentiments.

She linked her arm with his, a perfect chain. They each grabbed their masks and left for the gala.

Maddy couldn't recall whose masquerade they were attending tonight, whose home they now inhabited. Or how they'd even arrived. But they were here. Present and accounted for. That was the important part. They stepped through a doorway wide enough to allow an army passage, then entered a ballroom so lavish it made their own divine home resemble a backwoods shack. A chandelier the size of a small blimp hung from the ceiling, its weight threatening to crash down and puncture the partygoers. Dozens of them. Mingling, snacking on foods they couldn't pronounce, sipping on Dom Pérignon.

All of them hidden behind their chosen masks, some simple and tasteful, some pushing the limits of grotesquerie. Richard wore a lion-esque disguise that covered his face from brow to upper lip. Maddy had decided upon a basic eye mask, its upper corners pulled to points like vintage cat-eye glasses. Her sewn lips almost an afterthought.

Angelic music soothed these savage beasts, yet Maddy could not tell where the sounds came from. No live orchestra. No obvious speakers. The notes simply appeared.

Richard wasted not a moment once they had taken their first steps past the threshold.

"I'm going to see what that old bastard Howard has been up to. I'll find you sooner or later. Try to stay out of trouble. Please."

He patted her behind, just firmly enough to remind her that he was the master. Always so sickeningly obsessed with those fleshy curves. And the hole that hid between them.

Maddy moved through the crowd, blending in as best she could. Across the room a server spotted her and started to make a beeline in her direction, then disappeared among the masqueraders. Just as Maddy was about to give up and walk away, the server reappeared in front of her, holding out a silver platter. From afar he'd appeared to be of average height and build, but now it was clear he was a dwarf. Must have been standing a few steps up the staircase when she'd first seen him. He flashed her a rictus grimace, his fancy mustache following suit.

"Madame," the server said, "would you care to sample some bruschetta with prosciutto and olive oil?"

Maddy nodded, took one from the platter, and the server danced away. She held the bread to her mauled lips, took in the scent enough to taste it.

She met her first acquaintance within moments. Less a woman, more a living, breathing Barbie doll. Maddy could not recall her name, wasn't sure if she'd ever known it. The woman's mask was aquatic in nature, as if she had peeled the face from some deep-sea creature and pasted it to her own. Her gown was a near replica of the one Maddy wore, which should have filled Maddy with endless dread but instead brought her some strange sense of comfort. Barbie's silicone torpedoes bounced in unison as she spoke. "I'm not kidding. Dr. Onassis has been a godsend. I can't wait for my next treatment. Dear, I have to ask…it's been a while. Something looks…different about you. Have you had work done recently?"

Maddy nodded.

After Barbie left, a waifish man, his head a shiny cue ball, approached Maddy. She did not think she knew this man but clearly must have, considering the grand and sincere affection he showed her. A peck upon each cheek, then atop her hand. Like her, he wore a mask that only covered the space surrounding the eyes, though his was decidedly more feminine than hers, adorned with sequins and feathery strands sprouting from its sides. He went on and on about overseas stocks and upstarts and lucrative investments that she and Richard should seriously consider. His breath smelled like the inside of a whale.

Maddy nodded, wandered off without so much as a wave, the man still yammering on. Another server approached her, this one a woman, a double amputee in a motorized wheelchair. Each leg gone below the knee. With one free hand she navigated the crowd using a joystick attached to the wheelchair's arm. With the other she held out a platter of champagne glasses, all half full. Maddy took one, and the woman smiled and sped away. Maddy held the glass to her lips, poured the chilled liquid. It did not penetrate the seal. Not even a taste. Her attempted sip spilled to the floor. She set the glass down on a nearby table, worried someone might have noticed her faux pas. No one did.

Invisible as she was, Maddy could not seem to hide herself well enough. A portly woman cornered her without warning. Maddy knew this woman. Patricia something-or-other. Her mask came to an absurd point right at the nose, the progeny of Cyrano de Bergerac. "Roger and I missed you at the last gathering," Patricia said. "I do hope you're planning to participate this time." She looked down at Maddy's hand, practically salivating. Maddy followed her gaze. She'd forgotten she was still carrying the bruschetta. A useless prop. "Are you…going to eat that? May I?"

Maddy nodded.

After Patricia dashed off to hunt down her next snack, the devil came to Maddy. Or so his mask and accessories implied. Glittery horns sprouting from his head. His mask so thin and long it resembled a living scream. He held a champagne glass between the tips of his thumb and forefinger. His hair a perfect helmet, his seersucker suit devoid of any creases. He extended one lithe hand to Maddy. "I'm here for you. He asked for you. He's ready now. *They* are ready now. Are you game?"

Maddy paused, considered, nodded.

Somewhere deep in the catacombs of the vast mansion, the devil-masked man guided her into the darkness. A comfortable, private room. A bed the size of a small yacht. A single candle on the nightstand.

A half-dozen faces hidden in the shadows. Maddy did not, could not speak a word. Her silence became her consent.

The devil was kinder, gentler than the others in line that preceded and followed him. He left the mask on. But nothing else.

Coughing in the corner. Moaning. Maddy floated out of her body, watched lifelessly from above. She knew he was out there, observing her.

And soon the final curtain dropped. A voice spoke from far off in the blackness. "I'm finished, Madeleine. Clean yourself up. We're leaving now."

Weeks later, in the guest bathroom, her happy special place. The wide, endless mirror above the sink her closest confidant and her dreaded enemy. Without a drop of water or a crumb of food Maddy had somehow subsisted. As she always had.

The healing had been far more successful than she could have imagined. Under the dim light, barely a noticeable scar. Sutures dissolved, absorbed. Where lips once lived now remained a smooth, flat, blank canvas. She remembered some of her fondest dreams of youth. Her goals to achieve. Once, she had wished she would grow up to be a surgeon.

And, for a brief period, she had hoped to become a beautician. One who specialized in makeup application.

With a lip liner pencil she outlined around the perimeter of her chin, jaw, and nostrils, soon to transform into massive, exaggerated, puffy pillows. Sketch, sketch, sketch new cherry red lips.

Trading the lip liner for black liquid eyeliner, Maddy scrawled rows of vicious teeth within the pale void, jagged and sharp to ensure they could tear through multiple layers of meat with zero effort.

Behind the sealed wall of flesh, she could feel her forked tongue pushing against the façade, her new teeth gnashing, the metallic flavor of blood seeping from her gums as the enamel daggers formed. Grinding, vengeful sounds roared behind this perfect work of art. Stalagmites. Stalactites. Take your pick. Chew, chew chew.

But none of this was worthwhile unless it was allowed to be free. To be seen.

At first, it had seemed rational to begin the new mouth hole with nail clippers, slowly chewing away at the naked flesh until Maddy could almost whistle. But she was anxious. And she owed it to herself to be more precise. A pair of craft scissors did the trick, slicing and carving each shape with an envious attention to detail.

She did not speak. Nor did she scream. She wanted her first words to be perfect.

Once satisfied with her work, she unlocked the bathroom door, opened it quietly, shuffled barefoot along the hallway, toward

Richard's study. He'd be reading, engrossed in Margaret Atwood. Wouldn't expect her.

She continued to cut as she walked, opening the chasm wider and wider. So many stains. And no maid on the premises to address this awful mess.

By the time she approached Richard, she'd be blessed with a gorgeous, gaping maw, her impressive smile the last thing he would see. Soon this fresh mouth would have plenty to say. These new teeth would have so much to gnaw on.

the
new
music

"The bodies boogied in the sweltering summer of '85. The backbeat was the devil's own."

-Graffiti found painted on the window of the abandoned KNJO station

1.

Humanity's not through fighting. It's just temporarily hiding. Not everyone is prepared for their final fandango.

Sandwiched within the silent suburbia of Thousand Oaks, California, sits a once-thriving hotspot of sonic commerce, a beacon of licorice-laced civilization: Floyd's Records and Tapes.

Seven rows of rarely dusted medium-density fiberboard shelving units run symmetrically through the building, lined with forgotten gems from failed collections and crisply shrink-wrapped Would Have Been Future Classics. A gaudy pink neon sign proclaims "Listening Station." A pair of cheap headphones hangs haphazardly near a fingerprint-stamped Technics turntable. Sun-stained posters and flyers with curled corners crookedly adorn the windows, merely hinting at the aural possibilities that once existed beyond the store's doors. Lately, this whole town's a dead scene.

Literally.

Some might call it a recession of sorts.

FLOYD

Playlist: Creedence Clearwater Revival "Bad Moon Rising," Pink Floyd "Comfortably Numb," Led Zeppelin "When the Levee Breaks"

Back in '72 I purchased the double lot next to my house and decided to build this store from the ground up. Never looked back, just faced the dream head on. Sherry, my ex-wife, claimed I would fall flat on my face trying to open up a record store in a residential neighborhood about a dozen blocks south of downtown, but we made enough to get humbly by. We never had a lot of foot traffic coming through, naturally. This ended up being quite a blessing when you take these particularly apocalyptic days into consideration. Not that it makes things any less dangerous really, but I feel fortunate we're located in the spot we are. I can't even begin to imagine what Los Angeles must be like right now. The nickname "HelL.A." has never seemed more fitting. Just thousands of mindless bodies wandering around, with such a lack of individual thought that it almost crosses over into hive mind mentality.

I suppose that's not all that different from how L.A. was before the Dead Pride Parade marched through town.

When everything started getting *poco loco* a few weeks back, my employees came to the store for shelter. News-cum-rumors spread from D.C. that this was some sort of an airborne virus. We were instructed to stay indoors. Well, we learned pretty quickly that was a big crock, but if you're listening out there you probably know all of this already. It's got to be something less naturally occurring. Acid rain, maybe? I don't know...what exactly *could* cause an empty body to start hopping around again? There haven't been any official radio transmissions or television since the first week, so we're pretty much on our own here, trying to figure everything out.

The fact that almost all of my employees showed up here makes me actually feel wanted, no, *needed* for the first time in, well pretty much ever. 'Cause I tell you what…Sherry never needed me much unless it was to change a light bulb. Life's worthy of protecting and apparently I'm capable of the job. So far, anyway…never thought managerial duties would prepare me for real leadership at this point in my life.

In other news…the power's been out for quite some time now. The nights are dark.

Real dark.

I brought over this portable CB here from my garage. In the 70s I used to communicate with truckers passing by on the 101 or the 23…just a fun little hobby of mine. Don't judge. Kind of a long shot, but I'm hoping maybe we can track down more survivors. Hopefully there are still some other relatively civilized people nearby. We'll see if anybody answers back or if we're just making our best attempts at drowning out the static. I'm already starting to feel like a little bit of a jackass.

Got a generator, too. Plenty of gas stored in my garage for the time being. Means we still get to play some records in the shop. Keeps the morale up. The few bodies that have managed to wander over from the more populated areas don't seem to be too attracted to sound as far as we can tell. Still, we keep the volume a bit on the lower end. I'm just as worried about the looters as I am about the bodies, especially when there's no one left to protect us but *us*. Human beings and whatever the hell these redux versions are can be equally dangerous, just in different ways. Glad I've got a shotgun. Also glad I haven't had to use it.

Yet.

T.O. used to be one of the safest cities in America, but that's sure changed ever since the world went to shi—

Aw hell, who gives a damn if I curse on this thing? It's not like the FCC is regulating us. Fuck it.

2.

There's been a burly biscuit building in the air:

A mix of fresh baby shit, neglected personal hygiene, and week-old Brussels sprouts left in the microwave during an extended vacation. A faint sense of recently relocated earthen residue catches the easterly winds, soil wedged in the crevices of fingernails. A decayed set of teeth, festering breath. The threat of the afterlife made wretched flesh.

Once, perhaps twice a week Floyd and his loyal employees write their names on unused Ticketmaster tickets, then draw them out of a Los Angeles Raiders ball cap that had been sitting in the lost & found box for months. This decides who will make runs downtown to scavenge. The Ticketmaster station is otherwise useless at this point. The bodies outside are often less menacing to face than the seething wrath of the frothing customers that once slept overnight in their lawn chairs outside of Floyd's, just to secure front row seats, just to catch a glimpse of the near-moribund Mick Jagger's sweat.

And the record store clerks can't help but question:

What constitutes a corpse in this day and age?

JAYSIN

Playlist: Bad Religion "Fuck Armageddon...This Is Hell," Raw Power "Fuck Authority," Void "Time to Die"

Been staring at Chelsea's tits way too much. If anyone listening out there ever shopped at Floyd's before, you probably caught a glimpse of those pale melons displayed on the sale rack. I don't feel one bit bad about saying this. She's kind of a creep anyway so she probably gets off on my drooling. I'm not saying I wouldn't boink her. Even back before the bodies started cruising the streets I would have probably taken Lil' Jay for a dip. Doesn't seem like there's a lot of options anymore, so she's starting to look pretty pinup-ready these days. Whatever. Screw it. I'll just go jerk it to a picture of Joan Jett in the bathroom later. No harm, no foul.

So yeah…it took a day or two for the bodies to start showing up full force in the cities and for the crucial info to trickle down to us.

We the Peons of the United States…

Airborne virus my *ass*. If anything, this is like our very own government-devised version of Minamata disease that just got way out of hand. I bet that bastard Reagan was all sealed up and safe within five minutes, too. Bunkers for Bonzo. Enjoy your stockpiles of jellybeans, asshole.

What's really getting me wired up right now is thinking too hard about the status of the post office. At what point did the friendly neighborhood mailman actually stop delivering the goods? When the shit started soiling the city's pants I was skating a ditch that was closer to Floyd's than my apartment, so I came here. Didn't look like the buses were running anymore. Seemed like the safest close spot. But, what I really want to know is—did my mail keep getting delivered during that day or two of crossover from Then to Now? I was expecting some tasty platters to arrive that week. I mail-ordered a copy of the new *Cleanse the Bacteria* compilation straight from Pusmort, orange vinyl with a bonus 12". Probably would have been a doozy. A Fix "Vengeance" single was on its way from some dude I found in the MRR classifieds. *Christ*. Fuck my life. At least the mix tape that Geert, my pen pal from Holland, sent to me made it out here in time. Some new shit-hot Euro-rippers on this bad larry: Indigesti, Funeral Oration, B.G.K., Huvudtvätt, Jezus and the Gospelfuckers, Negazione, Terveet Kädet—not even sure if I'm pronouncing some of those right, but yeah…there's some good jams on there. Not like anyone else gives a flying fuck. Nobody in this stale bunghole of a town even understands what the hell this music means to me. The revolution is six feet under now.

Or, well, not really.

So I thought about taking a detour to my pad last time we went out for supplies, just to see if any of my packages made it, but there were too many bodies shuffling around the outskirts of north T.O. It would have been worth the risk to me, but Kenny put the kibosh on the idea. So who knows? Maybe my goods are all lost in postal limbo, stuck in some warehouse in Lovett, Texas, or some other ghost town? Does anyone out there even realize how much that screws with my fucking head? Aaargh…

3.

The dead have adopted a "Locals Only" approach. Zero contact with any living for weeks now, the former working stiffs at Floyd's wonder if they missed the metaphorical evacuation train. They grow restless, sick of the same despondent faces. The arguments over rations and turntable turns have begun. A copy of *Irwin the Disco Duck Dance Party II* lies shattered near the front counter. No one cares to clean up the grooved shards (they never will).

CHELSEA

Playlist: Joy Division "Dead Souls," Bauhaus "Bela Lugosi's Dead," The Cure "The Hanging Garden"

Jaysin's fooling himself if he thinks he's getting into my pants. End of the world or not, I'd rather swap spit with a corpse.

Actually, I probably shouldn't give them any ideas. Not nice to tease.

It's not like I'm some sort of virginal good girl…far from it, but a girl's got to have standards. If there's a need to replenish the human race at some point, then it's probably a novel idea to be selective about the gene pool. I doubt I even have that luxury anymore. If this is all that's left, then we're in big trouble. I think I used to want kids when I was a kid, but doesn't everyone want that at some point because it's "normal?" I'm not really looking to be the resident womb, even if the fate of humanity rests in my ovaries. How the hell did I end up being some sort of token "girl who works at the record store?" It's not just me, either. I know…*knew* plenty of other chicks hiding behind their boyfriends, with just as much musical knowledge as the guys.

Whatever. I'm so over sex. Who needs a dick when you've got the dead to worry about?

4.

"Hey, man, just because Floyd went all Samson on us doesn't mean I'm doing the same."

"It's a liability. If you get too close to one of the bodies, they could grab ahold of it. Same applies to loose articles of clothing, but that's a little less avoidable."

"Nah, no way. They're not even that interested. They're stupid. They barely know what they're doing. I've walked right past them so many times."

"Their behavior changes every time we go out. Haven't you noticed? It's completely unpredictable. We need to be prepared for any random factors, don't you think? They're getting hungry. Soon they'll be just as hungry as we are. They just don't realize it yet. And there's no advantage to having the ability to 'walk right past them' when surrounded by a group."

"Screw that, Marcus. I want to grow my hair all the way down to my ass. Like, I want to do my beard, too. I'll be like a wizard!"

"That's not very intimidating, Kenneth."

"Dude, it totally is. *Nobody* fucks with a wizard. Even Ozzy knew that. And don't call me 'Kenneth,' man. I mean, come on."

"What karmic crimes did I commit to deserve spending the end of days with you?"

KENNY

Playlist: Iron Maiden "Run to the Hills," Slayer "Hell Awaits," Metallica "Creeping Death"

I need a goddamn cold Bud. This room temperature shit ain't cuttin' it. Maybe some weed would be better.

Wouldn't kill me to score a Twinkie or two, either.

Fucking aliens caused this or something, yeah? These aren't dead people—they're pods! Corpse pods! Does the "why" really matter? Here's what's important to me—they showed up…we're toast.

Hey, Floyd—why the hell are you making me talk on this stupid thing anyway? I'm done. This sucks.

5.

Needles wear down on vinyl grooves like jagged teeth on virgin flesh. Armageddon has a soundtrack, but it's not ranking on the *Billboard* charts. Stale sweat forces moisture to glaze the windows. The outside world is like a murky fishbowl. The funny thing, though—it looks just as grim from outside to in.

MARCUS

Playlist: Lee Morgan "The Sidewinder," Ornette Coleman "Focus on Sanity," John Coltrane "Good Bait"

It is with great regret that I have made it through life on Earth long enough to see it crumble. Would it be out of line for me to argue it's long overdue? My daddy was a preacher back when we lived in Athens—Georgia, not Greece. In a way, he predicted the world would eventually ravage itself. He used to write out and save his sermons, and there's a portion of one he gave about ten years ago that I read over and over until I memorized it:

"When humanity has reached its darkest hour, the dead will come to rise and judge those who have chosen the unholy path. Our cries will be the songs of archangels, our flesh devoured, our blood suckled like milk from a mother's teat. Do not compare this to the sacrifice of Christ. We all deserve to have our sins eaten away, inch by inch."

My father, a modern day Nostradamus with jheri curls.

I wonder how he's holding up out there, and if God is guiding his path. I miss my mother dearly. This is the first time I've ever truly been thankful she passed when I was still in high school, and that her posthumous wish had been cremation.

Some used to say I should be bitter about how blacks have been treated in America, that I am entitled to hold a permanent grudge against the white man for what his ancestors did to my ancestors long ago in the past, and also in the recent past. I have never fallen victim to violent, oppressive racism and it appears that I likely never will, though my mother told me she was run out of her hometown for dating a white man before she eventually met my father. That's the G-rated version of the story. I will not attempt to lie and claim I have not personally experienced any form of prejudice. In fact, I dropped out of UGA after my second year when a professor used a word directed toward me that I could not prove and I shall not repeat. I simply choose to be the bigger man and take each situation on a case-by-case basis. Live by peace and teach by example.

Besides, the struggle is not about "my people" anymore. Only an ignoramus would not understand that these days there are only two kinds of people: those who still have heartbeats and those who do not. The "us" and the "them" are *extremely* clearly divided. They want to use our bodies as fuel, but for what purpose? There are no racial divides, and they do not discriminate between white meat and dark meat. They simply take their pick from the plentiful smörgåsboard.

Though, now that I have brought up the issue of race, I may as well state one opinion I do feel very strongly about: we *have* had the upper hand in music and culture for decades now. Hell, it's less an opinion and more of an indisputable fact. You want jazz? You want blues? You want to take rock 'n' roll and co-opt it to make it palatable for a white audience with endless disposable income? You come to the black man. You steal it all and make failed attempts to call it original. Elvis Presley was a sham. It feels good to finally be able to express that opinion with zero repercussions.

Hmm…maybe I *am* bitter after all.

6.

Hope no longer spreads from lyrical earnestness. What was once considered potent poetry is now a heap of mindless mantras, only suitable as failed attempts to assuage permanent fears. Power anthems become white noise. The dead and the living grow equally desperate. Billboards become dated, armchair critics severely jaded.

JAYSIN

Playlist: The Cramps "Zombie Dance," T.S.O.L. "Code Blue," Poison Idea "Give It Up"

So today, faithful listeners, we're reminiscing about in-store pranks. All the wicked fun we used to have in this store when we still attracted some living, breathing customers. Because…why not?

Exhibit A: The Fake Turd.

Take a big hunk of Styrofoam popcorn—about the size of a finger, melt a sizeable piece of a chocolate bar onto it and voila! You'll have a pretty believable brown baby to fit snugly along the inside of the toilet bowl. You may also want to add a few drops of hot sauce to make it more, uh, appealing. Anyway, we always knew there would be at least one unsuspecting customer asking to use the head on any given day, so sometimes the fake turd would already be waiting for them. Once some stupid girl from the Valley managed to accidentally find herself in our neck of the woods and needed to use the restroom to go douche herself for her big beau Bryce or something. She screamed the second she walked in! The best part was, no matter how much someone flushed, the shit would stick to the bowl. Tight fucking grip.

Exhibit B: Bread Mask and Shoes.

So there was some art fag who used to bring in all of this weird gourmet bread every couple of weeks. I think he had a crush on this kid Paul who worked here for a hot minute. He was kind of a seedy dude.

Get it? Bread humor. Hardy-fucking-har.

Anyway, one night Kenny and I were about ready to beat ourselves from boredom, so we sculpted a mask and shoes out of some of the larger loaves that were leftover from the last batch. I wore them out on the floor and helped a few customers. Kenny said it made me look sort of like Rocky Dennis. Man, you should have seen the looks on their faces. I acted like everything was totally normal. Which, of course, it was. Typical day at Floyd's.

Nobody ever ate that fucking bread. Tooth-breaking garbage. Sometimes we used to have food fights with it in the receiving room. What I wouldn't give for just one loaf now. Canned speckled butter beans are getting pretty old, you know?

7.

Green paper sits untouched in the register. That's all it is now: filthy, inedible spinach. It has no function, no purpose. It was once worshipped, deified. Now it is hardly worth using to wipe one's ass.

FLOYD

Playlist: The Jimi Hendrix Experience "Manic Depression," The Rolling Stones "Sympathy for the Devil," The Doors "The End"

Been thinking a bit about compact discs, the impact they might have had if they were given more time in the music world. We were starting to carry them right before we had to, well, prematurely close shop. A new, but not necessarily improved format. I was resisting even ordering any for a while. Don't get me wrong…I'm not some sort of technophobe. Not completely, anyway. I've never been a huge fan of the cassette format either. They're only a step above 8-tracks in my eyes, but they always sold steadily, and you could still play them in your car. But there was something not quite right about the compact disc format. The warmth of vinyl grooves just lost and left in the cold. The hands-on experience and intimacy that comes from flipping side A to B was completely non-existent with these discs. And then you need perfect vision to even look at the damned artwork. Sometimes convenience is just a nuisance. I'd hate to see if this is what the future looks like.

Or would have looked like, I guess. I keep forgetting…it's hard to remind myself that isn't even an option anymore. I suppose I should be careful what I wish for.

That gets me thinking more and more…this is probably it as far as new music goes. No new albums to be recorded and released, no concerts, just the same leftover sounds repeated ad nauseum. For us, I suppose that means as long as our generator keeps running. I've got to feel sorry for people out there without this luxury right now. I don't even want to begin to think about that eventuality. Music is such an important part of the human experience. Even though the sounds themselves count most of all, a select few of us are able to bond because of the physical products created from these sounds. What's life going to be like without that to look forward to? Was there ever a world without music? What did Cro-Magnon man use for his tunes…twigs and stones? Are our albums just going to become fossils that run the risk of never being rediscovered?

Probably no more rock stars either. Most of my heroes are already dead, but it's almost funny to think about some popular artist these days like Prince or Boy George trying to somehow blend in out there with the bodies. Or what about that one Michael Jackson video? It's like that boy had a goddamned premonition. There's not much to laugh about anymore, so I kind of have to accept these thoughts when I get them and allow myself a little chuckle.

Now, granted, we had a pretty good selection and a wide cross-section of genres in the store, so there really is plenty to keep our ears happy for a while. Maybe even some new discoveries hiding deep in the dollar bins. I also break into my personal stash next door from time to time, but it's still very disheartening to come to the realization that this is basically...

...it?

8.

"Stop sucking my nips so hard!"

"Can't help it. They're like little Everlasting Gobstoppers."

"Can't we just hurry up and get this over with already? I'm starting to get bored, and I sure as hell am *not* planning on using the grape jelly. So don't-—"

"But—"

"—get any ideas!"

"Just pretend I'm Scott Baio or something."

"*Ew*. Are you for real?"

"Do you think there are still any cats and dogs out there?"

"What the—concentrate!"

"No, I mean, I just haven't seen any when I've been out on runs. Seems weird. You'd think we would have seen at least a few strays running around or something."

"Can we wax poetic about domestic animals later? I'm trying to come, you dickwad!"

"Shh...I think I hear something outside."

"Fuck muh...muh—Fuck *THEM*"

"Shut the Christ up, Chels! You're being nuts."

"Everyone I care about is gone."

"You don't know that. Stop crying. Maybe they're—"

"No! Nobody loves me...everybody hates me."

"No way. I love you, dude."

"..."

CHELSEA

Playlist: The Smiths "Suffer Little Children," Siouxsie and the Banshees "Carcass," Christian Death "Romeo's Distress"

Well, I gave in and fucked Jaysin last night. *Ugh.* Call Colonel Sanders 'cause this chicken is done.

What's the use in caring anymore? We're running low on food. Marcus, Floyd, and Kenny have been gone for two days now. They took Floyd's Gremlin up to Camarillo and Oxnard to look for food since the well has pretty much run dry down here. They claimed it would be better to have more people scouting the unfamiliar ground. And Floyd knows the owner of Vinyl Destination up in Oxnard. He wants to see if anyone's there. We have no idea when or *if* they're even coming back.

So I got lonely. Sue me.

And Jaysin's not *that* bad looking, considering the options are dwindling these days. His lazy eye is actually kind of endearing. We just went back into the receiving room and did it right on the concrete. It was cold and hard, like doing it on a necropsy table.

Don't ask me how I know that.

I guess this CB is my diary now. Yay. Dear Diary, I've lost some weight. Looking like a trampy skeleton. I could really use some chili fries right now.

9.

"I don't understand, Floyd. Why did it look like there were bite marks on the records in that shop? Are the bodies really that hungry?"

"Search me. The better question is 'why the hell didn't they even sample the compact discs?' Not that they'd taste better, necessarily, but—"

"This is exactly what I've been talking about. If we're being rational—"

"Marcus! Look out!"

The bodies surround the Circle K next door to Vinyl Destination in an almost premeditated perfect formation, a post-mortem sense of gracefulness, gliding along sunbaked asphalt like novice skaters on an ice rink in dire need of resurfacing. Their jaws droop and drool like a discarded Dali piece.

Sacrifices have been made: cherry slush strewn and splattered like new blood, salty chips sweating through their under-packed bags, sinewy Slim Jims hardening from age, smeared puddles of melted, feculent chocolate.

The bodies shatter the panes, the glass tears the flesh, the pain threshold is a non-issue.

Floyd and Kenny: a tight escape made at the last possible moment.

A meal made of Marcus.

KENNY

Playlist: Black Sabbath "Children of the Grave," Venom "Raise the Dead," Motörhead "Dead Men Tell No Tales"

Marcus is gone, man.

Fuck.

(*incoherent noise blocking transmission*)

10.

Eulogies have lost their luster. Carl Orff's *Carmina Burana* echoes throughout the store, an acceptable funeral dirge. The employees mourn their fallen comrade. No one speaks, eyelids are anvils, sweet lullabies soothe.

JAYSIN

Playlist: Die Kreuzen "This Hope," Battalion of Saints "Doomed World," Discharge "A Hell on Earth"

Well, we finally confirmed the real danger of the bodies. I overheard Marcus predicting this a few weeks ago, and he was spot on. Proved his own point, the poor bastard. They're even hungrier than we are, if you can imagine that. I don't know why it took them so long to develop a taste for their former selves. I suppose there's something ironic or fucking poetic about that.

Nah. Just seems to be something we all have to look forward to. Consumers will consume.

"Young 'Til I Die." Never thought I'd have a pretty fair chance of taking that song title really fucking literally.

11.

The outside world resembles an old film, when the colors of the streets and the sky were almost indiscernible. A permanent humid dusk is all that remains.

A lone body has wandered from the city into the suburbs. Its eyes are scrambled eggs, its tongue bloated and black like a dirty gym sock stuffed full of spoiled ground meat.

It is the first of many.

FLOYD

Generator's pretty close to being kaput. We haven't had any luck finding more gas out there. Once the sun goes down we're only using candles. Need to save as much power as we can. No more tunes either…too many bodies exploring the neighborhoods now. There's no way they'll ignore the sounds. We're in desperate need of a paddle at this point, if you catch my drift.

The CB's been crapping out here and there, so this'll likely be our last attempt at contact. I figure we've been talking just to hear the sounds of our own voices the last few weeks anyway.

Sayonara, if you're still out there.

12.

Endless feet shuffle, marching with a staccato cadence. Cries of insatiable hunger fill the air, but there's no Bob Geldof left to bandage their wounds. The moans of the masses come together in unison, a ghoulish gospel.

No more need for radio waves, turntable twists, amplified chaos.

This is the new music.

"The Insomniac Gods of Blackberry Court"
(Chew on This - Blood Bound Books - 2020)

the insomniac gods of blackberry court

He should have worn gloves.

His calloused toes shoved in ratty slippers, a frayed robe tightened around his torso, but nothing to protect his hands. Typical.

More garbage bags are piled in front of the curb across the street today. He's certain of it. The heap is growing. But no one's been home at 747 Blackberry Court for days. This, he can only assume. Technically, he's never seen those particular neighbors out and about. Certainly hasn't witnessed them stacking their Great Wall of Refuse. But he's still new to the neighborhood, and he's yet to meet everyone who lives in the curves of the cul-de-sac. Or meet anyone for that matter. He's a man who prefers to keep to himself.

But he can't help but indulge his curiosity.

When he rips open the first garbage bag, he isn't sure what he's looking at. It should be filled with obvious disposables—rotting table scraps, shredded premature offers to join the AARP, empty bags of Fritos. Something similar to what he keeps in his own trash.

It comes to him slowly.

He bites back a shriek, bullies it into a whimper.

The husks of rodents, birds, perhaps a stray domestic animal or two. Each poor creature marked with an imperfect little hole in its head, as if a drill-headed worm had burrowed through its skull and removed a hidden treasure, stolen its most intimate, bestial thoughts. And—mixed among the animals—there's something else. Something his mind cannot comprehend because oh God no nothing like this could ever happen in his neighborhood, no not on his watch.

Upon first moving in, the appearance of the house across the street should have been a red flag. More than just a severe lack of curb appeal, more than owners who have simply gone above and beyond the call of neglect. It's a boarded-up bungalow that's seen better days, its structure's stomach deprived of sustenance. Once-white paint gone grey. The front yard an army of weeds at ease. Cracks on the winding sidewalk so huge that any passersby would, without fail, break their mother's back.

He wishes he'd never crawled out of bed. Never opted to snoop. Not today. This isn't his day. Realistically, it's never been his day. But today, least of all.

The moon is eager, the sun stubborn. As if they'd had difficulty finding this little nook in the neighborhood, the friendly local police have finally arrived at Blackberry Court. To little fanfare. No nosey neighbors. No lookie-loos. No emergency, it seems. It's nothing, really. Only a pile of crudely detached genitalia, left to draw flies in a heat-baked Hefty bag. An everyday occurrence.

He thinks he's going to be sick. But also wants to avoid being sick. If he vomits, his throat will be sore for days. And if he didn't lose his lunch upon the initial sight of the bag's contents—which he's still proud about—surely he's safe now. Except he can't shake the sensation that something might have crawled out of the garbage without him seeing, then found a tiny open wound on his arm to slip into, and was now traveling beneath his skin. Something had to be causing that incessant itching.

The door to the police car slams shut, sounding off like a quick gunshot. It's at this moment that he realizes no familiar sounds penetrate the street. No crickets, no hum of nearby traffic, no anxious buzz of electricity. Were they ever there before? He can't be sure. Again, he's still new, hasn't had time to adjust to the neighborhood's normalcy. And he's not sure he wants to anymore.

The officer—a cornstalk of a woman, her hair pulled back so tight it resembles the top of a rubber mask—questions him, asks if this is his home. The one he is standing in.

He isn't sure how to reply to such a preposterous question. A nervous chuckle spills from his lips.

Damned cop tries to look inside, doesn't believe a word he's saying, asks if this has anything to do with the pharmacies. The ones that were robbed. Without making eye contact with the officer, he points to the curb lined with garbage, where he found what he found, his finger vibrating uncontrollably. Without responding, the officer struts to 747 Blackberry and rifles through the open bag, her only reaction an extended pause. Then she steps a few paces back. The cop doesn't call for backup, only approaches the front door to the old, dead house, her hand at her holster.

From across the street, he watches the officer's every move, his nerves popping and writhing. He doesn't understand why the cop was looking at him the way she was. What did she see? Just a dirty room behind him. Furniture he harbored no pride for. Nothing more, nothing less.

A knock. A call to open up. A moment of waiting that defies the laws of time.

The door flings open, and everything happens so fast that he isn't completely sure it's happening at all. The police officer drops her gun and begins a scream that's never allowed to come to fruition. A fleshy blur pours onto the porch, obscuring his view of the officer. It's like a windshield smeared with bug guts when the wipers aren't working effectively. And then the cop isn't there anymore, the space her body occupied now a swirl of dust.

Then something reaches out for the fallen gun.

A hook. A cane.

A hand.

Maybe none of those things. It isn't something quite that simple, and his mind is far too beyond the melting point to offer any clues or legitimate ideas.

The front door closes. Not a slam. A careful motion, as if anything more aggressive will demolish the house. Attract more un-needed attention.

He bites his lip hard. Draws blood. Despite his best judgment, he approaches the house at the end of the cul-de-sac, keeps a cautious distance. But still closer than he's ever been before.

Every flaw in the structure is visible now. Every speck of dirt more pronounced. Every sign of disrepair digging at his dread.

And the heat of the day grows more oppressive the closer he gets.

Baby steps. No rush. He decides that approaching the front door is out of the fucking question no fucking way, so he steers himself to the west side of the building, once protected by a chain link fence that has succumbed to the elements. No need to hop it. He merely peels the layer of fence away from its posts like a slice of deli meat from wax paper. It falls to the ground with an explosive clang and he grits his teeth.

The sole window on this side of the house is set a little too high to peek into without the help of tippy toes. But even then, he can't see a damned thing. The glass is blacked out from the inside with what looks to be electrical tape, perhaps cheap paint. He considers tossing a rock to break the window, but it's far too early to make a decision so desperate. He eyes the backyard. Maybe he'll have more luck there, the weight of that luck yet to be determined.

A few steps before reaching what may have once been a nice patio suitable for guests but has since become an aboveground cem-etery for long-deceased wildlife, he stops. Not of his own volition but because his face smacks into something. Hard. He loses sight of the sun for a few seconds, trades it for stars.

He curses, massages his nose, wipes away a few trickles of blood. After refocusing his vision, he glances around for a pole or a free-standing plate of glass. Nothing. He feels the air in front of him, expecting a shock. He inches slowly forward until his hand connects with something solid. An invisible mass.

Convinced something is there but he simply can't see it yet, he places his hand flat against warm nothingness, reaches up as far as he can and discovers no obvious end to the illusion. He starts to trail his hand horizontally across the invisible partition, then stops when he realizes there's a chance it could go on forever. He can't even begin to deal with that possibility. Too heavy to bear.

He counts his own breaths. It's all he can do to keep the final thread of his sanity from snapping. Decisions must be made. Just bail out now, forget he'd ever left the relative safety and comfort of home. Rewind the darkening day.

Or allow his curiosity to take control, no matter how high the risk.

Options running low. An unseen wall blocking one direction. A dark window preventing a peeping tom's view. The front door, well he's seen the trouble that could lead to.

And the horror of that indescribable hand.

He decides the other side of the property will prove more fruitful. As he passes the front of the house with a wide berth, a low rumble vibrates from a direction he can't immediately discern. The irritated yawn of a giant hibernating bear that has overslept. He stills himself. The sound is coming from underground, a few feet away from where he stands.

A cellar door to his left. This is where the sound is coming from. And the door isn't locked.

He steps past the door to test a theory, this time with his arm fully extended. A few paces in, he jams his finger. The illusion continues on this side as well.

He approaches the cellar door. He kneels and lifts it slowly, peers into the gel-thick murk. An entire hell's worth of heat whooshes out.

The vacuum of sound is even more prominent here. His ears plug. He squeezes his nose tight and pops the pressure out. He really should just return home, crawl back in bed, and watch multiple consecutive episodes of *Jeopardy* in an attempt to banish this feverish dream.

Two choices. He can shut the door, scurry away, and do his damnedest to forget any of this ever happened. Or he can feign heroism. Save the cop who should have been saving him. Or arresting him.

Bravery. Stupidity. Twin sides of the same coin.

Only one choice will allow him to continue living with himself. He dips his toes into black soup, and soon he is consumed.

His initial thought: Cellars are known for being decorated with cobwebs. It might even be considered a prerequisite.

Also stains. Dampness. Signs of rodent activity. Something to indicate it's a space a rational person doesn't want to spend more time in than necessary.

Key word: *rational.*

Once he locates a light source—via a string he initially believes *is* a cobweb—he discovers the cellar is immaculate, its floor clean enough to use as a plate and lick up after.

Empty. No shelving, no tools, no storage, no stockpiled canned goods, no forgotten heirlooms. All this space, used for nothing. A total waste.

The rumble subsides, then vanishes. Silence dominates now that he's fully underground. He's swimming on the deep end of the pool, the only sensation of wetness caused by being in a space that could double as a sauna.

Then he sees something he hadn't noticed before. Or maybe he at first believed it to be an illusion. His eyes still adjusting.

A corner.

He moves toward it, hesitating inches away from the turn, unsure he wants to know where the next pathway leads. There's still time to turn back. He should call the police a second time, state what he's seen (and not seen). But they'd never believe him. There would be more questions. And fewer answers.

Holding his breath, he makes the turn. Sweltering wind daggers his face. A long hallway stretches too far to see where it ends. So much space. Far too much to fit directly beneath the house.

He digs a nickel out of his robe's pocket and sets it on the ground, carefully balancing it on its edge. He lets go. The coin rolls forward, continues until he can no longer see it. Then the sound of the nickel wobbling, giving up, and plinking on its side.

Something flickers at the far end of the hallway. Where the heat resides.

Despite his best judgment, he creeps toward it. With each step the ruckus rises again, growing louder and louder into an almost-growl. And someone speaking. A language he doesn't recognize. His heart jackhammers.

Another corner at the end of the hall, which he reaches much more quickly than he assumed he would. The ground is no longer concrete but tightly packed dirt. He allows one half of his face to peek around the corner, his bowels pulling in the opposite direction.

Piles of bodies stacked neatly in rows against the sheetrock. Some animal. Some—despite his best efforts to deny it—human. Some…perhaps neither. He can't make sense of the shapes. All he can discern is the one familiar feature they share—an imperfect hole drilled into the skull. A single trickle of blood oozing from each hole, relieving the pressure.

And there are people down here. At the far side of the vast space, their presence lit by a fire pit, its putrid smoke traveling across the room, seeking escape with no success. The people see him but don't acknowledge him.

He squints.

Tweakers.

Of course it's tweakers. He knows their kind well. They've come out of hiding from the valley, set up their squat here in this hellish cellar. They're all pockmarks and soggy hair and gum rot and infected sores. Standard mutants born of meth. Their mouths masticate and their lips slurp on something unseen. They're hardly human anymore.

He chuckles at the thought. A sentiment that feels metaphorical but represents the supposed reality. One of the tweakers in particular has undergone changes far beyond the reaches of methamphetamines, stretched the definition of what could still be considered a man.

And, naturally, this is the one who approaches him.

Warmth and wetness soak his leg. He's frozen in place despite his mind's protests. Before him, an indescribable mass. Long, shivering tentacles, at the end of each of them a begrimed hand. At first, he believes the being before him is a beached octopus struggling to find its way back to water, then he sees a man at the brink of giving up hope but who finally learned his true purpose. A second later, both are as one. Despair and confidence, man and mollusk, in equal halves.

Before he can regain control of his legs in order to run, the tentacle hands surround him, hugging his shape. An act of camaraderie, not of aggression, or so it seems.

He moves to speak, to ask. No sound leaves his mouth.

But vocalized questions aren't necessary. A roar, a voice bringing answers enters his mind. A voice with the cadence of human speech, its timbre ancient, its history unknown.

Let me show you, it says. Let me help you remember.

When they first arrived at 747 Blackberry Court, the tweakers hadn't expected to learn something so deep, so affirming. It wasn't their purpose. But every action, regardless how great or small, creates side effects, ripples in the stillness.

They were unable to sleep no matter how much they craved it. Nothing worked. The methamphetamines had performed their duties far too efficiently. And they couldn't stop cooking fresh batches. Consuming their untainted product.

Despite the poor Wi-Fi so far down below, one in their group dove rabidly into research on her laptop, didn't stop for days until she discovered what they all believed they were truly searching for. All sources, whether reliable or not, claimed melatonin to be the natural key to curing their chronic insomnia. So they came out of their cave and stole as many bottles of the substance from as many different pharmacies in the vicinity as they could manage. Far more milligrams than they ever should have needed. A stockpile. But it still wasn't enough. They guzzled it like water on the driest of days. And it was only a diluted piece of the puzzle. They needed to learn more.

It didn't take long. Determination prevailed. After further digging, they discovered the most natural, raw form of melatonin.

The pineal gland.

The regulator of circadian rhythms.

No need for much discussion. A unanimous decision to move forward.

Their addiction, their ascension, began with rodents, which offered the most structurally complex of pineal glands. They drilled to the spot as best they could, then sucked them dry before the poor creatures had time to perish properly. The last squeals of life kept the bitter pill palatable. Each snack no bigger than a grain of rice, and at first it seemed like it might be sufficient. They dove into deep slumber. And the dreams that came to visit brought clarity. They no longer had to squat in secrecy, worried they'd be discovered and have to relocate. Because their new life was coming directly to them. Collectively they conjured delirium after delirium, each hallucinogenic vision forming something incomprehensible.

Eventually, they settled on the nothingness, the invisible shield that made their new home appear empty, unoccupied from the outside. An illusion that dreamt itself real.

They weren't sure how they'd done it. More agonizing hours of research resulted. Only one answer made even a semblance of sense. Despite dissension among the scientific community, the pineal gland was thought to be ripe with the chemical DMT, causing psychedelic wonder. And the tweakers had managed to tap into the purest supply, so they assumed. But there was a problem that spawned further challenges. The rodent population ran to its limits. The tweakers then moved on to avian subjects, then local pets, of which there were few. But none of these lasted long enough to satisfy.

So they had to assess their options. And do what it took to achieve their ultimate goal.

The postman solved their problem. Even the ghosts who inhabit abandoned homes sometimes still receive credit card offers and grocery store advertisements. But his sacrifice only offered a temporary solution.

The tweakers soon realized the hallucinations were spreading, their unconscious will the cause. The DMT they'd been consuming impacted the closest residents, covered their free will like a thick fog, making them believe all was well on Blackberry Court.

And they would never have the chance to realize just how gravely wrong they were.

The voice continues in his head.

My name was once that of a man's, and I've already lost the letters that formed it. But soon I'll learn my true name. It's calling to me, and I can almost hear it. And it seems yours is calling to you as well. Yes. Can't you hear it? You've been searching for your identity as well, haven't you?

He nods in response. To all of it. The tentacles molest him further. He wants to move to leave to never return. At the same time, he wants to stay. There's a sense of comfort here. Familiarity.

If only we'd learned sooner, the voice says. What we'd find once we discovered the wonders of the human pineal gland. You see, we've made contact with another world.

Aliens? he thinks.

No. Not quite, the voice replies, now an inhuman gurgle struggling to form English.

He shrugs. What then?

A laugh. A bellow. A pause.

We've found god.

Or—as it may seem—many gods. All of them true, truer than any deity that may have been forced upon you as a child. And they've granted me the honor of merging with one of them. Offering my flesh as a vessel. Soon I will be assimilated into the mass. And I will lead the rest of our group to glory. The gods have removed all carnal desire, much more than even the melatonin had managed. And they asked for a sacrifice to prove my worth, which I offered with no protest. Certain organs no longer serve a purpose. They are merely a distraction. I believe you were the one who found the final remnants of my former self. Out there. My manhood. Soon the others will follow, offering their own respective parts. When they're ready to ascend.

The door to the other side has opened but a crack. And we are working to make room for those who once ruled our world but have rested for far too long. They no longer need to sleep. Not ever again.

But they do need to dream.

And now that you're here, you're fortunate enough to take part in their grand design. Better still, you have a choice. First, you can offer us the sustenance we need, your own delicious pineal gland, and be relegated to a mere footnote in the history yet to be made. Or, you can join us. Let the dreams of the primeval rulers form flesh.

He considers. Decides.

There is one other option, the voice says. Or, more accurately, another possibility.

Is there? And what might that be?

That you've been here all along. With us. A crucial part of our quest for sleep. Except for the moments when you weren't. You were gone for quite a while. We thought we'd lost you, that you'd been caught.

But we're so pleased to see you've returned.

party
guests

1. Now Not Then

Call me Geoffrey. Why? Well, 'cause that's the name Pops gave me. Also called me "Idiot Genius." Don't like that name. Sometimes I have bad, bad dreams. Red dreams. Real dreams.

Got four people collected in my house today—well it's more of an apartment, well it's more of a four-hundred-square-foot studio. Program helped me get a job over at the Dollar Tree so I can pay rent, buy Flamin' Hot Cheetos, lick the orange-red fire spice off my fingers. Watch dirty movies on my cable TV I paid for myself. Momma can't tell me not to now. Been gone a long time.

Sally's my neighbor, real pretty with hair color like pineapple upside-down cake. Rosie worked at my group home, then she was my job coach, now she's at my house. She's kinda chocolate in the face like Oprah, but she don't make so much money. Brought me my old video games. *Grand Theft Auto. Dance Dance Revolution.*

Met Kim and Daryl out in the community at the Taco Bell by the bus stop on 10th Avenue. Kim's got a nice double bubble. Don't usually invite boys, Daryl had to come 'cause he's her son. Hope he likes game shows. All that's on right now. *Family Feud. Super Password. Press Your Luck.* Big bucks, no whammy. No *Kojak* cop shows. No *Mi Vida Loca* gang shows. Not supposed to watch those. Too many red thoughts. No *Legend of the Overfiend* anime tentacle shows. Too many scream dreams. Too many surprise sex dreams. Too many dig-dry scab dreams.

One. Two. Three. Four. Piled on my floor. Need to get the table set. Shiny silverware. No spots. No dirt. No filth. Wash hands. Scrub hands. Bleed raw hands. Corpse friends.

Doctor says I'm autistic, but I ain't never drawn no pictures.

Like to spray sweet cinnamon scent when it gets real stale in here. Got a case of twenty-four cans. Lasts me a month or so. Twenty dollars, real good deal. Don't like urine smell much. Don't like rot smell any better.

One thousand five hundred twenty-three jellybeans in the jar. No eating black. Like the green ones.

Done some awful things in my life. "Today's the Devil's Playground," like Rosie used to say. Rosie's non-verbal now. Gotta get some treats ready. Like to serve appetizers. Nipple hors d'oeuvres. Tongue filet mignon. Intestine pasta with cream skin sauce. Blender was a good Christmas gift last year. Thanks Gramma.

Quick snack of eyes like seedless grapes. Not Daryl though. Still want him to watch TV with me. Like Kim's silky hair. Want to scalp her like an Injun would. Want to make her my girlfriend. Had a girlfriend once. Had sex once. Name was Yolanda, but she met another boy named Travis last year. Not supposed to talk about past events though.

Geoffreybadverybad. Had another scary dream last night, is this it? Not sure I can control it or if I care either way. Time-Out Room no fun.

Preacher says my moral compass faces south.

Stupid cable's going out again. Don't like snow. Real stuff's not supposed to be here. Why's it on my TV now making scratchy itchy noise? Need to change channel. Watch Rambo gun shows. Like Chuck Norris kill shows. Can't find remote control. Square root of 13 is 3.605551275463.

2. BusStopGo

Diesel fuel's in the same risk group as asbestos and arsenic. Bus number 15 stops two blocks from my old group home. Number 15 stops every 15 minutes. Turned 15 years old in the group home. 2925 Zephyr Road. 2+9+2+5= 18. Was 18 when Pops died. Didn't care much. Pops was a cock-knuckle. Mad cow. Necrotizing fasciitis. Drowned in the kiddie pool after too much vodka. Elephantiasis of the bunghole. Asbestos, arsenic, diesel fuel. Who knows? Not me.

Don't live at 2925 Zephyr no more. 744 Navajo now. Twenty-one years old now. Independent now. Big chief of my teepee. Tickle-feather teepee. Scratchy-leather teepee. Don't want to see Mary or Jacobus or Mondo or Alice or Keiko or Terry or no one else from my group home. Maybe Rosie though. Always liked Rosie. Treated me like a person.

I remember once Rosie says, GEOFFREY YOU'RE SUCH A BIG, HARMLESS, SQUISHY TEDDY BEAR. IT'S HARD NOT TO LIKE YOU. WHEN YOU'RE BEHAVING APPROPRIATELY, THAT IS. Also used to say I was a client, a consumer. Only to other people at the group home and the transition program though. Average 'merican consumes 85.5 pounds of fat and oil every year, 141.6 pounds of caloric sweeteners. Got that beat by a big, big lot. Shows how much Rosie knows. Not just a person, I'm motherfucking Superman.

Right?

Right.

Jacobus always called Rosie *N* word. Not supposed to use *N* word. Jacobus got put in Time-Out Room for saying *N* word three times. Don't like Time-Out Room. Cold, white pillow walls. Try to avoid Time-Out Room. Dingy, spotty window. Can't open, can't break. Tempered glass. Why you so mad, glass? Maybe 'cause last Tuesday, Nando Gutierrez smeared hot, brown shit on the Time-Out Room window. Don't want to think about what's prob'ly in the crackies of the pillow walls. Ain't mine.

On the bus now. Passing by the Bank of 'merica. Where I take my paychecks. Mucky, creamy stucco walls. Number 15 stops across from AM/PM at 55th and Maple. Gonna get a chili dog. Two chili dogs with onion, one with no chili. Maybe some nachos. Extra jalapeños, please. Tongue on fire. Spicy icy. Thank you, come again.

Bus stop again now. In front of AM/PM. Gotta go back the way I came. Save one chili dog in my pocket for later. Homeless man creepin' on the side of AM/PM with his pit bull doggie. Ain't gettin' my snacks. Fuck that noise.

Transfer to Number 10. Take me to Dollar Tree. Dollar Tree on 10th Avenue. Number 10 stops on 10th. Start work at 10AM. Maybe get ten tacos at Taco Bell for ten dollars. Five for first break, five for second break. Five minute breaks. Steal five packs of Little Debbie Swiss Rolls. No stealing tapes. No stealing tapes.

Got my Sony Walkman. Listen to my Willie D *Controversy* tape. Like the song "Bald Headed Hoes." Good music. Good words. Yeah.

**"Something must be done about these citizens.
You ask what will I do to support my fellow man?
I'm proposing a bill to Capitol Hill
to kill all bald headed women at will."**

You tell 'em, Will. I'm a damn good rapper just like you.

On bus Number 10 now. Young girl sitting across from me. Not bald. Hair like a firecracker explosion and red, red, red like Ronald McDonald. Chicken nuggets with honey dip. Yum. Girl's face real friendly. No, real scary to Geoffrey. Eyes. Black, black circle eyes. Target eyes. Dagger rings in ears. Want to pull them. Stab them. Purple-People-Eater lips. Want to pinch them. Itch them. Funny look says she don't like my rapping though. So what? Want to know what her mushy mounds taste like. Want to know what her bad parts look like.

NO!

Rock back and forth, Geoffrey. Do the pigeon dance, Geoffrey. Just listen to the Willie D tape Geoffrey. Don't look at scary, cutie young girl, Geoffrey. Probably got three boyfriends anyways. Maybe use another one? Don't mind. Free for all kinds of naked, pumpy time. Hand gets tired. Rub, rub raw.

Young girl's shirt torn and light black and says, CHARGED G.B.H. Look it up later on public library computer. Thirty-minute limit. Leave ID at front desk. No hentai. No penetration. No nudes. LOL. Look up CHARGED G.B.H. Computer's got pictures of peacock pogo hair men. Music sample. Noise sample. Singing/screaming. Axing/playing. Beating/pounding. Computer says, "Grievous Bodily Harm." Like the idea. Scribble it, put it in my pocket. Probably good didn't mess with bus girl. Cotton candy prison witchy or somethin'.

Not Geoffrey's type. Someone better out there to love. Someone better to keep in my pocket.

3. Chalupa After Work

No damn tacos for Geoffrey today.

Motherfucker Fat Register Bee-yotch says, WE'RE OUT OF SOUR CREAM.

Asked for soft taco with no meat, add beans, no lettuce, extra cheese. Fat Fucko don't like that order, yells at me. Don't care. Just keep rapping. Waiting for Chalupa, waiting for Cinnamon Twists. Drinking Mountain Dew Code Red. Refills. Threefills.

Feather hair sexy lady comes in. Motorboat. Cunnilingus. Make Whoopee on *The Newlywed Game*. Little boy comes in too. Who cares? I ain't no Michael Jackson.

"The kid is not my son."

You tell 'em, Mikey. Don't want no stinkin' baby neither.

Lady and boy see Fatty being all mad, yelling at me. For taking too much fire sauce. Out of mild sauce. What do they expect?

Lady says, SO WHAT? LEAVE HIM ALONE! Then she whispers and says, "can't you see he's special?"

No high frequency loss on the audiogram test. Got ears like a barn owl. Hoot! Hoot!

Then Lady says to me, ARE YOU OKAY? YOU POOR THING. WHAT KIND OF AN AWFUL PERSON WOULD YELL AT A BIG SWEETHEART LIKE YOU? I OUGHT TO COMPLAIN TO HER MANAGER. She says that last part in a dragon voice while lookin' all mean over at Fatty.

Thought she was gonna pull an Auntie Betty and pinch my fat ass cheeks. Guess that'd be okay. As long as she don't jiggle my jellyrolls. Hate that. Scratch that.

I say, YEAH. I'M COOL. I'M GEOFFREY. YOU'RE PRETTY. PRETTY *NICE*.

Lady laughs. Maybe 'cause Geoffrey's smooth, maybe 'cause she gets the joke. Turns all blushy, then says, THANKS, GEOFFREY. I'M KIM AND THIS IS MY SON DARYL. CAN YOU SAY HI, DARYL?

Daryl hides under the booth and says, HI DARYL, then plays with dumb robot toy and says, DANGER WILL ROBINSON!

I say, WHY'S HE WEARING A SUIT? IS TODAY CHURCH DAY?

Kim sighs and says, WELL, GEOFFREY—DARYL'S SPECIAL. SORT OF LIKE YOU. HE HAS TOURETTE'S SYNDROME. DO YOU KNOW WHAT THAT IS?

I nod, I shrug. She don't notice. Just keeps yapping.

She says, IT'S NOTHING TO BE ASHAMED OF. HE JUST DOESN'T LIKE TO WEAR ANYTHING BUT BLUE SUITS. RE-FUSES, TO BE HONEST.

I say, OK FAIR ENOUGH.

Daryl says, BUTTERMILK! FUCKERMILK! maybe three times before momma shushes him.

She says, AND HE CURSES. A LOT. DO YOU NEED ANY HELP, GEOFFREY? A RIDE SOMEWHERE?

I say, MAYBE.

Eating my Chalupa. Finally. Damn. Kim and me talk about poli-tics. The government. Budget Christmas. *HA!* No we don't. Stupid. Don't watch the news. Too busy for the news. Gotta catch up on watching my *Street Sharks* tape. Stole it from Amvets. News bor-ing. Don't care about president. Geoffrey's got a life. Watch Charles Bronson *Death Wish 3* instead.

Wanna feel Kim's soft, soft silky follicles in my fingers. Wanna tear real quick like a Band-Aid. Wanna see the itty-bitty red drops on the bald, bald scalp. Take 15 hairs, mix and match the shades. Find the longest one. Put it in my pocket, save for later on Bus 15.

Invite Kim and Daryl to my house—well it's more of an apartment, well it's more of a four-hundred-square-foot studio. Can't come. *Damn!*

Daryl got homework, therapy, something. *Damn.* Give me a ride to my house anyways. Not far. Better than Bus 15. Stop by the AM/PM first. Get some Pop Rocks. Put the Pop Rocks in my Mountain Dew Code Red. *Boom!*

Drop me off. Take my phone number. Gonna answer their call on my Marvin the Martian phone.

"Oh, I can hardly wait till Hugo finds him. Hugo will be so thrilled, he will probably smother him with love."

You tell 'em, Marv. That Daffy Duck is a damn pussy.

Say they'll come by this weekend. Bring me lunch. I say, OK.

Wonder if it'll be an Ultimate Cheeseburger. Or a meatball sammich and Funyuns. Or a breakfast burrito. For lunch.

4. Did You Know?

Monday's the most popular day to kill yourself in the Netherlands. Today's Tuesday. Where the hell are the Netherlands? Is that near Disneyland? Fuck Mickey. No. Wait. Fuck Minnie. Little slut mouse. *Ha.*

'Proximately 178 seeds on a McDonald's Big Mac bun. 1+7+8=16. Was 16 when I had my first Shamrock Shake. Green ass tongue. Grimace is my homeboy.

Cockroach heads can live for days—no, weeks—without fucking bodies. Prob'ly true. Kicked one once. Hard. Body stayed there.

Head and two front legs kept on truckin'. Sucka had somewhere important to be.

Almonds are members of the peach family. Aw, nuts.

Ear, eye, gum, jaw, hip, arm, leg, toe, rib, lip. All human body parts. Three letters long. Three guests in my house right now. Daryl don't count.

Ketchup leaves the bottle at 25 miles per year. Red, red flow slow. Be 46 years old when ketchup's done spilling. 4 times 6 is 24. Three pretty ladies in my house. 24 minus 3 is 21. 21 years old now.

Thirty minutes up?

Screw you, library lady.

Be back next week anyways.

5. Won't You Be My Neighbor?

Little Miss Sally likes to sunbathe on the patio. Undoes her bikini top so sun can fill in white, white holes, make her back all dark like J. Lo. Sally from the block. Sally on the chopping block.

Thanksgiving turkey. Take your pick. Dark meat, please. *"Different flavor means different savor,"* like Gramma used to say. Mashed mashy taters with butter and gravy. Squirt, squirt, squirt in the sausage stuffing. Soft, squishy crescent rolls like baby legs. No green bean casserole. Tastes like hot, summer ass-crack.

Sometimes get out my X-Ray Specs, peek through the blinds. Sally's already naked, what's the point? Make-Believe Land. Funfunfun.

Gristle missle, blood flood, bone moan.

Give myself the Bad Touch. Gramma would slap my behind red, red, red if she knew about the Bad Touch. Gramma died last month. Can't say much now. Tombstone talk.

Sally's hair hangs off the side of her chair. Can't count from here. Blondes average about 140,000 strands on their heads. Means 383.561643836 hairs every day this year. Works for me. Keep me busy. *"Idle hands do Devil's work,"* like Rosie used to say. Can't help myself with the Bad Touch. Makes me miss Yolanda. Not really, though. Played Dr. Salami with Yolanda once. Just once. Real good time.

Told Yolanda, I DON'T WANT NO BABY CHILD.

Then gave her a little slap in the eye.

Yolanda's non-verbal. Don't know her opinion. Who cares? She can tell it to her PECS Book.

Guess everything worked out. No damn baby. No damn squirty, crying, stinky shit trashcan brat. Yolanda got her menstruation. Likes to eat her menstruation blood. Fresh or dry. Don't matter much. Bad, bad behavior. Not appropriate. Has to wear Ripstop Jumpsuit for a few days. Maybe stupid Travis will 'pregnate her later. Good luck, Travis. Gonna need it.

Can't make baby with Bad Touch Special Time. Phew!

Maybe Sally wants baby. Maybe not. Worth risk of nookies and cookies. Want to rub her double bubble. Wash hands clean. Brush teeth. Floss teeth. Dig in fingernails with scrub brush. No fingerprints on soft, soft skin. Lick, lick leather. Rub, rub raw. Shave with grain. Against grain. Grain matter, grey matter, brain matter. Teeny, tiny toilet-paper spots sop blood drops. Leave mustache to look like *Magnum, P.I.*

Sally goes and gets dressed. Go knock on her door five minutes later. Gotta let the woman have her time. Takes forever. Two forevers. Gotta look presentable for Geoffrey. Look across the street while waiting. What's goin' on? Man mowing lawn. Sweaty ass. Severed grass. Green, green blade make clean flesh flayed.

Sally opens door. Looks like a cupcake angel. Has a tank top that says LOVE PINK on it. Shirt has purple/white stripes, though. Don't get it.

Sally says, OH. HI GEOFFREY. HOW ARE YOU DOING TO-DAY?

I say, SALLY WHAT YOU THINK ABOUT BABIES?

She says, ARE YOU KIDDING? O.M.G. I'M TOO YOUNG TO THINK ABOUT THAT, GEOFFREY. I'LL WAIT UNTIL I'M MARRIED. I DON'T EVEN HAVE A STEADY BOYFRIEND RIGHT NOW.

I say, DAMN SHAME SALLY. STUPID MEN. THEY BLIND. YOU DON'T HAVE A HUSBAND IN FIVE YEARS GIVE ME A CALL. DON'T LIKE BABIES MUCH, THOUGH. JUST SAYIN'.

Sally laughs and says, OKAY, GEOFFREY. THAT'S, UH, SWEET OF YOU TO SAY. I'LL KEEP THAT IN MIND.

I say, YOU GOT MY NUMBER, RIGHT?

Sally nods. Then I say, CAN YOU COME OVER LATER, HELP ME WITH MY CHECKBOOK? GOT MY PAYCHECK TODAY. GOTTA PAY CABLE. BILLS MAKE ME CUCKOO FOR COCOA PUFFS.

She says, I THINK SO. I CAN TRY TO COME BY AFTER I GO TO THE GYM, IF THAT'S COOL.

Don't know who Gym is. Don't like him very much already.

6. Goodboy

One time, when I was ten or eleven or twelve, Pops gave my behind a real good swat. Found me playing with some neighbor's roadkill cat on side of the road. Cadaver. Cataver. Shitty kitty. Poked it with a dead, dead stick. Eyeball all gravy gooey. Peel back the furry layers like Velcro. Pops beat me real good. Never messed with no dead cats again. Too much trouble. Plenty of other dead things to play with anyways. Pops would be proud. *No he wouldn't.* Don't care though. Pops was a dicksicle. Sent me off to group home— 2925 Zephyr. Made me go to special school. Goldberg Education Center—67 67th Street. Coincidence? Hell no.

Teacher says to Pops, WELL, ACCORDING TO DR. SORI-AN, YOUR SON IS VERY GIFTED IN MANY WAYS. FOR IN-STANCE, AS YOU PROBABLY ALREADY KNOW, HE HAS THE ABILITY TO PERFORM A VARIETY OF COMPLICATED MATHEMATICAL EQUATIONS IN HIS HEAD. Then she whispers and says, "he also has severe autism and has been diagnosed as being e.d."

But I hear that shit. I say, NO WAY. I *HATE* REESE'S PIECES.

Teacher looks all shocked at my superpowers and says, GEOF-FREY, I'M NOT SURE WHAT YOU THINK YOU HEARD, BUT I'M MERELY TELLING YOUR FATHER THAT YOU'VE BEEN DIAGNOSED AS EMOTIONALLY DISTURBED. IT'S OKAY. IT'S NOTHING TO BE ASHAMED OF. Then she turns back to Pops and says, WE'LL PLACE HIM IN THE REGULAR ELEMEN-TARY CLASSROOMS FOR NOW. WHEN HE TURNS EIGH-TEEN HE CAN ENTER THE TRANSITION PROGRAM, AND THEN HE'LL GRADUATE WHEN HE TURNS TWENTY-ONE. WE'VE GOT SOME GREAT PROGRAMS TO HELP SOMEONE SPECIAL LIKE YOUR SON LEARN HOW TO FUNCTION AND ASSIMILATE INTO SOCIETY.

7. Come on Barbie Let's Go Party

Rosie says I shouldn't look at porno. Plastic women. Placid flaccid. Caught me once on computer when we were at my group home. Not my apartment. 2925 Zephyr. Not 744 Navajo.

Penetration shot. Porno clown lick, lick, licking all over naked nipples like a wannabe Gollum. Money shot. Monkeyshine. Midget ass.

I say, CAN YOU FIT A WATERMELON IN ONE OF THOSE?

Rosie says, NO GEOFFREY. THAT'S NOT APPROPRIATE.

Once, when Rosie was my job coach, we were at Dollar Tree. Working. Dusting shelves. Dust is made of dead skin cells, dried feces, desiccated corpses of dust mites, and tiny fibers of clothing. Stealing dusty 3 Musketeers. Love, love nougat.

I say, ROSIE DO THEY HAVE NUDIE MAGS HERE?

She says, NO GEOFFREY. THAT'S NOT APPROPRIATE.

Rosie didn't talk much, talks even less at my party. Kinda liked her. Never called her *N* word.

One time I said, ROSIE, THERE'S A PARTY IN MY PANTS. YOU'RE INVITED.

Rosie didn't get the joke, didn't work with me much for a little while. Tried to transfer to the adult program site. Threatened to take away my games. *Mortal Kombat. Paperboy.* Had to apologize. Later. Much later alligator.

Still good friends, me and Rosie. Like a decoration friend, not a roommate friend.

8. Gay Nando Commando

Nando Gutierrez tried to kiss me. No way, buddy. Don't play that sloppy-ass, man-tongue game. Never even let Yolanda kiss me. Hate lips. Hate spit.

I say, NANDO, CUT IT OUT.

Nando says, I'D LIKE MORE MILK, PLEASE.

Nando Gutierrez scream, scream, squawks like a Macaw. Don't like that much. Not the best guy to talk to. Don't take no for an answer. Oh well…

Nando Gutierrez eats Cap'n Crunch with no milk instead of doing his schoolwork. Task avoidance.

I say, NANDO, WHERE'S YOUR MILK?

Nando says, MORE EGGS, PLEASE.

I say, NANDO, I GOT A SIX PACK OF SURGE IN MY ROOM. TRADE YOU FOR YOUR DISCMAN.

Nando says, SURE, GEFFY.

Nando Gutierrez don't like to haggle much. Like that about him. Ain't invited to my party, though. Don't want boys there. Farmer John's Sausage Fest. Nando can stay at home and watch *The Electric Company* for all I care.

Nando Gutierrez run, run, runs like a wing-flapping fool. Jacobus or Keiko laughed about something else, made Nando have a behavior. Nando's about as giant as a black rhinoceros. Good luck getting Nando in prone position. Rhino horns are made of keratin, a fibrous protein that forms the structure of hair. Harder to count than pretty lady hair though. Or easier? Don't know.

Glad I'm high functioning. Glad I'm independent. Lucky duck.

I say, NANDO, YOU AIN'T A BIRD.

Nando stops. Seems kinda normal. Just for a second.

9. Little Buddy

Daryl's on my big comfy recliner. Suit could use a wash. Lookin' a little lousy. Lookin' like a tiny business elf that just got fired and sauced and picked a scrap with a fake, orange-fingernailed, toothless ho.

He says, WHERE'S MY MOM AT?

I say, SHE'LL BE RIGHT BACK. JUST WENT TO VONS TO GET GRAPE JUICE OR SOMETHING.

Daryl says, BUTTERMILK PANCAKES! LICK A DICK! GEOF-FREY, MY HANDS HURT.

I say, DON'T WORRY ABOUT IT DARYL. WANNA WATCH *DOUBLE DARE*? IT'S A MARATHON.

Super, sloppy, oozy slime. Creamy grime. Ice-cream time.

10. †††

Had another scary dream last night, is this still it?

Shitshitshit. Spray my cinnamon cans all over the apartment. Last can. Empty can. Need to buy more. Better still be on sale. Smells real bad. Like someone dumped in here, then ate it, then puked it all up, then spooged on top of it. Copper smell. Salty bleach smell. Wonder why? Had a dream last night. Broke into a foxy, fucky girl's house. Surprise sex dream.

Red dream.

Kill dream.

Skin dream.

Don't know if I could control myself if it was a real dream.

"The Heretic Lambs"
(San Diego Horror Professionals: Volume 3 - Grand Mal Press - 2017)"

the
heretic
lambs

They're not really ghosts, they say. *They're just innocent children, not demons, for the love of God,* they say. *They only want candy…where's the harm in that?* they say.

They say, they say, they say. Who are "they" anyway? Squawk, squawk, squawk. All the chicken talk in the world won't save the children now. Besides, they were stolen and replaced long ago. Something else inhabits their tiny bodies now. Something from beyond. Something from below.

This Elsa knows.

The children, the voices, they all think they have her fooled, but Elsa Stone, widow of THE Roger Stone, mother of no rotten stinking brat—stands for no funny business. Not on the other glorious 364 days of the year, and certainly not on this—the unholiest of unholy days. She can see behind the masks the children wear and there are gaping holes where there should be souls. Black matter hovering behind cheap latex. No substance fattening their fidgety flesh.

Except they are not children, have not been for God knows how long. Perhaps they have always been fiends incarnate, waiting in the shadows for autumn to arrive and set its pretty leaves aflame.

Rotten stinking things want rotten gooey candy for their rotten rank teeth. And, oh, they'll have some. All they want. They'll come to Elsa's house and gobble up their sugary goodness. And they'll enjoy it, savor it when they get home and realize it's their last, when they understand they won't live long enough for it to be shat out a day or two later. When they choke on chocolate, make nooses out of nougat. When their fluids shift and their throats constrict and their eyes roll back to fish belly white and they seizure while mumbling in unknown tongues, they'll have Elsa Stone to thank. They'll remember her, even in death. Even when their half-grown bodies are nothing but premature husks crumbling under the weight of untended soil, when their heads are abandoned projects for blind, destitute grubs.

The devil's children, all of them. They're coming tonight, to celebrate their father's favorite day. Armed with pillowcases and glow sticks and fictitious innocence, all in the name of collecting more and more of the devil's delicious drugs. But Elsa's ready. She knows what truly burns behind those dark, mischievous eyes.

Rotten stinking pagans. All of them. How dare they question her truth? How dare they question the glory of God and celebrate a day that mocks the death and the rising of his one true son? Extol a dark night that spits in the face of the Almighty. Carving pumpkins into false idols, extracting their guts—

"...and you will suffer severe sickness, a disease of your bowels, until your bowels come out because of the sickness, day by day..."

Shoving sugar down their gullets rather than savoring the sweet body of Christ. Calling it blasphemy is letting them off easy. Halloween. A Hollow Win.

Elsa first noticed the children last year, this year, next year. She can't quite remember. After Roger passed. Before he was buried or cremated or wasn't. After the doctor's words. After the Lewy bodies. Gooey bodies. The demoniac brats had the nerve to come to her house. After dark. Asking for *candy* of all things. As if she would even think to have such a terrible thing in her home! She had screamed and slammed her door in their rotten faces. But she is no longer afraid. They'll get their candy this year, next year, last year. The evil brats will pay on their dirty holiday.

Days ago, minutes ago, perhaps tomorrow, Elsa sharpens two tiny blades, scrapes them back and forth. The sound makes the nerves in her teeth tingle, her inner ear tickle. She chops the fine powder. Crushes the glass, tears her tissue paper skin. Tiny red drops seep through the pores in her fingers, like sweat dipped in food coloring. She does not feel the sting. The granules dig deep into the crevices of her prints. She is numb, inside and out.

And now—the voices call to her again.

Are you certain, Elsa? they say. *Do you think you can go through with it?*

She wants to be certain. With God deep inside her, she believes she can win this battle, but the war will continue to be waged long after her soul has left her body and her body has become one with the Earth. Who will God appoint to win the war?

She is realistic. She knows praying only helps so much, that she bows her head and bends her knees and whispers to the Holy Spirit more to soothe her own emotional wellbeing than for actualization. God demands action. He does not coddle. He demands His soldiers to prove their worth. And she is more than worthy. She has always known this. She has never known this.

She wonders where the demons have come from. No—not Hell. Not exactly. Hell is only a ruse created to throw the righteous off the devil's scent. Hell is a hidden place on Earth, but God will soon expose it and the devil will dance in his birthday suit, his shriveled, burn-scarred balls bared to the world. Earth's own Hell will be razed and erased from the history books.

Have the devil's children only come to torment her, to steal her soul, to suck the breath from her lips and pass it on to Lucifer, their one and only king, with a sweet puckering kiss? She cannot allow that to happen.

What if they seek more souls beyond just hers?

Of course they do, they say.

What if Halloween is just the beginning?

Of course it is. It is the beginning as it is the ending.

What if they want the world?

They do want the world.

But they cannot have it.

That's precisely why you must stop them first.

Yes. The downfall of mankind must be thwarted at Elsa Stone's doorstep.

Elsa cannot just sit idly by and let the devil win. And, oh, what a trick he has pulled, using the guises of children. A feint to fool the weak and make them even more susceptible to the devil's lies. It is exactly like in the blasphemous movies she boycotted in 1973 and 1976 and 1984, when she and the righteous few banded together to purify a world that wanted nothing but wickedness served to them on the silver screen, to defeat those who wished to sell evil to mal-leable minds. And to use children as their vessel…the sickest, cruel-est joke of all. Both in film and in reality.

Both are the same, just different forms of reality.

And these are not children. Elsa must remember this.

Remember what?

The evil—it has now returned. Another year, another rotten holiday. The mold has been altered ever so slightly this time around—so many hidden hormones in processed foods leading to premature puberty these days. Menses at age 8. Bush, beard, and B.O. before First Communion. Needing their own precious phones when they have nothing of substance to discuss, brand new devices to communicate their nonsense. Preteens pretending to be heroes and whores, and some even finding success in their make believe worlds.

But! If the devil is anything, he is consistent. Predictable in his unpredictability. His tools come prepackaged with the promise of progress. He can be beaten. The devil will choke on his hubris.

The sun is sinking. Slowly. Elsa itches. Scratches. Paces like a caged panther. Peers through the dusty drapes and the stained, smeared windows and watches the last pure rays of precious sunlight vanish. A gust of wind lifts a patch of orange leaves, creating a colorful cloak that dances in mid-air. Elsa wonders if she will ever see the sun again after tonight. She wonders if she will remember what it looks like if it never returns. She wonders if this is her final chance to burn the beautiful sun into her brain. The darkness has great power. It is a thick, black tar that threatens to engulf her frail body and remove it from this world as if it never existed. It is an anvil atop her very soul. A tempting embrace. A lascivious lover.

Elsa hears singing, playful screeching in the distance. The festivities have begun. It is only a matter of time. But she is ready. Almost ready. Not nearly ready. Not even close.

She has begrudgingly decorated the outside of her home to attract the little ones. Such simple work for simple beings. Like smearing peanut butter on a rat trap. Cutesy witchies and baby ghosties and googly skullsies taped to her windows and speared into her lawn. Symbols of Pagan evil designed to corrupt the once-innocent youth. The false idols make Elsa's gorge rise. To defeat the devil, she must first become one with the devil. She must become a faux-facsimile of a department store, selling what the masses desire. She must fool the devil into thinking she is his for all eternity. But she will be purified of her rotten peccant behavior. God always forgives the righteous. His soldiers are impervious to ultimate sin.

She has sprinkled a thin trail of salt across the threshold of her front door. The demon children cannot enter. They must not cross over into her holy space. Her efforts transcend mere superstition.

But she will risk stretching her arms beyond the threshold to hand them candy. As much as their pasty hands can shove into their fat little faces. She will pass it to them gently while wearing a saccharine smile. Sweets to the sweet.

The phone rings. Elsa hears it, but does not hear it. The ringing becomes an endless droning loop.

The answering machine speaks to her like an estranged friend. She tunes it out. The voice is a *Peanuts* adult.

"Good evening Mrs. Stone…Alice from Med-Check…reminder to take…Dr. Chatsworth…recommending 10mg…donepezil…please call to confirm…"

Click.

She will get to it later. To what? To something. For now she must remain focused. Distractions are the devil's tactics. He tries to speak to her through the masked voices of the familiar. He wants her to go ask Alice. To toss the pills or toss them back? Idle minds control idle hands in the devil's rotten playground.

Elsa thinks back to the important preparations she made yesterday, next week, this morning:

She slides the delicate skin of her fingers and hands into a pair of blue rubber gloves. They are surgically sterile, tight like a constrictor's coils. She winces at the pain deep in her joints, almost faints from the throbbing in her cartilage. She breathes deep. She understands those who perform heroic deeds must sometimes suffer. But she must show her mettle, must wield her mighty sword for God.

Her right hand trembles uncontrollably. Pins and needles attack her legs. She shuts her eyes, bites her lip softly. It takes minutes, seconds, hours, but the tremors eventually cease.

She sits at one end of a long and lonely dining table, where meals only meant for one have been served for so long. A sole candelabrum, decorated with long-abandoned cobwebs, sits dead center, its ancient candles burned to the bottoms of their wicks, the hardened wax in a permanent menacing drip. Blades and bottles and candy are meticulously stacked in front of her like a model of a planned city. She takes a blade from one stack—carefully, so as not to disturb the sleeping city, and tenderly cuts a near perfect circle from the bottom of a bite-sized peanut butter cup. She opens a package of 20 mm lithium coin batteries, pushes one up into the soft peanut butter center, dabs some superglue on the chocolate bottom, and sets it back in place. She slides the peanut butter cup back into its crinkly package, dabs a drop or two of glue and applies slight pressure. It is almost seamless, as if human hands have never touched it. She repeats the ritual again and again. She is a one-woman assembly line.

She pinches a piece of wax bottle candy, slices the tip off like a veteran *mohel* performing *brit milah*, lets the psychedelic syrup trickle out into a disposable paper bowl. The feral cats that frequent her yard can lick it up later, long after her deed has been done. She takes a syringe filled with antifreeze, injects the green liquid into the open slit in the wax. The color is vivid, even more attractive than the original syrup. The children will love it, consume it, gorge themselves on it. She glues the tip back on. Repackages. Cuts. Drains. Injects. Glues. Repeats.

She opens a package of Pixie Stix, empties half the sugary powder from each stick into a Ziploc bag. She tweezes a tiny funnel between her fingers and barely fits it into the opening of the first stick, taking care not to tear the paper in the slightest. She wants to leave no trace of interference. She pours in 500 milligrams of arsenic trioxide, closes the opening, shakes it lightly but firmly. She wants to be sure. Has to be sure.

She opens a box of rock candy crystal, white as ice. She tosses a few shards of glass into the box, bits no bigger than her pinky nail, and some miniscule granules for good measure.

She unwraps a caramel apple dipped in chopped nuts. It reminds her of autumn carnivals from her childhood, of good, wholesome fun unravaged by the heresy of Halloween. With a brand new blade she slices off a small square of caramel shell. She takes a second blade, sharp and dipped carefully in strychnine, slides it into the side of the apple, pushes it in deeper with the first blade. The apple may as well have been a stick of butter. She holds it up to the light for inspection, to ensure no edges of the blade show, then spreads glue on the caramel and presses it back into place. She leaves no trace. The tainted apple is a work of art.

And now:

She feels like she has been going about her preparations for hours, but that cannot be possible. When was the last time she slept? She cannot remember. It may have been since yesterday, today, tomorrow.

You can't do this, Mother, the voice of her daughter would have said, if she had ever birthed a rotten stinking brat. She is not quite

certain, but she has good reason to believe a daughter never existed. Not in Elsa's womb, nor abloom, nor resting in a tomb. *There
will be consequences. Forgiveness is fickle. Forgiveness only exists in fair weather.*

The phone rings again. Elsa grabs a large, rusty pair of scissors
and snips the line, then pulls the answering machine's cord, swings
the machine overhead, lets loose a war cry, and throws the machine
across the room as hard as she can, as if it makes a difference at
that point.

Elsa's heart beats faster than it should. Her soul was almost
in the devil's grip, but she remains in control. She must return to
God's blessed work.

She knows the children will be coming soon. Those who wish
to stop her. Those she must try to stop before they proceed to poison the next home and the next and the next. She knows there is
only a slim chance they will taste her tampered treats right away,
that their terror might be thwarted before they have a chance to
carry on with the devil's duties. The souls she saves will be those
of the future, souls that will never be able to thank her because
she knows it is only a matter of time before she is snuggled in
Heaven's loving embrace. Elsa has resigned herself to this fact.
She can only do so much. She is just one ancient woman in God's
great army, far from mobile enough to go door to door and warn
her neighbors, much less the world. She must do what she can in
the here and now and pray to the Lord the souls next in line after
hers will be spared.

She is willing to sacrifice hers if need be. God will understand.
He will have a place in Heaven reserved for her. A warm soft pillow that some call a cloud. A halo for her honor. Wings for her
wholeheartedness.

Elsa thinks she feels pressure on her left shoulder, a tickling in her ear. She believes the floorboards are creaking softly behind her. Cold, humid air surrounds her.

"Roger, darling. Are you still here? The monsters are on their way. Do you hear them? Will you tell them to go away, please? It's not too late to cancel Halloween. I don't think I can handle the devil's devotees today. I'm very tired."

Of course you can handle them, dear. They're only children. Or—well, you know what I mean.

Elsa's jaw droops. A tiny trickle of drool slides out the corner of her lips. She wonders why Roger sounds…different today. His voice seems wrong. Less masculine. It must be the wine. Too much wine makes him womanly. She places her right hand to her left shoulder, expecting to link her fingers with Roger's, but he is gone now. He has always been gone. She hopes he will bring her some of the wine he is having. Or anything at all. Husbands should never hoard wine when their wives are parched. Her tongue feels coated in fur, but her bottom is glued to the chair, her feet to the floor.

She whispers to Roger even though she knows deep down he was never there. "Yes, of course. I will remain strong."

She places her doctored candies in a swing-handled wicker basket. Gently, as if they are eggs containing precious golden yolks. She must get up soon. They are approaching. Soon she will be forced by the will of God.

She thinks of the misguided years of her youth, so many decades ago, when she wore silly scary costumes as well. She succumbed to peer pressure then, had her fill of rotten tooth-decaying candy. More than her share of pretty little rainbow pills. But never again.

The difference between Elsa and the other children, both then and now: Elsa is not evil. She has remained pure and free from the grip of Pagan gods.

The chattering of the children comes closer. They are next door, perhaps two houses down at the most. Elsa's hearing has always been sharp, a tool gifted to her at birth from God. She suspects she will hear whispers throughout the graveyard one day. And she will call back to them, warning them to tread lightly over the soil, over the souls that deserve eternal rest.

Elsa breathes deeply, as much as her withering lungs can take. She is ready. She must be ready. She is not ready.

But she has no choice. Her hands, her actions, her intents all belong to God now.

Muffled giggles and maniacal shrieking vibrate the front door. They are here now. They have always been here. Within the walls, inside the mind, inseparable from the flesh.

A ring, a knock. Elsa is not sure which. Such similar sounds.

She stands up, her spine feeling as if it might snap, her femur feeling as if it might turn to dust. She picks up her basket and shuffles toward the door. But there is no door. In front of her there is only pure, flat white. A pounding, a ringing comes from the direction of what was once the door. It grows louder. Elsa's brain pulsates. She feels dizzy, nearly drops the basket of goodies. She slides closer toward the white, thinks it must be Heaven calling her home. She has already fulfilled her duty and the Lord will take it from here. Another soldier sent from above will carry her burden. She is exempt from blame. She feels relieved. She can finally rest.

But then she squints and sees the outline of the door once again. It was not there seconds ago, but it has rematerialized. She reaches toward it. Slowly. She is uncertain if she wants to see the monsters waiting behind it. But she must follow through. She must be brave. The world is counting on her.

Something shifts near her feet. Something white, mindless, and wriggling. Little lords of carrion. Maggots peppered across the threshold like someone's leftover steamed rice gone to waste.

No.

She will not be the devil's fool. She must confront his wicked warriors at her door. They have come for her soul, but they cannot have it. They have no clue who they are up against. She shuts her eyes tight until they throb, until her eyelids are crushed and sore. She opens them, and the larvae are magically gone. Only her trail of salt remains.

Elsa reaches for the doorknob. Her hand swats at the air in slow motion, as if the flesh from her fingers cannot keep up with her tired old bones. The knob is miles away, inches away, galaxies away. The knocking, the chanting, the ringing grows louder and quicker. She shuffles forward and her hand connects with cool brass. She twists the knob for a lifetime.

The brisk night breeze enters Elsa's home. She welcomes it, beckons it, breathes it in. She is not a tall woman—though she has always wished she were, and she does not need to look down far to face her adversaries. She almost drops her basket. She clutches it before it can slip away and crash to the floor, before her glorious work becomes squandered.

The children stand before her:

A rotten stinking corpse, faux flesh falling from its face. A drooping boar's head, dark button eyes, greasy black hair draped over its ears. A chubby clown, its grin stretched from temple to temple, its melting pale makeup oozing down its face, its teeth black with plaque and sharp as a shark's, its rainbowed attire smeared with feces, graveyard dirt, perhaps both. A reaper, its hood filled with cold, empty blackness, tiny red eyes burning from the back, its scythe poised for battle.

They chant for tricks or treats, but little do they know that what Elsa offers covers both requests. She sees behind their masks, their true faces. She always has.

Lights explode behind the creature children. Elsa winces like a vampire witnessing its first sun. Near the flashing lights, she thinks sees Laurie Calvert from church and Rosie Wilkes—Reverend Isaac's accountant. Yes. It *is* them. The young women clutch cameras. They snap photos like crazed paparazzi.

For a moment she experiences what she once knew as clarity, in a former life so long ago that was barely hers, perhaps never truly was hers. An Elsa who no longer exists, an Elsa who may have only been a dark thought dreamed by the Elsa breathing on this Halloween night. She sees children below her, their pudgy faces yearning for sweets, androgynous eyes awaiting instruction, soft, feathery hair begging to be tousled.

But then these images vanish. The lights flash again, lightning from the devil's fingertips. The faces of the false innocents fade. They are replaced with grinning, horrid skulls.

It's time, Elsa, the voices say.

The demons hold out their pillowcases, their plastic pumpkins, their paper sacks. They sing like rotten baby angels.

Please don't, Elsa, they say.

Elsa stares forward. Her face is pure poker. She reaches down into her basket, fondles the fate of the children with her fingers. The demons will be fairly rewarded for their undying efforts.

And so will she.

i
am the
taxidermist

The head of Johnny Thunders hanging on the wall, an inch above the door, attached to a cedar mount lined with rusted studs. His expression preserved as if just finishing a particularly stellar set at CBGB, his eyes rolled back in a heroin stare.

This was the first thing David Maher noticed upon passing through the unmarked doorway and entering the warehouse. He'd dragged himself to a shit part of town, the absolute toilet. The gallery wasn't officially open yet. He'd been invited to a special viewing, a party of one, save for the host. Jimmy Gilman. The famed taxidermist.

"You like that, huh?" Jimmy said, nodding toward the disembodied head. "He was my first. I hadn't, uh…mastered my craft at that point. And didn't have all the proper instruments yet."

David opened his mouth to question if his host had made an intentional music pun, but decided against it. Jimmy didn't read as being intellectually clever enough to have any success with subtle humor.

The taxidermist fidgeted with his hair, a single, thick dreadlock that had matted into a beaver's tail down his back. His mouth full of busted piano keys. A tattered Discharge t-shirt hung from his slight torso, the threads threatening to snap and leave him topless, exposing his grime-covered stick-and-poke tattoos. He stank of patchouli oil and fried tofu.

David reached toward the Johnny Thunders display, but Jimmy shook his head. No touching.

"He still looks alive," David said. "Aside from not having a body, that is."

"True heroes never die. Hell, he can even hum a few bars of 'Born to Lose' if you ask nicely."

David eyed Jimmy, expected his host to crack a smile, spit out a laugh. He didn't. The game already growing stale.

"Come on, there's so much more to see." Jimmy beckoned David with his entire hand and led him forward into the heart of the gallery. The lights dimmed to twilight, the temperature two degrees shy of an igloo. Music drifted from unseen speakers. Something familiar yet foreign. Adolescents "Kids of the Black Hole." A cover version. And not a very good one. The Agnew brothers' guitars replaced by synthesizers, the lyrics sung in Farsi.

They strolled through reproductions of icons from every era and subgenre of punk imaginable, from death rock and power violence to ska-core and crossover. All international regions represented, a collection of unsung heroes frozen in time. Some who had passed in their prime, others reworked to appear as if they'd been forever trapped in relative youth. Members of bands David had grown up listening to, some he'd been lucky enough to share a stage with, and even a few he'd never heard of. Newer bands, he guessed. Punk hadn't died when he'd moved on. It had kept evolving and raging, leaving him covered in dust. Despite his teenage convictions to never surrender, never give in, he'd traded his combat boots and studded jean jacket for dress shoes and a matching tie before age thirty. Almost two decades had passed since then, and he'd grown old. Irrelevant.

"Check these ones out," Jimmy said. "They're a lot less, uh… leathery than Mr. Thunders."

And so the narrated tour began.

First came Siouxsie Sioux (*"Millions of midnight creatures wept the night she faded into the fog,"* Jimmy said), then Wattie Buchan (*"Everyone thought it would be a heart attack that did him in, but he ended up just falling down some stairs."*), then next was Ian Mackaye (*"He still doesn't smoke, doesn't drink, doesn't fuck—doesn't do much of anything anymore, to be honest."*), followed by Pig Champion (*"This one was a real pain to stuff."*), and on to Justin Pearson (*"Choked on one of his own snot rockets. Can you believe it?"*), and finally Sakevi Yokoyama (*"My business partner never came back from Japan after securing this one and shipping it to me. Don't ever cross the Yakuza. Holy shit. Just sayin'."*). This was only the first room. No organization. No rules.

"You wanna drink?" Jimmy asked. David nodded, and his host hobbled off to the far end of the warehouse.

What David really wanted—no, *needed*—was a coffee, but the taxes on beans had skyrocketed to an unaffordable level following Martin Shkreli's short-lived presidency. He'd have to take what he could get, and hopefully it had a decent kick, hold the side effects.

Impossible and paranoia-driven as it was for the sensation to burrow into his mind, David felt the taxidermied husks watching him, their glassy eyes judging him for selling his soul without putting up so much as a squeal of protest. A steady salary and an impressive pension had been all it took to turn in his membership. So few punks did the distance, truly lived the lifestyle and set an example for the next generation, so why the hell should he be singled out among the thousands of others who had made similar choices? Adulthood had brought new priorities, fresh challenges.

As much as he hated to admit it, he missed his records, sold long before they were worth anything beyond sentimentality. After the Great Sonic Cleansing of 2033, vinyl had become so rare in the remaining states that he'd be lucky if he could spot an album in a museum, protected by multiple armed guards. Even then it'd be something vapid like Bon Jovi or Culture Club rather than Christian Death or The Dicks. He missed his homemade mix tapes as well, each carefully crafted to provide the perfect soundtrack to a day of skateboarding or a night of hard partying. They were likely taking up space in a landfill now. More than anything, though, he missed being on stage, microphone clutched in hand, sharing sweat with the crowd that screamed along to his lyrics with more conviction than he could have ever mustered.

He closed his eyes, ran his hands across his fresh buzz cut. Things change, forever in flux. He couldn't recall the precise moment when he'd accepted that notion as law. Time had claimed him as its slave.

A few moments passed, and Jimmy returned. He handed David a mason jar half filled with a piss-colored liquid. David sniffed it, made sure.

"I think you'll dig this," Jimmy said. "It's hard stuff. Swallow, don't savor."

David nodded, funneled the drink down his gullet. A cleansing, flavorless burn that temporarily blinded him. He hacked uncontrollably, half-expecting a lung to detach and fly out of his mouth.

"Yep," he said, wiping his lips, "that's what I was hoping for."

Jimmy laughed. "Killer stuff, huh?"

David looked at his empty jar, then set it down on a nearby table. He eyed Jimmy. "You're not joining me?"

"Nope. I quit a few months ago. And then a few weeks ago. And then again a few days ago. Hey, I'm tryin' at least. Success isn't always the point."

David nodded. Been there, failed that. "So why taxidermy? And be real with me. I scanned an interview with you in some chipzine a while ago called…shit, what was it called?"

"*Do Punks Dream of Black Light Sheep*?"

"Yeah, that's it. Look, I know a bullshitter when I see one because I'm king of the bullshitters. You don't seem like the type to take on a hobby like this. Home brewing, maybe, but stuffing empty corpses? Come on…what's your real motivation here? And don't tell me it's only 'art,' because that's just piling new crap on top of the old crap."

Jimmy's face went fox. "Hey, let's get this straight. I didn't invite you here for an interrogation."

David's teeth tingled, as if his beverage had penetrated the enamel and was now wetting the nerves. "Sorry. I didn't mean to—"

Jimmy slapped him on the back, laughing. "Damn. Lighten up, man. I'm just fucking with you."

David grunted. "Okay, well why *did* you bring me here, then? I can only assume it's because of my past and—"

"Bingo. I find out Davey Kross from The Copulation Police lives in my town and I'm not going to offer him a sneak preview of my life's work? Yeah, right. A no-brainer."

"I haven't thought about those days in a really, really long time." A lie masked as humility.

"Dude, I saw you guys in Bakersfield back in, like, 2029. One of my first shows ever. I was just a wee little shit. Man, it was killer. Massive. I lost a tooth at that gig. Reunion tour, but still…"

Bakersfield. Former home base for The Copulation Police. Nothing left of the city now. Or the entire state of California. Not for several years. The Nostradamus-worshipping crackpots had been right after all. Nevada had become a hotspot of oceanfront properties.

"So you're a true diehard fan, I guess."

"Fuck yeah I am. I honestly didn't think you'd come when I sent the invite." Jimmy turned away, motioned to David to leave the first room. "Glad you did, though."

David couldn't take his eyes off the displays as they entered the next room. So many legends lost to time, preserved here for posterity. Jayne County. Keith Morris. Don Bolles. Jerry Only. Kathleen Hanna. Screaming Mad George. The list went on. The ultimate who's who of punk rock history. The loved and the hated and those in between.

"Pretty good collection, huh?" Jimmy nudged David with his elbow. "Still missing one or two special surprises to make it perfect, but I'm almost done. I'll be ready just in time for the official opening."

"Hey, so I'm not trying to be rude or anything," David said. "This really is pretty incredible, but…"

"Aw, man. Always a 'but,' isn't there?"

"…but what's the point? *Is* there a point?"

Jimmy beamed, a joker's grin. "Can't keep any secrets from you, huh? Okay, you know what? Screw it. I'll tell you everything. Might as well. Time bomb's tickin', and at this point I've got nothing to lose."

David's head felt like a fish tank that hadn't been cleaned in weeks. He'd been overworked lately, overstressed. Too much action. And too much tedious paperwork. Maybe time to get on the wagon and stay there. He did his best to shake off the sensation, promised himself a nice hot bath tonight, followed by a solid seven hours of sleep mode. Turn off his brain and take no calls.

"All right," Jimmy said, "so you're going to have to suspend your disbelief a little bit, but just trust me, dude."

"Sure. Trust."

"So all of the taxidermy stuff. It's totally legit. Took a lot of trial and error to get it right. Like, years and years. I learned a lot from the old guard. They were working on this project even before I joined up. I don't know if you know this, but human skin doesn't preserve as well as other animals."

"Sure. Pretty sure I've scanned that somewhere before."

Jimmy's beady eyes somehow became beadier. His voice dropped to a whisper, as if someone might be eavesdropping from the next room. Recording. Taking notes. "The truth is…and keep this between you and me, but not all of these punks I've got here are the real deal. I mean, they're real people. For sure. Just not all of them are the people you think they are. Not technically. Some of them are really solid lookalikes."

"Hm. Okay. Makes sense. I thought something was a little off. Some of these date back to the 70s. You weren't even born then."

"Shit, man, I wasn't even sperm in my daddy's donger until the turn of the century made it well into its teens. But here's the thing—the bodies—the shells, they might not all be authentic, but the souls are. One-hundred percent bona fide. Transferred and secured into their forever homes."

"Wait—what? Souls? I'm not sure I follow."

"Okay, so Mick—my partner. The guy I said never made it back from Japan? Anyway, he figured out a way to extract and preserve the essence of each person's…I don't know…raw talent I guess? Some assholes still think punk's just a bunch of noise, but I've got a firm finger for them and they know where they can stick it." Jimmy cackled, a little too long for David's comfort. It made his head throb even harder.

David stared at Jimmy blankly. He wanted to kick his own ass for wasting so much time with this loser. He could be curled up on his couch right now, sucking on synthetic root beer barrels, scanning the latest chip of *Shepherds & Dobermans Monthly*.

"Look man," Jimmy continued. "It's not a *soul* soul. Not really. Religion ain't punk, right? It's just what we started calling it. Mick left notes behind. Thank Biafra. But whatever the hell it was that drove the musicians to write and play the songs they did, that's what Mick honed in on. And all he had to do was keep it bottled up until he needed it. Here's the real kicker though: didn't matter that they were dead. See, Mick was crafty enough to go grave digging once he figured how out the magic worked. The trick. Fuck it man. Let's be real. The *science*. If the corpse was still there and more or less intact, which it almost always was—he told me once about a desecration incident with Ian Curtis' grave. Not pretty. Point is, if the corpse was still there, so was this alleged 'soul.' Fucking wild, right?"

Jimmy's words blurred into a slur in David's head. "Hey, do you, uh…is there somewhere I can sit down? Maybe I need to hit the bathroom. I'm feeling kinda dizzy."

"Sure thing my man. Follow me." Jimmy licked his sandblasted lips, then turned and walked off. David trudged behind, and Jimmy led him to a small, barren room. "Warned ya that stuff was potent."

"Mm-hmm.

"Just spread out there." Jimmy pointed to a caved-in twin mattress. "Hope you enjoyed the tour, bud. It'll all be over soon."

David stumbled into the room, hand braced against the wall, his eyes adjusting. "Wha? Wha you mean?"

Next to the mattress—a table. Tools stacked neatly atop it. Scalpel. Hack saw. Awl. Caliper. Surgical gloves. Staple gun. Scissors. More items David couldn't identify, intoxicated or not.

David's chest tightened. So did Jimmy's face.

"What a chump," Jimmy said, grabbing an apron off a hook on the door and wrapping it around himself. "Coming here all alone. Didn't they train you proper in the academy?"

"I don't—" He tried to will himself to run, charge at Jimmy and tackle him, but his legs went marshmallow.

"I know what you are…what you became. Fucking traitor. Scum-sucking pig. You make me sick." He spat at David's feet. A green, viscous mess.

David locked eyes with Jimmy. The realization smacked him. He tried to hold out his hands but couldn't lift them. "No. Wait. Please."

"Collection's almost complete."

The door slammed shut. The room, the whole world went black.

It's beyond dark on a Saturday in mid-October, and the night people have come out to play. The daylight's too bright and they've slept too late, but they're here to drink and celebrate opening night. The Big Reveal. The soiree to end all soirees.

Every faction of punk imaginable in attendance. Rigid skinheads arm-in-arm with wispy goths. Clean-cut straight edgers joining forces with filth-caked crusties who have dragged themselves from the gutter. True unity achieved in the year 2045.

A holographic sign accompanies each exhibit, meticulously labeled to ensure all attendees are aware of who they're gawking at. One display in particular has attracted a considerable crowd. He looks authoritative, almost alive. Some guests hawk loogies on him, some pour their drinks over his head. And it's okay. It's allowed. This is what they paid their admission for. Jimmy is right alongside them, egging them on.

The host looks on proudly. The final piece to his puzzle, finally in place. Adorned in a crisp, dark blue uniform, a silver badge shining from his lapel. A crude mustache drawn on his upper lip. The holograph sign reads:

DAVEY KROSS - THE COPULATION POLICE

THE ULTIMATE SELLOUT - PUNK TURNED COP

acquired taste

Uncle Ray peels back the first layer or so of his thumb and drops it in the frying pan, adds some cayenne pepper and liquid amino acids, says those two things get wedged in the creases of the fingerprints and spruce up the flavor real good. He wraps up his thumb tip in a previously soiled cloth bandage before the wound has a chance to take a deep breath. He doesn't even wince. Hunger pangs trump traditional pain. He adds a few hunks of Yukon Gold potatoes with the skin intact and some slices of white onion and stares at the sizzling meal.

Jess Tyler watches from across the room, her bantam body curled up in a cracked plastic Adirondack chair. Jess is not old enough to sign the Eat Treaty yet, so her Uncle Ray has to take care of all the feeding duties around the house, which he has proudly done ever since the secretive flesh sharers across the nation were finally permitted to publicly declare their beliefs.

The Tylers had some leftovers of Mr. Martin from next-door out in the spare freezer in the garage, but those are gone now. Jess thinks Mr. Martin was a good neighbor, a good friend, hell…a good American. He knew about the worth of sacrifice and what an honor it was to be consumed, absorbed, and shat out. *From the earth and back to the soil,* Uncle Ray had said when he took his first nibble of Mr. Martin's sautéed cartilage in between two stale slices of ciabatta. The true cycle of life. But their neighborly feast was cut short because some jerks broke into their garage a couple of nights ago and took what was left of Mr. Martin, what would have been enough to feed Uncle Ray and Jess and her big brother Jojo for at least a week. Normally they have Jojo guard the garage 'cause he's built like a fortified prison, but Jojo was out sharing some flesh with his lady friend last night. Sharing some flesh in both the biblical and the modern sense. Jojo came home this morning with fiery bloodshot eyes and a soaked bandage around his left forearm. He said they were spreadin' 'round some blood like may-o-naise. Must have been quite a party.

Poor stealing from the poor, just like before, Uncle Ray says in an unintentionally poetic cadence, followed by a few indiscernible obscenities directed toward the thieves. Jess doesn't know much about "before." She was less than two-years-old when The Great Reverence passed into law in Black Briar (and the rest of the country, for that matter). Even now, at fourteen, she can barely grasp what eating meant in the old world, what a typical meal might have consisted of. How it played into the family dynamic. How the now sacred flesh of sentient non-human beings was ravaged and disrespected. The concept is like a dream that never existed, a wraith of the recent past.

Uncle Ray likes to spout off about how Aunt Nickie used to be such a great homemaker and made the most delectable peanut butter cookies every Sunday. From scratch. He licks his lips as he describes how she used to make crisscross impressions in the tops of the cookies with fork tines. But what does anything about Aunt Nickie matter? She passed through multiple colons months ago, and none of that flavor was even remotely close to peanut butter.

Uncle Ray finishes frying up his thumb layer and veggies, takes out a butter knife and slices the skin sliver in perfect thirds, sprinkles some sea salt and freshly crushed peppercorn on it. They each crunch on a meager piece. Uncle Ray *Mmm mmm mmms* all the way to Christmas and Jojo releases a belch like a whale queef, but Jess just forces a grin. She's had worse and she's had better. She feels grease tickling her lip and reaches for a napkin with her right hand, forgetting that the fingers are barely healed stumps, sacrificed for the greater good of nutrition. Just because Jess can't legally sign the Eat Treaty doesn't mean there aren't some loopholes to be found courtesy of Uncle Ray. The phantom pains are still fresh, wiggling like invisible, bony worms and Jess feels the sensation may never go away. She switches hands, uses the napkin, and washes down the family flesh with tepid grey water. She anticipates there will be ice cream for dessert, still does not know for certain what the creamy, bitter substance is made of, shudders to think of the possibilities. Sugar and coconut flavoring can only mask so much, and sexual education during class time has robbed her of at least some smidge of naiveté.

When the family shows up to Worship the following morning there are three animals strategically placed on the stage: a Saanen goat, an albino cow, and a Flemish rabbit. The goat will not lift its head from its water bowl, the cow is wearing a muumuu for some unknown reason, and the rabbit is extra twitchy. The church is not the animals' natural environment, yet somehow they look like they belong. Jess was hoping for the appearance of a gharial this time, just as she always does, but reptiles are a rarity at Worship and Uncle Ray has promised her again and again that those ugly shits went extinct prior to The Great Reverence. He's sure of it. Jess ignores Uncle Ray's rudeness. She believes the gharial is a creature of beauty, of wonder, a crocodile designed as if God had taken design tips from Pablo Picasso. One-hundred-and-ten teeth, and yet Jess has read in some old dusty encyclopedia in the Black Briar Library that there is not a single documented attack on a human. She does not believe they are truly extinct, though. How could there suddenly just be none of something one day? Just like that, snapped out existence? Would the last one even know it was the last? Who would allow any of God's innocent creatures to pass from this world, and will humans one day be a part of this list? If so, who will be around to take note of it?

Jess will find another gharial. She knows it is her destiny to see one in the scaly flesh. The image of the gharial comes to her in her dreams some nights, smiling its elongated smile, gazing at her with reptilian wisdom.

Jess keeps leaning over to Uncle Ray, asking him in a whispery voice why they can't eat any of the animals that pass naturally in the world. The ones that were treated like part of the family, bathed weekly, passed around as community idols, medicated into euphoric states. Not that Jess even *wants* to eat them exactly, but it seems like a waste, she thinks. When Jess's gerbil Herman went to that Great Runabout in the Sky two months ago, his empty husk was placed on their mantel and a shrine was constructed to honor his sweet life. The smell eventually became too much to bear and Herman was given a proper burial in the side yard, the topsoil sprinkled with lye. Jess always asks Uncle Ray about this waste of perfectly edible meat, and Uncle Ray does his best not to act irritated when he responds. Jojo tells Jess to *Shut up 'cause she's a stupid know-nothing ingrate brat*, and Uncle Ray says not to question the decisions of God and Government. All will become clear at adulthood. Jess has heard some stories in between class times about those who broke the laws of The Great Reverence, and those weren't all that pleasant—they made tales of the Spanish Inquisition seem like a senior citizen cruise in the Bahamas, so she thinks maybe she should just listen to Uncle Ray. He's no dummy. He used to be a senator or a manager or a janitor or something useful like that.

There's a portly preacher man up on stage with the animals. He's whiter than Frosty's taint and he's blowing hard about respecting their superiors, the sentient creatures that have put up with human abuse for so long. His purple robes are tattered and unwashed. *Looks like a homeless Grimace,* Uncle Ray whispers to Jojo. Jojo bites the edge of his hand so that he does not disrupt Worship with his laughter—drawing blood even, but Jess does not get the joke. Uncle Ray just tells her it was something from before her time. Jess wonders if this Grimace was an Old God, one that will soon return to spread his mighty gospel.

Some short little cotton-candy-haired old lady in a crinkled paisley tunic kneels in front of the goat, then rises, then brings its damp beard to her lips. Her face is full of glistening tears. It looks like someone filled up a water balloon with her make-up inside and threw it at her face to see how it might come out.

Jess wonders what makes the preacher man pick a particular member of the audience and match them up with one of these beautiful beasts. She simultaneously wishes for and fears this privilege. Will she ever be chosen? And if so, how will it change the course of her young life?

Jojo finds the jokers that took the Mr. Martin meat. Right under their noses, two blocks south on Slater Street. The scavengers had eaten about half of it, including the private parts (which every pamphlet seems to claim are the most nutritious bits, but Jess refuses to try them). The Tyler family passes through a door that is not only unlocked, but barely hanging on its hinges. Uncle Ray and Jojo take the back end of a hammer to each of the thieves' heads while they are laughing the night away in their mildewed basement, lit up on some homemade hooch. A bootleg videotape plays in the background, some ancient banned television program where an adorable wisecracking alien puppet tries to eat the family cat. Jess observes the scene from the top of the stairs without a sound and feels nothing. Jojo curses about the blood splattered on the new unworn blue jeans he just bartered for.

Uncle Ray and Jojo will not face any prison time for this murderous action. In fact, should they even bother to inform the proper authorities, they might be rewarded with a medal and a meal of choice from the Gourmet District, where the wealthy have many untapped resources and prison slaves. Meat theft is punishable by death, not regulated by the state, so says the Eat Treaty. But Uncle Ray is a humble man. He only wants to provide for his family and keep his home safe. Jojo—not so much. He will likely leak the information to his source at the Print Shop and get his picture in next Sunday's pamphlet.

Now the family has rescued the rest of Mr. Martin, the added the bonus of the thieves, plus some other flesh of indeterminate origin that was crammed in the back of the thieves' fridge. The mystery meat is scaly and scabby, but unquestionably human. Any potential disease or contamination will cook right out, any foul tastes can be masked with cumin and garlic powder. The Tyler House freezer is so full that the door barely closes. Jess wonders if—in the old world—it had been a crime to steal from thieves, to reclaim what had been unjustly taken? Jojo tells Jess that Robin Hood was probably gay, because why else would he be worrying about stealing and giving back to the poor when he could just be boinking a babe like Maid Marian? That even in the Disney version, she was a real fox. Jess just shrugs, another reference from the old world lost on her.

Jojo is guarding the stash with his life now. He can forget about his little lady friend for a while unless she stops by for supper some time. Supper in the traditional sense. Traditional in the post Great Reverence sense. More important matters to attend to here. Duty calls.

On an overcast Sunday afternoon, Jess and Uncle Ray make a trip to the farmer's market. Chickens trot freely amongst the people as if they have their own shopping agenda, so many crowded into some spots that their loose feathers in the air appear to be the result of an impromptu pillow fight. Their clucking is metronomic, trance-inducing. Jess stops at a booth where a husband, wife, and son are selling their family flesh. Each of them is missing some piece that was once aesthetically necessary or even quite useful, but not essential to survival. An earlobe, the tip of a nose, a tongue, a finger or two. Jess stares at the son. He is around her age and, strangely, is missing exactly the same fingers on exactly the same hand as she. She feels something stir within her, a kinship-gone-crush that she refuses to vocalize, but they at least exchange crooked smiles. The boy has only a handful of teeth left. Enamel is a precious bargaining chip in these times.

Jess spies an old woman behind the family, what remains of her slumped in a wheelchair. She is a quadruple amputee, also missing much of her face and appears to have had a double mastectomy. Now that Jess's own breasts are beginning to develop, she wonders if and when they will be large enough to become a useful commodity. To offer the purest of milk to all those who seek it. Uncle Ray has already been underlining passages from the Breast section of the Eat Treaty. A cream-colored substance oozes from the old woman's nasal cavity and a fly hungrily rubs its legs together in the curve of her remaining lip. The fly seems to be well aware that the old woman cannot swat it. Jess studies the woman clinically. She presumes the family made a decision that Gramma had lived the longest life and therefore should be the first to be sold off at the market so the rest of the family might thrive for a few more weeks. Jess knows this because her own Gramma went through the same process when Jess was still a toddler. She does not remember this, but Uncle Ray brings the fact up more than is necessary.

Jess sees an emaciated, androgynous child peddling professionally bagged samples of rat droppings. She barters a piece of flesh that once belonged to the thieves, a tiny, lean patch that she has hidden from Uncle Ray all morning, knowing that trading for this bag of droppings will put her in Jojo's good graces when she gifts it to him. Jojo and his girlfriend snort the precious droppings on special occasions, and their anniversary is coming up. The droppings offer some strange level of high that Jess is curious about, but not curious enough to pilfer any of the droppings for herself. Her body is a temple and no waste shall enter its gates.

Uncle Ray purchases a bag of oranges because he claims Jojo has been deficient in his Vitamin C consumption lately and is at risk for scurvy. That is all the currency they have for today. As they leave the market, there are true vegetarian protestors politely picketing off to the side so as not to actually obstruct any foot traffic.

They wield signs that say ALL MEAT IS SACRED—DON'T EAT SOMEONE WHO COULD BE THE NEXT EINSTEIN OR MLK OR POL POT and A WORLD WITHOUT MEAT=A WORLD REALLY NEAT. Jess is curious as to why they would not picket the entrance, as people leaving have already made their purchases and made up their minds. But she sees worth in their cause, will sneak away from home one day when Uncle Ray is in a drunken coma and come attempt to learn more, maybe even join in the protest if she feels it worth the effort.

Jess attends Worship by herself the following Sunday. Uncle Ray is taking care of Jojo, who has come down with a case of something that may or may not be chicken pox. She stops by the market to speak to the meat-free protestors, but is disillusioned by the fact that most of them appear to be taking a break and drinking some milky beverage made of flaxseed. So she moves on for now. At the church, the pews are near empty, perhaps because there is a Sacrifice Lottery on the other side of town. Everyone wants to know who will be next obese denizen to be consumed in the communal feast, but Jess just rolls her eyes at the thought.

The purple priest is reading rewritten Leviticus passages, practically singing them in a bouncing ball cadence. He has an almost beautiful and soothing voice, like an angel's harp that is slightly out of key. Nothing matters until the animals are brought out to gaze upon. An alpaca with its fur dyed blue, a Pug/Shih Tzu mix in a too tiny pink t-shirt that says "Lil' Princess," and—

Jess's solo attendance today is like sweet serendipity, for the third animal that now sits on the stage is everything she has hoped for. She immediately recognizes that long, thin maw lined with jagged razors, that cold stare that burrows into her soul.

A gharial.

The last gharial, or one of many—this does not matter at this moment. What matters is the existence of such a creature at all. Extinction is a myth that can be disproven with just one subject.

The priest notices Jess's excitement, makes eye contact with her, and beckons to her. It is as if he has been holding out for this very moment, taunting her for months upon years with the fact that she was not worthy. That there are not many attendees to choose from this particular Sunday is beside the point. This is Jess's time to shine.

She approaches the stage. She is trembling, but she does not give a single damn. The gharial is indifferent to her approach, but Jess expects this. A gharial is not a Golden Retriever waiting patiently for its human companion to return home so that it may lick upon his or her face. A gharial is cold and calculating, but it is still beautiful.

It is the closest thing to God that Jess has ever known.

Jess reaches out her hand with the missing fingers, knowing that the likelihood of losing the fingers on her other hand is slim, but still possible. Those teeth do not lie.

The old scars along her arm are stripped in perfect indented lines like tribal tattoos. She reaches, she approaches. The gharial seems to be almost sleeping, probably dreaming of the gorgeous swamp it calls home and the plentiful fish that only it is allowed to consume without repercussion.

Jess kneels before the gharial, her finger stumps twitching, her destiny fulfilled.

"The Perfect Playground"
(Creature Stew - Papa Bear Press - 2015 & California Screamin' -
Barking Deer Press - 2017)

the perfect playground

Headlights glaring on a Cimmerian midnight, tires grinding the asphalt of a lonely urban road in Chula Vista, in a part of town where rural illusions sometimes still exist. A lone driver at her most vulnerable. Eyes heavy after a wild hangout session at her girlfriend's pony keg party in Eastlake. The mostly-finished bottle of her fifth strawberry daiquiri wine cooler rolling back and forth on the passenger floorboard like a man trying to put out a fire on his own body. Misty mouth that would undoubtedly fail the Breathalyzer test. Thinking about that moderately cute boy with the sideburns that she *almost* kissed. The stereo blares. Her off-key voice wailing alongside Smashing Pumpkins, truly believing that today is the greatest day she's ever known, too buzzed to care about the occasional sound of reflector bumps beneath her wheels.

Until—

A form sprints across the street. Not something as easily explainable as a clustered clowder of feral cats, or—as some have argued their eyes have tricked them into seeing—a naked man seeking suicidal freedom from the hardships of modern life.

Tall as a street lamp. Androgynous features. Thin as a mantis. Arms and legs like broken yardsticks. Sheer skin like laurel vellum.

It dashes in front of the quick-moving turquoise VW Jetta, a flash that the driver's eye only thinks it sees between the soft cracks of the frosty mist that decorates the windshield. On a night more fortunate than this, she might have encountered this shape elsewhere in the city, witnessing it in her rearview mirror while the vehicle was stationary and relatively safe in Terra Nova Plaza, waiting in the drive-thru of Jack in the Box for her two-for-a-dollar taco special. A brief encounter, before the form lunged into the bushes. Into the hills.

But that option never did and never will exist for Heather Chapman. She will never finish her unfocused Associate's Degree at Southwestern College. She will never lose her virginity to that Dylan McKay wannabe in the bed of his truck pulled off to the side of the road in Proctor Valley. She will never hit twenty.

A pair of middle-aged women wearing neon blue jumpsuits, out for their weekly power walking session, will discover Heather's husk the following morning. One will be yammering about her *husband that absolutely must attend every Padres game*. The other will turn to the side of the road and scream *OhmyGODthere'sabodydownthere*, then vomit up her Wheaties. She cannot stand the sight of blood. The women will both head quickly back to the comfort of their nearby tract homes located somewhere along the not-so-seamless border of Bonita and Chula Vista proper, gaining more exercise than they initially bargained for. The woman with the stronger stomach will phone the authorities. Police vehicles emblazoned with the City of Chula Vista logo—a sun rising above a mountain and rippling water—will surround the accident-gone-crime scene. The blood will only be a figment of the vomiting woman's imagination. The paramedics will later determine that all traces of sanguine fluids were somehow removed from the body. Forensic experts will comb the cracked, dying grass for hours, never finding a speck of evidence. This information will be intentionally omitted from any and all news articles, so as not to disturb the safe sanctuary of suburbia.

No, Heather will certainly never live to recount the tale of the unnamable thing she somewhat saw. In a split second decision, she swerves at the sight of the mad runner, loses control. Her car flips once, rolls down a steep hill next to the road, and lands in the vicinity of a soon-to-be-built storm drain. Seatbelt never clicked. Airbag never activated.

In the distance, the unknown creature dances a mirthful, epileptic jig, gyrating like a Sea-Monkey in heat. It tiptoes on bare, wiggly, bendy feet, closer and closer toward Heather's strained calls for help. Giggling, lip licking, it inhales air into its toothless, tubular mouth hole. Humming with insatiable hunger.

"Saved by the Bell sucks ass, dudes. Turn that shit off. I'm bored. What else are we doing tonight?" The sense of mischief in Chase's voice was as infectious as an STD.

"Ah, you're just mad 'cause you got caught trying to egg Mario Lopez's house that one time." Gabriel knew how to make Chase shut up, at least temporarily. "I say we go spray paint some shit on the library at Hilltop."

"*Trying* to? What the fuck do you mean by that? I hit the door twi—"

"Hey you guys!" Danny said, somehow managing to defeat Chase's decibel level. He began rummaging through his tornadoed closet. "I don't think I have any spray paint, but if no one else has any good ideas…I've got some of *these*."

He whipped out a half-used bag of assorted water balloons, a seemingly innocent possession just bursting with teenage trouble-making potential.

"Sounds as good as anything else, I guess," Gabriel said. "We could cruise down Telegraph Canyon on our bikes and hit joggers or something."

Danny laughed and almost choked on his third dose of Jolt Cola. "Remember that time we shacked that old fart right in the nuts? Classic!"

Chase made a jerk-off motion with his right hand and rolled his eyes. Been there, done that.

"Okay, fine," Gabriel said. He gazed into space, like he was trying to guess if the answer to an algebra problem was "A" or "C." "How about we launch 'em at cars from the hills out on East H Street?"

"Yeah, yeah, let's do that," Danny said. "Let's call up that lame-fuck Mark Torson. He can drive us."

Chase protested with gestures that somehow managed to be even cruder than his earlier motions, then leaned back, his body now nearly immersed in Danny's waterbed.

"Screw that," he said. "Mark's about as fun as a full pineapple rotating in my ass."

"But he can totally borrow his mom's car," Danny said. "Who else—"

"On second thought," Chase said, sighing, "maybe we shouldn't do that tonight anyway. I just got off restriction after that stupid fight at school with Shaun Ramsey. If we get caught, my dad's going to beat my ass raw and take away my Game Boy again." He absently picked at the corner of Danny's Faith No More poster.

"Chase, can you stop fucking with that? My dad just bought—"

"You got any nudie mags, Danny?" Chase asked.

"Nah, my mom found the last stash and flipped her wig. I've got—"

"Aw, come on dudes," Gabriel said. "Let's get out of here. It's been forever since we've done something like this."

"Mark. Sucks. Hairy. Nuts." Chase was always quite clear about his sentiments. He raised his body up from the waterbed coffin, peeked through the blinds, looked out at Danny's detritus-infested swimming pool.

"Well, we don't really have any other options, do we?" Gabriel asked. "He's the only one with a license. I don't know about the rest of you jerks, but at this point I don't feel like fucking walking *or* biking all the way out there tonight."

"Yeah, no way," Danny said. "Let's just call Mark. You *know* he's not going to be busy. That limp dick is probably just watching *Alf* reruns."

"Okay, okay," Chase said. "But if he gets even slightly annoying I'm going to smack him in the head so hard that when he wakes up he's going to think he's watching *Star Trek* instead."

"I like *Babylon 5* better," Danny said.

"Are you fucking crazy?" Chase's face looked primed to kill. "Dude, just shut up. That's not the point anyway."

Mark had promptly picked the rest of them up in his mother's car after informing her that he was "going to Ben Christian's house for a Biology study group," being the lameoid mama's boy that he was. The boys parked in a cul de sac on Camino La Paz to take the back route to their chosen spot. The streets were lined with respectably priced vehicles guarded by dim lighting.

"You think it's safe to park here, guys?" Mark asked. "My mom's gonna shit a pig if we get broken into or anything."

"I dunno, man," Chase said, waving him away. "I heard all the vatos from VCV live on this street."

"What? But I thought—"

"Don't listen to him, Mark," Gabriel said. "He's just fucking with you."

Mark looked like a shamed puppy.

"Gabe, you dick," Chase said, "you never let me have any fun, dude."

They got out and trudged through thick bushes and lemon trees, Gabriel leading the way with a yellow industrial flashlight. Mark and Danny shared the burden of a mid-sized Rubbermaid ice chest stuffed with a small arsenal of balloons that were filled with a mixture of water from Danny's backyard hose and half a carton of milk. The ground was lumpy, but bearable. They had only been walking for about a minute, but Mark was already huffing and wheezing.

"Guys, can we take a break?" he asked.

"Oh, come on. You've got to be kidding me," Chase whispered incredulously.

"Here, just let me carry the other handle," Gabriel said, grabbing the Rubbermaid's plastic handle from Mark's clammy hand. He grimaced and wiped the sweat off on his pant leg. "Keep moving, though."

After a few more minutes, they reached the clearing that led them to a small hill that overlooked East H Street. They faced sporadic lights on the opposite side of the road that highlighted the future Rancho Del Rey shopping center. Not far off to the west, Gabriel could see the outline of the Brunswick Premier Lanes building and wondered if it was Cosmic Bowling night. They briefly turned away from the lights and back toward the trees, only seeing varying shades of green patterned against the dark sky. A small lemon fell from the nearest tree and bounced off the top of Gabriel's head.

Their hiding spot was decent, but lacking a certain perfection. Not quite close enough to touch their targets, and the cover of night and surrounding foliage was barely sufficient to shroud the four of them. A large green generator decorated with the illegibly tagged signatures of *Dopey* and *El Shaggy* (the latter of which had "*FAG*→" permanently carved next to it) sat silently and hid them mostly from view. Cars sped along the street at an average of forty miles an hour. The timing for a toss had to be impeccable, and was based more on sheer luck than any sort of precise mathematical calculation.

Target practice proved to be mostly uneventful. Only Chase had any natural physical abilities to speak of, so only his balloons ever managed to make a splash on any passing vehicles. Even those successes were rare—they typically hit the corner of the trunk or a tire, likely unnoticed by the driver. They did their best to keep their eyes peeled for familiar vehicles. The last time they tossed water balloons from this spot was a few months back, and they had the misfortune of nailing Gabriel's mother's car. Gabriel would never forget the guilt he felt the morning after that incident when his mother unwittingly said to him, "I'm so thankful I have a good son who doesn't do awful things like that."

"Hey, you guys want some Doritos?"

One other good thing about Mark: not only was he a convenient chauffeur, but he always had some salty snacks in his tattered backpack that he never left home without. There were certain fringe benefits to having an overweight, junk food-obsessed faux-friend.

"I got, like, two kinds. And a couple of Chocodiles, too. We can split those if you want 'em."

Danny didn't bother responding. He was busy attempting a double-fisted toss of balloons, both of which came nowhere near the intended car.

"Do I?" Chase responded. "Do I? Does a Mexican pick lettuce? Does a beaner shop at Pic N Save?" He knocked on Gabriel's shoulder blades with his knuckles.

"Hey, fuck you Chase." Gabriel shoved Chase away, gave his shoulder and his pride a quick massage. He knew his friend was just being a cretinous jerk as usual, acting out of insensitivity and ignorance rather than malice, but that didn't stop Gabriel from being at least a little crushed deep down, since he was half-Mexican and had already swallowed his share of racist jokes.

"Yeah, fuck you right back, Gabe. With a used dildo." Chase threw his next balloon. It exploded prematurely. "Gah!"

"Guys, we're running low on ammo already," Danny said. He looked worried. Then again, he always looked worried. "We'd better get a good toss in soon."

Chase made a farting sound with his mouth. "Wow," he said. "*Big* surprise this night's a total bust."

"Ooh…lemmedovisun," Mark mumbled, his mouth stuffed with Cool Ranch. The savory crumbs tumbled with each word from the corners of his pudgy mouth.

His eagerness was obvious to the other boys, and they all groaned. According to Chase—Mark "threw like an African whore." Chase was not the World's Greatest Scholar. In his mind "whore" was spelled "hoar," and he only marginally understood what the word meant (as in, "Your mama's a hoar walking on Broadway").

"Mark, you're just gonna waste the balloon," Gabriel said. "You haven't even made one to the bottom of the hill yet."

"Lasswon," Mark said. His mouthful of chips had now formed a thick paste. "I pwomith."

Mark pulled a balloon out of the cooler and stood up, swaying with anticipation, waiting for another vehicle to pass by. His Metallica shirt was about a half-size too small. His marshmallow belly peeked out the bottom of the hemline.

Mark cradled and cupped the balloon tenderly like it was his first attempt at fondling a date's breast in a near-empty movie theater.

After the longest thirty seconds in the history of time, the engine of a car could be heard in the distance, the first signs of headlights inching their way around the slight curves of the road. Mark geared up for the throw, his tongue protruding from his mouth in intense concentration.

The balloon soared clumsily, like a Japanese beetle that had just woken up.

Mark didn't just have plain dumb luck with his throw—he was a bona fide leprechaun. The balloon smashed on the windshield. It looked like God blew His load all over the glass. The boys' mouths were agape and Mark was officially, though temporarily, initiated to be One of Them. They were barely able to control their cheering, belly bursting, and high-fiving.

Then—a screeching halt.

"Oh, shit!" all the boys whispered in unison, though there were likely slight variations of the expletive.

The car erratically pulled over to the side of the road. A man stepped out of the driver's seat. Short, balding, disheveled looking. Wearing the defeated attire of an oversized grey pocket tee and green sweatpants. Despite his severe lack of intimidating qualities, his adult status was enough to make the boys darken their undies. His anger multiplied that power exponentially.

"You goddamn kids! I see you up there!" he hollered, shaking his pudgy fists in their general direction. He began to walk toward the hill. "When I get up there I'm going to teach you—"

The boys were about to attempt the arduous run back across the canyon to the car when a sudden strange burst of movement came from the center divider of the wide street. The angry man was tackled by what appeared to be another, considerably more svelte, man. Chase bleated out a half-laugh.

"What the hell? I didn't know it was football season," Danny said, a goofball chuckle slipping from his lips. "Go team!"

The driver was pinned to the ground, but the boys had trouble viewing the second man. His movements were quick and jarring, disconnected and flashing like he was a living strobe light. Disorienting, pale green flashes from a twilight dream. A wind dancer from a car dealership on a "This Weekend Only" sale made bizarre, terrible flesh.

The motions gradually slowed, and the boys were only slightly able to process what was occurring from their vantage point. Gabriel turned on his flashlight and cast the light toward the street. The skinny being peeled back epidermal layers on each of its long pencil fingers—creating a flower bouquet effect on each hand—then moved them up near its mouth, facing the sinewy stubs outward with a taunting gesture.

Nanny nanny boo-boo, it may as well have been saying. *You caan't catch me.*

The wiggling digits coalesced into an unfathomable proboscis. Writhing and squirming like the foulest eels in the depths of undiscovered oceans.

"Um, guys…do you see—" Gabriel had always prided himself in the fact that he had been blessed with "five better than 20/20 vision."

Chase cut him off.

"Holy fuckwad. What the shit is that?"

"Guys," Mark said, his mouth now finally clear of all edible interferences, "we gotta help him!" He started to stumble down the hill a bit.

"Mark, what the hell are you doing?" Gabriel yelled.

He tried to grab Mark's shirt as he followed him down. Mark's backpack tumbled down the hill, the contents littering the side of the road. The beam from Gabriel's flashlight cut through the night like searchlights advertising a stereo blowout sale.

The creature now straddled the driver. The newly formed tentacle tube penetrated the poor man's mouth like a freshly forged sword fitting into a virgin leather sheath, muffling his terrified screams. Crisp sounds of sucking, squishing, and flatulence drowned out the pleading noises of human struggle.

How many sucks does it take to get to the center of a full-grown man?

The answer is three.

The victim's name was Howard Denney. He will never finish reading *Gorky Park*. He will never turn in his most professional grant proposal to his superiors on Monday. He will never make it home to finally confess to his wife that he was having an affair with her less attractive cousin (though, truthfully, he never would have confessed anyway).

The flashlight illuminated the creature's face just as it finished its midnight snack. It stretched out a pocket of flesh on the side of its newly distended belly and squirted some indeterminate creamy pink bodily fluid into the pouch, as if it were saving something special for later.

Gabriel felt his bowels in danger of loosening when he finally caught a good glimpse of the finished man-smoothie and its deadly drinker. The freak creature honed in on Mark and Gabriel with a hawk's accuracy. They reacted like living Munch paintings, with added sound effects.

If H.R. Giger had been the chief art designer of a Saturday morning cartoon, he might have come up with a character that bore a slight resemblance to what was now effortlessly gliding along the endless rows of ice plants toward them.

"Jesus shit! Run!" Gabriel yelled.

"But…my backpack…" Mark obviously did not have his priorities straight.

"Fuck your backpack! Let's go!" Gabriel tugged at Mark, then dropped the flashlight and grabbed the car keys out of Mark's hands like an aggressive designated driver, intending to get the car started despite only completing one driving lesson two months ago.

Gabriel sprinted up the hill. His fearful eyes were enough to make Chase and Danny haul ass alongside him. Mark's preference for snacks over life caused him to fall behind the other three.

The other boys soon heard his curdling screams. They chose not to look back.

The car was in sight, but not close enough to give them any relief. Their pace quickened. Branches and brambles whipped and sliced at their faces and any other exposed portions of their bodies. Fallen lemons exploded beneath their feet like overdue pimples. Gabriel tripped over a small rock or log or some other obstruction that could not be seen clearly in the dark. He dropped eight feet into the canyon, landed on his left arm, howled in unimaginable pain. Contrary to their own selfish interests, Danny and Chase doubled back to help him. He *did* have the car keys, after all.

Gabriel's adrenaline forced him off the ground, but his arm now hung horribly, a Dali reject.

The three remaining boys ran on, the sound of a straw slurping the hard-to-reach remnants of a root beer float lurking closely behind them. Followed by silence, then crunching leaves, bestial grunts, and gleeful singsong laughter.

Danny was hopping bushes like an Olympic hurdler.

Chase muttered a botched version of the Lord's Prayer. "Our Father Art's up in Heaven. Hollow Bee's his name. When the kingdom comes, you will be done…"

Gabriel held back tears and did his best not to take quick glances at the half-inch of cracked bone protruding from his forearm, a glistening white in the moonlight. He turned around to see how close their pursuer was. A few feet behind Gabriel, the creature somersaulted like an amateur gymnast. It hopped back to its feet and skipped playfully in a zigzag motion, then suddenly sat in the grass in a pretzeled yoga position for a few moments—its head bobbing back and forth like it had "Kumbaya" stuck in its brain on a loop. It picked up a handful of lemons and juggled them like a trained monkey, then stood again, performing a mock rain dance to unseen gods before jumping back to its feet and resuming its pursuit.

The boys were beyond exhausted by now. Despite the creature's initial speed, it had not caught up to them yet. Gabriel had collapsed out of shock and the others were dragging him as best they could. The monster seemed to be taking a leisurely stroll now, toying with them. As the boys neared the car, the creature seemed to grow bored and slowed its pace, not really even following them anymore. It rubbed its belly and belched like an infant, then skipped off in an unseen direction.

The boys kept their pace.

The car alarm disarmed.

They drove off in terror, eventually ditching Mark's mother's car at the corner of Madrona and Del Mar, a block from the Torson residence.

They made a pact to never tell their parents where they really went that night and that Gabriel "broke his arm trying to clear a set of ten stairs with his bike."

Mark Torson will never get himself into acceptable shape via a half-assed attempt at a gym membership. He will never design a top-selling video game called *Heavy Metal Cyborg Zombie Soldiers From Hell.* He will never have a curt fling with an out-of-his-league woman that accidentally ends up carrying his sole heir.

Mark's face will eventually decorate a milk carton. His body will never be found.

Years, months, weeks later, the further expansion of Chula Vista births the wealthy exclusivity of Otay Ranch.

On an overcast day, in a section of nature yet-to-be-developed into another crispy clean shopping center, a group of innocent, unassuming children play Tunnel Tag. The fuzz of dead dandelions clings to their play clothes. A pig-tailed girl spies a distorted form twisted and tangled in the tall grasses a few feet away from her frozen spot and decides to break the rules. From where she stands, it resembles a faded chalk outline from a long-forgotten murder scene. As she inches closer, she discovers that the form has volume. Her curious fingers confirm it is tactile. It feels like false flesh, a rubber body suit left behind from an unfinished Roger Corman shoot. It glides along her fingers, the slick, pythonic texture almost moving of its own volition. Dancing. Green residue marks her fingers as she allows the shed skin to float to the ground.

Mesmerizing.

The safe confines of suburban retreat stifle imagination. The perfect playground for the unexpected.

Children are not the only creatures that enjoy games.

lacunae

One: Fluids, Fluidity

It began innocently enough—an STD scare that turned out to be a razor burn. Or so Clay thought. A week after the double misdiagnosis, the insignificant spotting on his inner thigh had coagulated into a thick, crusty paste the size of a silver dollar. And now, a month after the growth's discovery, it looked like a patch of fake vomit from a gag shop was growing on Clay's skin. Any attempts to scour it off had proven fruitless. He still couldn't figure out where it had come from, why it had continued to swell. Worse—why it one day had become capable of moving. Each day that followed, inching its way closer to his knee. And growing. A blossoming dahlia.

Clay teetered at the edge of his motel bed, munching on stale ginger snaps. The news fought its way through the beginning sands of television static. Coming up after the commercial break: a feel good story about a father who'd convinced his daughter that her pet pony was actually a unicorn. Clay already knew for a fact that the father would be featured in the news again tomorrow, arrested for animal cruelty because of a poor decision involving a hot glue gun and a waffle cone.

He'd seen the story run its course already.

The newscaster continued babbling, his head shifting diagonally, as if the top half were trying to escape from the bottom. Clay whacked the top of the television with the side of his fist, attempting to Fonzie the reception back into a normal state. Defeated, he fell back down on the bed.

Through the window, "VACANCY" shined its dark light down upon him. To the left, "NO" flashed on and off in fluorescent pink, so many times that Clay could not be sure if the room he inhabited should have been legitimately rented to him.

His leg twitched. Incessant itching, irritating like a scourge of mosquitos. Using an overgrown fingernail, Clay dug at the late bloomer birthmark. Applied pressure with an ice pack. Then a heat pack, for contrast. Poked and prodded with tweezers. Pus seeped out of the center, the color of watered-down honey mustard. No pain, which was disconcerting. Actually feeling something might have helped him cope. Frustration got the better of him and he let loose a bellowing man-scream.

Before he could complete his roar—a knock at the door.

"Who is it?" His attempt at politeness came out closer to a snarl.

"Oh, 'ello. Is this Clay's room?" A thick British accent, almost a parody.

"Yes," Clay said. "Who's asking?"

"It's me…Lorraine." Her name spoken like a question.

Clay peeked through the peephole. Staring back at him—a fisheye lensed version of a woman squeezed into a frilly red blouse and black pencil skirt. The glaring streams of early sunlight surrounded her figure. He could have sworn it had been nighttime mere minutes ago.

"Just a second."

A sweaty panic possessed him. He scrambled for something to cover his marred leg. Nothing within convenient reach aside from his filthy trousers, streaked with the dry flakes of either semen or cinnamon roll frosting. He brushed the pants off as best he could.

He opened the door, squinting at the full force of the sun. Once his eyes adjusted, he got a true look at his visitor. From a brief glance at her silhouette, her face mimicked some B-grade actress from the 30s that he couldn't quite place. Her face turned slightly to the front, modernizing her look and changing Clay's opinion. A single streak of grey weaved its way through her tangerine hair, belying her otherwise youthful features. Her outfit hugged her in all the right places. Her heels were just high enough to say, "I'm an absolute monster in the sack."

I know I didn't order a hooker today, Clay thought. *Did I ever? No, get it right. This never happened. Not yet anyway. When does Lola arrive…tomorrow? Damn! Why can't I keep my timelines straight? It's been too lo—*

"Clay. You there, love?"

"Hello," Clay said. "I'm sorry…I'm not sure who you—should I be expecting you?"

"Oh…you don't remember…yesterday at Gemini Station? When you almost fell right into the L train's path?"

The L Train? What is it with the letter "L" anyway? Why is it haunting me? Loop, lewd, larva, leech. Limbo, lager, loneliness, liminality. Love? Has to be some connection.

Lorraine continued. "You told me you were staying here and that I should pop in this afternoon. You seemed like a fit bloke, so I decide to take a chance and swing by. Have to make your own luck, right?"

Clay's face formed a confused prune. He hadn't even left the motel yesterday. He was scheduled to give a Power Point presentation at the Rustic Furniture convention this afternoon. The whole day had been devoted to organizing and preparing his final touches. He didn't have time for this. Unless…

Unless the time had been granted to him.

"I realize this is rather brazen. May I?" she asked, gesturing to the inside of the room. She did not indicate any awareness of the space smelling like sweets and stale sweat beyond the threshold. The haphazardly strewn notecards may as well have been perfectly stacked, the dirty laundry pressed and folded. Clay invited her in, perished all humility.

As Lorraine drifted by him, she winked with gauche provocativeness. The adhesive to one of her fake eyelashes failed her and came loose, drooping in front of her eye, an intoxicated caterpillar.

"Oh, dear, this is all so embarrassing," Lorraine said. She hiked up her skirt a few inches, an apparent distraction from the eyelash. "I promise I'm not a cheap tart."

The diversion was also a bust. Clay turned his gaze back to Lorraine's face. A pulsing in the corner of her eye, something beneath her skin lifting the lash back into its place. A milky green substance seeping through the surface of the sclera, trailing down her cheek. He glanced down at her midsection. Something was crawling underneath the side of her skirt as well, struggling to free itself from the skintight tweed.

"It's alright, love," she continued. "Let me just go to the loo, powder my nose, and I'll be the bee's knees. Promise."

Clay's rational mind told him to force Lorraine to leave so he could continue preparing his notes. Unfortunately, he was also irrevocably erect.

Doomed, once again.

Two: A Test

To say the woman seated at the opposite end of the bar from Clay was hideous would have been a crass understatement. Even a blind satyr wouldn't have gone to bed with her. Thankfully, Clay had no interest in wooing her. He was merely hoping to rid himself of his affliction. And she might be his savior. Nothing to go on now but faith.

He silently scoped her from afar, then slithered his way to her. The dim lighting did her no favors. Clay motioned to the bartender. "I'll have what she's having. And another for her if she's ready."

The bartender shot him a baffled look. "If you say so, pal."

The gruesome woman stared at Clay as if he were a figment of her imagination. Her pig nose wiggled.

"Yes, I mean you. Do you see anyone else around?" Clay touched the woman's hand just lightly enough to avoid seeming like a threat. He grasped her lithe fingers, giving them a softly presumptuous caress. They were the only attractive quality about her, a set of symmetrical buoys afloat in a foul, polluted sea. He introduced himself. The woman gave no indication that she could tell Clay's face had broken out in hives. He'd sloppily caked it with pale mineral powder. To her undiscerning, tipsy eyes, he just looked a tad peaked. So he hoped.

"Oh…well, hello then. I'm Linda. I guess I'm just not used to men approaching me." She released a snort that made Clay's ears itch.

"Pleased to meet you." *And I truly am sorry for what's about to happen. I wish I could let you walk away from this. But it's not my decision anymore.*

Clay's touch almost instantaneously affected the crevice between her thumb and forefinger, the skin quivering like fleshy Jell-O. Linda remained oblivious.

Good God, I'm an awful, awful specimen of a man. But I didn't ask to be this way. I promise to be better if I—No. When I get well again.

"I'm sorry, would you excuse me for just a moment?" Linda asked. "I need to go powder my nose."

Clay cocked his head.

Someone else just recently said the same thing to me, no?

"Going to the…*loo*, is it?"

She shot him a quizzical look.

No. No, this isn't her. I don't think that's actually happened yet.

"Never mind." He waved her off. "Take your time."

"Don't you leave. I'll be right back. I really would like to take you up on that drink."

"Wouldn't think of it." *Oh, except I'd* so *love to leave right now, but I'm somehow stuck here and none of this, not the motel or the rental car or my meals, not even the damned drinks I just ordered, are on the company card. So, yes, I'm staying.*

As if on cue, the bartender slipped Clay two mint juleps in pewter cups. Once Linda was clearly out of sight and the bartender had found a new patron to poison at the opposite end of the bar, Clay grabbed Linda's drink, raised it near his lips. He extended his tongue, now bloated and adorned with a colorful assortment of blotchy pustules. He hesitated, then squeezed the head of one that was begging to burst. It drooled into her drink, and he used the skinny straw to swish around the fetid globule until it dissolved. He thanked the gods for pitying him—the lighting in the pub was pure shit, and thus the few lost souls who had come to drown themselves could not witness what he'd done.

Just as the jukebox finished excreting a botched electronica version of The Who's "Boris the Spider," Linda returned from the restroom, distress smeared across her face. She took her glass with the hand that Clay had not touched earlier, promptly swallowed the filthy ichor. Her mutated hand remained at her side, mannequin stiff.

"Oh…pardon my manners," she said, lifting her near-empty glass. Her words read calm, but her eyes screamed with internal terror. Some sort of moisture—tears, perhaps—had caused her eye makeup to go rogue. With a grimace, she said, "Cheers!"

"Yes," Clay said, his grin gone crooked. "*Salud*!"

Linda polished off her drink. She burped, did not apologize.

Pity. Clay was actually starting to enjoy her company.

Three: Little Buddy

You want to boink her, don't you?

A voice searing though his brain. A *Sesame Street* reject running a used car lot.

"Wha-what?" Clay awoke, feeling as if shards of dry ice were raking his back. "Who said that?"

It's okay. Just admit it. Even after all that's already happened, even in her current state, you still want your John Thomas to go steady with her Muffy LaRue. That's cool. No judgment. It's only natural. She's got that kind of off-brand appeal, makes a man want to poison his wife and sell his kids into an Armenian sex trade.

Clay's limbs went static. His body felt like it had been through a weeklong imprisonment in a coffin two sizes too small. A mild tingling sensation just below his epidermis reminded him he was still alive.

Listen. Take my advice. Don't believe everything What's-Her-Face says. Her real name isn't even Lisa or Lucille or whatever. Or maybe it is. Look, the point is—I'm not going to hurt you, okay? This partnership ain't permanent. I just need to borrow your body for a bit until I can build up the strength to detach myself.

"What the hell is going on?" Clay was incredulous. "Why should I even—"

Well, you don't really have a lot of options, do you? We're in this together for now, whether you like it or not.

"But…my Power Point presentation…"

Don't worry about your precious little seminar. In the revised version of the upcoming week, a suitable double for you has been manufactured. He's been thoroughly trained in the Power Point software and is currently taking care of business so you don't have to worry about losing your job. Relax. This has already taken place and will also soon take place and is completely under control. Plus, I saw him run through the presentation a couple of times, and to be honest he's doing a much better job than you would have.

Despite its illogical nature, that response satisfied Clay. He'd already had enough experience accepting nonsense as nothing short of the truth. This new development—just more of the same.

"But, I don't underst—where are you? Why do I feel like I'm hearing you speak directly to my mind, not through my ears?"

That's 'cause you are, my gracious host. I can intrude upon you whenever I feel like it. Sorry 'bout that. But it gets lonely in here. Took me a while to pick up enough of the cadence of human language to begin communicating with you, though. The Boob Tube's actually good for something. Who knew? Myself,

I don't care much for the BBC like a certain you-know-who. But think of all of this as a larval stage. I'm just—

Clay realized with madhouse terror that the speech was coming from the growth on his leg.

"No! NonononoNO! This ends now! I want you off my body!"

Sorry. No can do. Not yet.

"Please! I'm begging you…I have a wife and kids."

No you don't, Pinocchio. That's part of why I hooked up with you. I'm not completely heartless. Give me a little credit. Sheesh.

"But I'm a decent man. I've never hurt anyone. At least I don't think I ha—"

Oh well. Too late. Now you have.

Clay's eyes finally adjusted to the dark. Realizing he was completely naked, he shivered, then sat up and surveyed the room. Concrete walls and floor, no windows, a stainless steel door reflecting a mangled image of his face. His hives resembled freckles that had gone horribly wrong.

To his side—the remains of a woman. Half a face. One breast, its fatty contents held together by an extra large twist tie. Both legs, the end of each severed thigh sloppily sewn to the other. Definitely the gargoyle he'd seduced at the bar the previous night. Likely exploded after the mandatory intercourse that Clay thankfully couldn't even recall.

Or did this happen tomorrow? It's becoming more and more difficult to keep track anymore.

It's happening right now, Clayton. Tomorrow's when you meet Lola, remember?

"Shut up, you. I wasn't addressing you!" Clay slapped at his leg, but his hands only stung his chilled flesh. He looked down at where his unwelcome guest had been before. The growth had moved from between his thigh and knee to just shy of his hip. It was now roughly the size of a small medicine ball.

Hey, see? I can move around on your body anywhere you want. You just let me know where it's comfy.

"Off! Off is where I want you!"

Clay's throat became a desert, his voice its silent sands. He swore he saw the pulsing purple lump grin up at him.

Can't do that, unfortunately. Gotta let the gestation take its course. Won't be much longer. At least I don't think so. Haven't you ever wanted to be the world's first pregnant man?

Just kidding.

No, actually, I'm not kidding. Is that what you want? I hope so. Clay?

Hey, buddy. You there?

Four: Tricks and Teats

Clay bit through the prostitute's nipple. Not cleanly—it took a few tries. She'd been injected with such a heavy dose of Quaaludes that she didn't even notice. Clay gobbled the nub up, his molars savoring the treat like the head of a Swedish Fish.

He scowled. Not as appetizing as he'd hoped, but maybe it would finally rid him of his ill ways. Probably not, though. Not if the alternative occurrences he'd been experiencing in other time frames were trustworthy hypotheses.

"Don't worry, Lola. You'll be fine."

"Stop…calling me…Lo…name's…Erika." She finally passed out. From the perceived pain or the pills, Clay could not say.

Clay lifted the prostitute's eyelids. Her eyes had rolled back as far as they could go. She would be out for at least a few hours. He summoned a sudden moment of ill-timed kindness within him and placed a cross of adhesive Hello Kitty bandages over her mutilation. Still, that was going to hurt like the cruelest bitch in the morning once the effects of the drugs wore off.

He left her a generous tip.

Five: Blender Dysphoria

Crust caked Clay's eyes. He peeled the gluey substance off. Back in the cold, empty room. Again. He adjusted his hazy vision to view the feminine form before him. The woman looked distinctly different from the next time he would see her, her hair currently a pale grey with one red streak. Dressed in low budget fetish gear and holding a scythe. A HELLO MY NAME IS sticker above her left breast. Scrawled below the printed portion was her alleged name: LAURYN.

"So what you're essentially telling me is that I'm in danger of becoming pregnant?" Clay asked. "Do I have that right?"

"Well, yah, dontcha know," Lauryn said. "Ahem. I mean—no, of course not. Well, er, not exactly. It's a bit more complicated than that. Men can't be inseminated. Not by traditional means anyway."

"I think this is something that warrants some clarity."

"Here…drink this, love." Lauryn's British accent had fully returned, after a brief foray into Upper Midwestern.

Or this was probably when she first developed the affectation. It's even more cartoonish, less practiced than later on. When the hell am I?

Clay reluctantly obliged. He was parched. The steel cup was frostbitten, but the liquid was room temperature and tasted like a tepid mix of orange Kool Aid and vodka.

"I'm going to do my best to give you the gen," Lauryn continued. Her stern eyes darted back and forth between Clay's face and the growth. "Your—er—attachment, it's not from here. And it has a name—Lux. It's what you might call a parasitic symbiote. I realize that's a bit oxymoronic, but there really isn't any better way to describe it. It needs—"

"A *what*? I'm not sure I follow."

Lux inched along Clay's thigh, uncomfortably close to his groin. Clay lifted his hand to slap at it. Lauryn whipped her scythe out, placing the pressure of the blade on his wrist.

"Don't be daft. Wouldn't want to agitate it any more than you already have, love. Anyway, I can't be arsed to spell everything out for you. We aren't graced with infinite time here."

"You sure about that? Seems to me time's been a little more relative lately."

The dominant fiery hue of Lauryn's hair had returned. She sucked in deep, preventing her inflamed face from bleeding into the hairline, then continued.

"Can we please focus on one issue at a time?" Lauryn asked. Clay nodded, gave her the go ahead. "Lux needs samples of your marrow in order to thrive. It feeds off of your Y chromosome. If given enough time to feast, then yes—you probably wouldn't have much use for your todger anymore and we might have to construct a temporary canal for the offspring to exit. Oh, don't make that face, please. It'll all be taken care of in time. I promise you have nothing to worry about."

"So says the only person in this room who's not in danger of an identity crisis."

"Darling, you do know that you are so unfathomably wrong about that, don't you?"

Clay shrugged. "No. I've never known. I realize that now. And I'm not about to start today. It *is* today, isn't it?"

Lauryn turned away, offering no answer.

Six: Progress/Regress

Moon/sun/moon/sun/moon/sun/moon. Twilight, dawn, whatever existed between. Space and time—all a blur.

Lauryn shook her head like a disappointed mother. "I see that pesky little bugger has begun developing its limbs. This is definitely not good."

"You're telling me," Clay said. His throat sounded full of crackers, the tone barely recognizable as human anymore. Suctioned tentacles had grown from his hips. They whipped around in a poor imitation of helicopter blades. "This has gotten so much worse! Nothing you've been doing is even slightly helping to make this go away."

"Well, love…I never technically promised I'd be able to help you."

"I beg to differ. You *specifically* promised that very thing!"

"No, I believe that was the fourth lass whom you spoke with on the adjacent Sunday. Lily? Lindsey, perhaps? I just need to figure the proper way to prevent Lux from becoming full-grown. Look on the bright side, though…at least you're not going to be preggers anymore. Now put a sock in it, will you?"

Clay thought about the last time he had eaten but couldn't remember. Before he could ask his captor if they could call for takeout, he spewed the contents of his stomach onto the concrete. Bile, minuscule chunks of convenience store snacks, a handful of half-digested acetaminophen tablets. His hip-tentacles deflated like post-coital pricks. The vomit rapidly coalesced into something the consistency of pancake batter.

Only—pancakes weren't generally known for moving autonomously. Nor for having partially developed eyes.

The vomit squished and squelched and slid across the floor. Clay glanced down at his leg. The bulging growth had vanished, leaving his leg resembling a bruised fruit. Wanting to cheer but not possessing the energy, he grinned with the tiniest glee he could muster. Thick beige drool slipped down the side of his face, and he promptly passed out.

"Ah," Lauryn said, grinning down at the puddle. "Well, hello Mr. Lux."

She cracked her knuckles, spat off to the side.

"Right," she continued. "I think it's time we had it out."

Seven: Head Games

Clay exploded.

In her haste, Lauryn had lunged at Lux and missed, eviscerating Clay. She'd hit a sensitive spot in the man's body that triggered the blast. His shiny new tentacles decorated the floor, a gourmet sushi dish that had fallen from its plate.

Lauryn huffed, frustrated. The man's death was a bit of a waste. Lux was still squirming with life. It had taken control of what was left of Clay's severed head and was now bouncing madly off the walls, leaving Rorschach splats of hair and grue at every corner.

"Stop that, you little ponce!" Lauryn tried to grab the head, using the curve of her blade as if it were a Vaudeville hook.

Lux spouted garbled gibberish. Without Clay as its living host, it was having trouble forming the same phonetic sounds as human beings. Lauryn thought she faintly recognized the dialect. Unfortunately, she'd spent so much time in her various human shells that hearing it gave her a minor migraine. It would come to her. Eventually.

Clay's head finally kissed the floor. For a split second it appeared as if life still glistened in his eyes, but then the orbs were gone, sucked back into their sockets. Two red antennae poked through the empty holes. A crooked claw reached from underneath the dangling viscera. It lifted the husk of Clay's Halloween mask and tossed it to the side, revealing a malformed cyclopean crustacean.

"Well, Lux," Lauryn said, "you certainly have nil chance of winning any beauty contests. Tired of fighting yet? Ready to give up and let me kill you already?"

Lorelei…wait.

Lauryn paused, her tongue stumbling. "N-no! Don't you *dare* call me that!"

You'd think that as long as we've known each other, it'd be acceptable to do away with formalities. Did you forget where you come from?

"Why am I able to understand you now?"

Because I'm part of you. Always have been. You just don't remember.

"You get out of my head now, damn you!"

Technically I'm in Clay's head. Literally this time.

Lauryn shrieked. "I will *not* let you attach yourself to me!" Her accent began to lose its character.

Please…a truce. Before it comes—oh shit. It's…coming…now.

"What? You sodding little turd…what do you mean it's coming n—"

Eight: The Joy of Birth

Lorelei covered her face as hot wind bellowed from the gullet of the Clay/Lux hybrid. Its breath smelled like freshly hatched brine shrimp. The hybrid's scales shimmered and reflected off the blade of Lorelei's scythe, temporarily blinding her. She repositioned her body so the shine no longer burned her eyes. Lux's remaining tentacles that had not been hacked to bits now wiggled to life, mesmerizing like the snakes on a Gorgon's head. Its body had grown to the size of a pygmy elephant, and its single eye glared at Lorelei with vengeful rage. For a moment they both remained silent, waiting to see who might attempt the first move.

Clay's muffled cries for help came somewhere deep inside Lux's body.

You want out, Clayton? I'd like nothing more than to be rid of you for good. You're all calories, no nutritional value. Diet time starts now.

It stood up on its hind legs, then bent into a squat. Flatulent sounds that might have been humorous in any other situation now became ominous. Iridescent excrement birthed itself from its backside, followed by a head, hands, torso, ass, legs.

Clay.

Whole and unscathed. Born again from scat. Naked and shimmering with sparkling fecal lubricant.

Now, Lorelei…we can have a fair fight. One that you'll lose, naturally. Nothing personal. It's just that I'm considerably superior. Don't be jealous. Some of us are just lucky that way.

"You little bugger," Lorelei said. "I'm more than happy to oblige. If you think you're leaving this room alive, you're more daft than a horse taking a tour of a glue factory."

Clay cooed in the background, a dreaming fetus expelled too early from the womb.

And the ones from elsewhere lunged at each other.

Nine: All a ~~Dream~~

No, it most certainly absofuckinglutely is not, Clay. This is real, more fucking real than real has ever been.

Or maybe it isn't. What defines "real" anymore?

Stop it. Get your shit together. Right now is when it all matters. When you finally get yourself out of this mess and you can save the world. Believe it and make it so.

Or—it's possible you've got the day wrong.

Wouldn't be the first time.

Ten: Welcome to the Kaiju Revue

The edge of a jetty, on a beach neither Clay nor Lorelei had ever visited before. Not in this version of life. Or on this construction of Earth. Lorelei now wore a candy striper's outfit, Clay a bathrobe and fuzzy slippers. Very different attire from the next time both of them would be here. In the adjacent life.

Waves crashed around Lux's skyscraper-sized body.

"Well, this has gotten a tad out of hand, hasn't it?" Lorelei asked.

Clay grunted back, stroked his smooth face. The shit baptism had restored his normal complexion. He felt ten years younger. Maybe he was.

"You think maybe it just wants to go home, or is the water going to cause even more problems?" he asked.

Lorelei cocked her eyebrow at him.

"What?" he said. "You never had any of those grow monsters when you were a kid?"

She didn't answer.

"Were you ever a *kid*?"

Lorelei chewed the corner of her lip. The ocean grew darker, a storm brewing beneath its surface.

"We may be in for a real shite week," she said.

"I don't see how this could possibly get any worse."

"It depends. I don't think we'll know for certain until the events of the second yesterday occur."

"That's very specific."

"Precisely."

"At this point, that means nothing to me. I've completely lost track of the timeline."

"The irony, love, is that the window of time for that particular experience to cross your path hasn't actually happened yet. I'd know."

The water bubbled below their feet, taking on a life of its own. Clay puffed on a clove cigarette. He couldn't remember lighting it. Lorelei gently removed it from his fingers and took a drag. The smoke formed a salmon cloud.

"Clay?" Lorelei asked. "What's your surname?"

"Lowdermilk. Why?"

"Interesting."

Lux howled in the distance. Its tentacles whipped bullets of salt water toward the shore.

"What…why?"

"Oh. No reason."

"You can't just ask me a question like that and then give me an answer like that and expect me to ignore its significance."

Lorelei grabbed Clay's hand and squeezed it. She rubbed between his thumb and forefinger.

"What are you doing?" Clay asked.

"Isn't this what your kind calls comfort?"

Clay raised his eyebrow. "Yes. I suppose it is."

Lorelei released his hand and tiptoed along the rocks of the jetty. Clay watched her but did not follow.

"Why the letter 'L'?" he said, raising his voice. "What does it even mean?"

She spun, responded just as the waves crashed against the jetty. Her lips parted, but Clay couldn't discern if she was laughing.

Or simply lying.

coyote christmas

1. Bad Mother

I'm on my way, Maxie-boy.

Maria Leone zipped among the winding mountains at just past 2am, her 1985 Yugo throwing a huge fit. The road belonged only to her. Her eyes stayed focused on the twists and turns of the pavement, but her mind was committed to apocalyptic visions clouded by a mundane reality. She was alone. All she had was Max, waiting patiently for her at home. Her parents had been worm food for years, so she wouldn't be seeing them anytime soon, and her only real human friend was likely already fast asleep back in Solvang.

To be perfectly honest, she was a little miffed at Suzy. Why on Earth had she thrown a Christmas party on a Wednesday anyway? So what if it was actually itty-bitty baby Jesus's big special day? Was Suzy not going to be accepted into heaven if her goddamned Christmas party took place the weekend before or after? Sheesh.

Had it been worth the inconvenience to receive a sloppy, intoxicated kiss beneath the mistletoe? And from a guy named Kent to boot? Well, it's possible his name might have been Ken. Maria had a hard time deciphering the smeared name and number he had passed to her on the backside of someone else's business card. It would probably look like an even bigger mess when she was able to scrutinize it under her harsh fluorescent kitchen lights.

And of course it had to be raining tonight, too. Not a lot, but enough to be a nuisance. It wasn't enough that Suzy's house had been a 45-minute drive from Santa Barbara. No bones were being tossed in her direction. Maria was starting to regret taking the 154 instead of the 101. She wished she could roll the window down and allow the cool California winter air to force its way in, blow her hair into an absolute mess, and help her stay awake. She was definitely calling in sick tomorrow, spreadsheets be damned.

No. She couldn't do that. Not with the big promotion being dangled in front of her like a baby carrot. Not with competition from that insufferable prick Gary from sales. Besides, she knew at least two other employees would be calling in sick the day after Christmas. Law of averages. Murphy's Law. Something with "law" in it. Her brain was too beat to process anything complex, anything beyond the sheer force of driving. At least tomorrow (or, technically, today) would be Friday Eve, and she was going to remind the rest of the office about it with a fresh bottle of cheer. And also with the chocolate cream cheese cupcakes she had made this morning, currently cooling in her fridge. If she wasn't able to make everyone else feel better about trudging through another week, well, they could just sit on it and spin.

Maria's eyes shut for a split second. Her body jerked. Her heart jumped. She slapped herself in the cheek twice, felt the vibrant sting of skin on skin.

She hyperventilated, then sipped on a reheated pumpkin spice latte that had already gone lukewarm but was still doing its best to dull her wine cooler buzz and keep her alert. It tasted like elephant shit laced with nutmeg, but less good. And she was still yawning, so it wasn't even worth the affront to her taste buds. She also had a sneaking suspicion she was going to have to pee soon. Perfect.

The beams of her headlights reflected on the wet foliage, creating distorted shadow puppets out of the sparse brush. The shapes danced and swayed and leaned, and Maria almost felt like they were watching her, that they were preparing to lunge into her path, a spirited prank taken much too far. She didn't spook easy, though. Ghosts were just vivid memories, the dead trying to live on through the people who were barely hanging on in the corporeal world. And shadows, well they were no more than ghosts that had long since given up.

Still, she slowed down. Just a tiny bit. Not enough to get a gold star from a highway patrolman, but enough to appease her exhausted mind. She shifted the weight of her bulldog frame. Her seatbelt felt just a little tighter than it had any right to. She made a mental New Year's Resolution: more CrossFit, fewer Hostess Cupcakes.

And then, just as her wheels crossed the threshold of the Cold Spring Canyon Bridge, just as she was taking another sip of her lukewarm latte, one of the shapes did step into the road. But this shape was no shadow, no trick of the headlights. Maria had a split second to register that it was a wolf or a dog or a coyote or maybe none of those at all, its emaciated form creeping in a nonchalant trot, in no real hurry to cross the road. She screamed and swerved recklessly. The creature made no attempt to run for cover.

Driving 10 MPH over the limit despite the fact that wet bullets were falling from the sky, operating on a younger woman's sleeping habits, the soothing sounds of smooth-fucking-jazz on the stereo, Maria never had a chance. The tiny Yugo leaned at a 45-degree angle and rolled on two tires, as if it were trying out for a stunt show. Her drink spilled on the passenger seat, and she briefly worried that the stain would never come out, no matter how hard she scrubbed, before the car flipped over the edge of the bridge. Trapped inside, Maria plummeted 400 feet to her doom. The flight was about as graceful as a grade school ballet recital.

She only had time to think one pure thought before impact:

I'm sorry, Maxie. I'm not coming anymore.

2. Wag Alone

On the evening of December 26th, Max's final true excrement consisted of thin slivers of leaves from an indoor fiddle leaf fig plant, strings from a rope bone, and a stale, dusty baby carrot he had managed to paw out of the crevice between the kitchen counter and the refrigerator, all of which were promptly re-eaten.

He probably should have rationed it out.

The future looked grim for Max. His favorite chunky human woman friend was way damned late this time. She was never exactly punctual, but this was an all-time low. If Max wasn't served his breakfast promptly at 7am and his dinner at 5:30pm, something in the house got ruined. Guaranteed. And his stomach made for one hell of an internal clock. His main source of food was locked away in a plastic tub, seemingly miles away in the garage, an impenetrable door preventing access. He was upset, to say the least.

Max had felt unsettled throughout the day. He had lain patiently by the front door, breathing the fresh air through the tiny crack between the panel and the jamb, spraying clear wet snot whenever he felt the need. He knew he'd have plenty of time to move out of the way when his human returned because he'd hear the jingle of her keys as she unlocked the door. He really hated those damned things. But he'd wag, get that tail moving like never before. He'd use that tail to beat the shit out of his human's leg with love. And he'd promise her he'd never dig up the garden again.

After a few hours of whining that wasn't getting him anywhere, Max decided to take action. He had been holding his pee for way too long, and he had already soiled his sole potty pad earlier in the day, then shredded it in a fit of boredom. He trotted over to the corner next to the pad, lifted his leg, and let loose on the baseboard. When he was finished, he shuffled away, his tail between his legs, his ears pinned back tight against his head.

After a few more hours of whining near the front door, Max gave up and curled up on his ratty bed, but not before shoving off the blankie his human had folded on top of it.

The second morning, Max was certain he heard the mysterious human who sometimes came midday and sometimes brought the little boxes containing the tiny treats he hated but made him stop itching. He heard loud steps and a creak and a slam. His ears perked up and shifted back and forth like waving princess hands. He barked and howled to no avail.

The third morning, Max wasn't able to take it anymore. His stomach felt tight and dry. He sniffed by the Christmas tree, knowing there had to be something there for him, just like every year. His human thoroughly enjoyed watching him tear up a gift or two just so he could get to the prize, which was almost inevitably edible. Even when it wasn't, he still did his best to swallow it.

He had to knock through a few presents in the front of the tree and force a few ceramic Disney ornaments to commit suicide before reaching the special package. It was way in the back, on the other side of the tree where his human thought he wouldn't be able to reach. Well, she sure had been wrong about that. How many years had they been living together? He could have taken this anytime, but he was a good boy most of the time and he liked hearing all about it. Being a sneak just wasn't worth it. He already knew he was in trouble for pissing—and now shitting—in the corner, so he figured opening his gift a little early wasn't going to make his stern talking-to any sterner.

And that hunger thing, it can be a real motivator.

From the smell, he already knew what it was before opening it. Jerky. Glorious chicken jerky, loaded with glucosamine and chondroitin. There were some other assorted treats as well, and a rubber chew toy that looked like a mouse on a penguin's body, but Max lived for the jerky.

Max ate all of the edibles in the package within an hour, as well as some of the less-than-edibles.

The next few days were as follows: a drinking binge from the toilet (thankfully his human never left the lid down), a spiteful bout of Hershey Squirts on the couch, somehow magically removing his leather collar for a rather chewy but not-so-tasty treat, howling for the nonexistent neighbors. They were apparently gone for the holidays. Gone, baby, gone.

3. Feast for the Famished

Sharp, piercing jaundiced eyes peer through the brush, like fading flashlights from a tired search party. One by one, the pack appears beneath the soft moonlight, their patchwork fur like a threadbare quilt, shit kings of the shit canyon. The rain has given up for the night, but the air is still damp. The pack smells like mildew in motion, like festering bacteria on an unearthed corpse.

They creep close to the wreckage, as cautious as coyotes can be, which is to say not very cautious at all. Hunger trumps fear. Near the piles of twisted steel and flayed rubber and something considerably more enticing, tiny bonfires flicker in the dry brush, then are doused by the drizzle. But even a full forest fire would not keep the pack from the meat.

The bottom half of the body is crushed beneath the weight of the car, the front severed and ripe for the picking. There is enough to go around for the entire pack.

The first coyote steps forward, rips through the fabric and into the flesh, then carries away a sloppy, dripping hunk of limb. It hangs from the coyote's mouth like a cradled cub.

Another slinks toward the broken body, does not hesitate to dig its maw into the face. It tears an eyeball from its socket, which then explodes when squeezed between the coyote's incisors. It goes back for a sliver of cheek, then trots away, allowing another to savor its chosen treat. They exchange looks as they pass, looks that only their pack would recognize.

Teeth scrape against bone, tongues explore gristle and offal, once-vibrant life disappears down skinny gullets. Life becomes sustenance becomes excrement. From the soil and back to the soil.

A light blanket of snow falls, only into the canyon, only for the pack to witness and enjoy.

They are ghosts without sheets, killers without malice.

The pack howls in unison, to keep others away, to protect their magical, precious holiday gift. To rejoice in the circle of life.

4. Hope for the New Year

Nothing left to consume.

Not a scrap of lint, nor a stray cricket or spider, nor a crumbling treasure hidden deep in the crevices of the couch. The remaining water in the toilet was getting harder and harder to reach, and Max's body wasn't agreeing well with his attempts to stretch.

Loyalty was a cruel bitch.

Max's spirit had weakened exponentially each morning, each complete day. He couldn't control his panting, his whining. Perhaps hours ago, he had strained to squeeze out whatever might have been left in his bowels, huddled in the last clean corner of the tiny house. All that came out was a glob of mucus and few drops of thick, black blood.

The meat on his leg, buried deep beneath the coarse fur, grew more appetizing by the moment. Like any animal, his instinct was to survive, even if that meant sustaining himself on the only available resource: his own body. Or, rather, the parts of his body he could actually reach, which were few and far between. Whether that was an unfortunate or merciful circumstance, Max would never know.

Still, he had to make a choice.

He threw caution to the wind and bit into his leg, then stopped immediately when he felt a jolt of pain. He hadn't expected that. He cried, even though there was no one available to offer him sympathy.

A few minutes later, he tried again. He whimpered while doing so and made it just a little farther, breaking the skin. On the third attempt, it took some effort, but a chunk roughly the size of a quarter finally came loose, which Max swallowed without contemplation. The flesh was raw, rough, and gamy. He'd had worse in his life. Despite his human's best efforts to spoil him rotten, despite his desire for delicious flavor, Max had consumed a laundry list of bland, barely edible items. A button, a used maxi-pad, a tiny geode hunk, a discarded bird's nest. He wondered how long it would take to make the meat on his legs taste good.

Unfortunately, Max was all out of gravy.

the fabulous and tormented life of a serial extra

You're in the comfort of your own home, an almost empty bottle of stale, warm beer balanced between your legs, watching the final sweet smooching scene in a tepid romantic comedy called *Farrah's Wheel*. Blinding brightness explodes from your screen like God's brand new headlights. It's a picture-perfect park on a clear and radiant day. Families are picnicking. Children are frolicking. All are sticking to their assigned roles and doing the Screen Actor's Guild proud. The two leads quarrel and quibble, their eyes are buckets filled with gallons of salty tears—there's no way this relationship will work itself out in time before the credits roll. The music crescendoes in an edited attempt to make you—the viewer—connect with the scripted romance. And then comes the magical kiss. All is well in the cinematic world. Fade to black.

There's one little pinch, though: you've just seen *him* again. That meaty whale of a man.

No fucking way.

Think back to just shy of five minutes ago, before sheer shock forced you to ignore the peaceful roll of credits:

There it is again—that same fat familiar face you've noticed in more films than you care to count. He's now lurking, peeking from behind a cypress tree, tongue lolling, confused eyes staring directly into the camera—no, directly at *you*. There's no mistaking his intent to lock you into a staring contest. He lacks constant motion, giving off the impression of a cardboard cutout placed in the background for practical joke purposes. But he does move. Eventually. He always moves. And the movements are always slightly different each time you rewind for another viewing. A shift, a vibration, a quiver that seems unnatural no matter how slowly you track the images on your VCR. It's an optical illusion. It must be. This time—in this particular movie—the fat man clutches something in his left hand. It looks like his digits are twisted around vines of greasy hair attached to a severed head, but that wouldn't make a lick of sense now would it? There was no subplot in this film about an ax-wielding murderer let loose from the sanitarium. That would have been just plain silly (though infinitely more interesting than what transpired throughout the drab ninety minutes you just toughed your way through). Yet there it is.

Maybe.

Below what might be a not-so-cleanly-sliced stump, which had once been connected to a healthy set of shoulders, are occasional drips. The extreme brightness of the foreground masks the color of these drips, so you can't be certain, but it wouldn't be too much of a leap to presume this escaping liquid could be blood. After all, what else would you expect to be drizzling from a severed head? Perspiration? Fondue sauce? Of course, there is always the chance your brain is confused again. It's possible the man is just holding a grocery bag in which his jar of salad olives has shattered and the vinegar is now leaking from the bottom. It's a mundane, yet somehow interesting story, isn't it? A clever one, like the type of business you might come up with for one of your own background characters when you're on set.

In his right hand, the butterball man holds a sign made of what looks to be off-white construction paper. The penmanship is worse than what might have been attempted by a preschooler. You squint and read the text, then re-read.

I KNOW THAT YOU KNOW THAT I KNOW

FIND ME BEFORE I FIND YOU

As ominous as this message seems, your main concern is that you were not given a callback for this particular film. You would have been perfect as the sweaty jogger or the pigeon feeder or the miffed boyfriend.

For professional purposes, you become invested in the lives of the insignificant souls who inhabit the background, where they go after their bodies briefly enter the pivotal moment in the main characters' lives, before they become one with the silver ether. These seemingly arbitrary individuals still have lives and important business to attend to. You wonder how they might have impacted the scene had the director chosen to use them to greater effect. The stressed businessman bustling through a busy New York Street. The restaurant patron ordering a favorite meal. The barbaric warrior suited for battle. The corner whore far too beautiful to be anything less than a private escort.

Some are serial extras, popping up in more scenes than your eyes can process. Expert chameleons, using their mastery of disguise as the only art form they are allowed. An extra is not required to be engaging, but you feel it is your personal duty to bring this to your unsung roles.

Someone important might be watching, after all.

This portly man you've just observed for the umpteenth time, his raw talent does not go unnoticed by your discerning eye. He kills it in every version of the scene.

You wonder if a serial killer has ever succeeded in murdering extras across multiple films. Like the homeless, like forgotten street urchins—no one would miss them.

It just might be the perfect crime. Or the perfect film. You're not sure which. You scribble a note to create a pitch for this later and toss it into the steadily growing pile of papers you refer to as "Killer Ideas."

You first noticed the enormous extra in a low budget romp called *The Dead Come to Delaware,* which, as you later come to find, is actually his most recent appearance. A difficult film to take seriously, but this extra stands out among the group of parading ghouls. He offers the sort of commitment usually reserved for marquee names. You wonder if he is a method actor, if he has spent the nights prior to filming this scene in meditative preparation—clawing his way up from six feet of worm-ridden soil, filling his fingernails with roots and remnants of bugs, gasping for precious breath. Though most of the special effects look like they have been assembled with a combination of marmalade and papi-er-mâché, the entrails that pool below his hungry grin could have been lifted from the local morgue or donated by a friendly butcher.

You have always felt authenticity is an underrated quality in your craft.

The next time you see him, you do not realize until after the film has already ended that it is the same man. In fact, you can't even prove it at that point. You just know. Clear as cubic zirconia. This time it is a gangster movie called *Bullets for You.* The rotund extra wears a small badge that is only noticeable in one flashing frame. It reads:

THE SOUL IS SWELL WHEN YOU'RE TRAPPED IN HELL

Your eyes are immediately drawn to his face, naturally shaped like a villain from a Dick Tracy comic. He puffs on a cigar the size of a baby's arm and caresses a Tommy gun like a disinterested lov-er. His skin is pink and creamy like a baby mouse. You assume he must be some sort of albino, but without hair or eyebrows it is dif-ficult to tell. His eyes are tiny seeds. One of them faces the camera, staring directly at you with strong determination. The other eye is dead, lazy at best—it drifts like it has an agenda of its own. The extra is doing more than just chewing the scenery. He is savoring the scene like it is fine tobacco and rocketing it into a spittoon. Once you deduce this man is the same from *The Dead Come to Delaware* (it may be a guess, but it is at least an educated one), you decide you have a new favorite actor. If only you knew his name.

If only you could work with him.

If only you could pick the hidden nooks of his brain and learn the ropes from a true master.

In the next film, the man is naked, charging through a crowd at a college frat party, carrying what is presumably a rubber fire ax in one hand. The ax is splattered with what appears to be a combination of red paint and fire extinguisher foam. In his other hand, he is swinging what looks like a small intestine. You can't be sure because you've never seen a small intestine before, except in books focused on human anatomy, but you assume it is just a truncated version of a large intestine. His bloated belly may as well be with child and there is a quick uncut glimpse of his exposed genitals. You pause this moment, just as he passes by the Jacuzzi, and note his package resembles a shriveled up peach. It is so unsettling that it is able to distract you from enjoying the following scene in which one of the nerds at the party accidentally walks in on a topless blonde applying her makeup.

The extra's appearance might have been even more jarring had it appeared in any other film, but this is a wild teen sex comedy titled *Sorority Slumber Party Sunday,* the kind that revels in a surplus of random cheap gags. After arguing with yourself for a moment, you remember that you also appeared in this film. In fact, you were in the same scene where this maniacally meaty fool stole the show. Sometimes the films you have appeared in begin to blur together.

How did you miss this moment? Too much complimentary champagne and rice cakes? Too busy ogling the women paid to act loose?

You wonder why this unsung genius has never landed any speaking roles. Surely he must be adept enough to at least become a recognized character actor. You are of the opinion this man has the "it" factor, but you are not a casting agent so your opinion amounts to zilch.

Over the last year you have watched dozens upon dozens of movies and this man has weaseled his way into nearly half of them. He must be non-union. What is especially fascinating to you is these films span at least a decade, yet the extra does not appear to age in the slightest.

You shrug, pause the video, and masturbate to a close-up of massive untrimmed bush.

It's another dull night, and your girlfriend (let's call her Bailey) has begged you to rent *Farrah's Wheel* from the International Haus of Video again, but now she's burying her sleepy head in your willing lap, leaving you to suffer through the film solo. It is difficult to process the imagery on the screen. Why would the director not have noticed this man breaking the fourth wall? The scene could have been reshot with little effort. Who is the extra trying to communicate with? Do you honestly believe it's you he seeks? And what exactly is he holding? No, not the sign. The head. It can't really be what you think it is, can it? You rewind. Watch. Rewind. Watch again. The background is blurry and you are in the midst of a cheap buzz from even cheaper booze.

You have always been prone to wild imagination, even before you discovered the wonders of alcohol and recreational amphetamines. When you were six-going-on-seven, you used to see things in your house that were not supposed to be there. Empty things you falsely judged as corporeal. You would tiptoe along the barren hallway to your bedroom and swear you spotted something out of the corner of your eye, something dashing through your door before you could beat it there. Something bendy like a pipe cleaner. Something toothy like a goblin shark. Something tenebrous like a shadow on a moonless night. Something wet and tangled and glistening like a mass of kelp in a shallow ocean.

This was not your imagination, not as you remember it. It was truth. Understanding.

Bailey stirs and starts to wake up, her puffy eyes gazing up at you like they are stuffed with cotton, her headband marking her forehead with tribal fabric patterns.

"Did I fall asleep, Shane?" Just for argument's sake, we'll call you Shane. But you knew that was your name, didn't you? Sometimes you need a reminder. These are the things in life that are tangible. You must cling to them. At this point, the mundane is all that keeps you grounded in reality. Mundane Shane.

"Yeah. About thirty minutes ago."

"How was the rest of the movie?" Bailey reaches over to your bag of unshelled peanuts and selects a particularly large one. Inside you glare, outside you ignore.

"You didn't miss much."

"Did they fall in love?"

"I don't know."

After this night, you never see Bailey again. You do not call her. You take your phone off the hook, change the locks, and sleep at your mother's house twice a week under the guise of "doing the laundry." You are used to Bailey calling you on a daily basis and coming over at least three times a week, but you have managed to avoid her. You do not bother checking up on her. Sometimes you think you catch the shape of her boyish breastless body hovering just beneath your sheets, but it is probably just your leg run askew. You hope that is all it amounts to.

She no longer exists. She is an extra whose scene was deleted, the ancient work print decimated to ash.

It doesn't matter anyway.

You have more important matters to attend to.

What if he's you? The egregiously obese. The corpulent corpse. A future you…a you-that-might-have been. You are beginning to put on more weight than you prefer due to a recently acquired passion for apple fritters, so you suppose you could eventually fatten yourself up enough to match this man's weight, that you could pat on enough pancake makeup to resemble an exhausted eidolon. But not only would none of that be feasible due to a lack of time-traveling abilities, it would also be a twist more yawn-inducing than the worst cliché found in the most contrived of all horror movies. You wish your world could be so simply explained. Your "Terrible Ideas" pile dwarfs your "Killer Ideas" pile.

You have made fast friends with a casting director named Bradley. You hope one day he will be able to land you a speaking role, and you send him updated headshots on a monthly basis even when he does not request them. Bradley is a mellow cat. If he thinks less of you because of this, he is doing a stellar job of hiding it. Sometimes you and Bradley converse about creepy urban legends revolving around certain films. The ghost boy of *Three Men and a Baby.* The hanging Munchkin from *The Wizard of Oz.* You want to debunk this bizarre new myth about the fat extra before someone else notices it and the rumor has a chance to spread through the public like a deranged game of Telephone. You then remember Bradley cast the extras on both *Farrah's Wheel* and *Sorority Slumber Party Sunday*, including yourself in the latter, and so you ask him if he recalls a portly fellow in the buff, a fearless trooper caked in a variety of sticky substances.

"Of course," Bradley answers. "That was Barnabas Cross. He was a real card."

"Wow!" you say. Even this extra's name has the ring of a legend. You assume Bradley must know Mr. Cross intimately, that he can introduce you to him at some point, perhaps even cast you together in the background of a future classic scene, one that might involve sharing a bite to eat in a diner or watching a crucial game in a sports bar or being wrapped in fresh clean towels in a steaming sauna. Even better: the chance these activities can occur in real life. Wouldn't that be a grand turn of events? You begin to make plans in a corner of your brain reserved for irrational thoughts and then say, "Wait…what do you mean 'was'?"

"He's dead, Shane. He passed away last year."

"Oh." You consider the proper manners regarding this situation—querying about the death of an individual you have never met but intended to. You ignore social mores and say, "I'm…uh, sorry to hear that. How, if you don't mind my asking?"

"Did you see *The Dead Come to Delaware*?" Bradley does not pause to wait for your answer. He knows you have seen it. Of course you have. He'd have trouble naming a movie you *haven't* seen. "Tragic how it went down, really. Severe food allergy. Something the effects team unwittingly mixed into the mock intestines he was chewing on, I believe. I can't recall offhand what the foodstuffs consisted of. No one realized he was choking until it was too late. The makeup was already so pale and he was so committed to the role. It was such a chilling scene that the director decided to leave it in. I'm glad he did. For art's sake."

You nod in agreement, assuming Bradley can see this motion over the phone. A warm whisper of fear tickles your neck like a vulture's tail feather.

You thank Bradley for the information, for the conversation and end the call.

You can't help but think he is lying.

Fucking rotten liar.

Beau at International Haus of Video cracks jokes to you because you're renting *The Dead Come to Delaware.* Again. He thinks you should just buy the damned copy because it would be cheaper in the long run, but you have a strong aversion to the idea of hoarding. You've never liked Beau, not even a sliver. He has a smug face like a rat you just can't seem to trap. He smells like fish sticks thawing in the tropics.

You study the scene featuring Barnabas Cross, possibly his finest filmed moment. So fitting you recently learned it was his finale. Out with a bang, leave 'em wanting more. The appearance lasts less than five seconds, but you feel you can invent a convincing back-story for this character's pre-ghoul life based on the emotion Cross has graced the screen with. You would claim the living version of this character was a master plumber, a widower of five years, a father of a teenage boy with an affinity for reptiles.

You later find out from Bradley that this was the actual life of Barnabas Cross. He only worked as an extra to help pay off his varying debts. You truly are a master of guesswork. You are also upset his mystique has been tampered with. Mystery is the meat of the man.

You rewind. Watch. Rewind. Watch again. You notice something odd about each progressive viewing: the rot on Cross's face seems to spread just a tiny bit further each time you steal a glance, like grape jelly leaking from the smashed crust of a sandwich. It is as if the ghoul's deterioration is inextricably linked with the life of the videotape. It is like a modest pimple that dreamt of becoming a nougat candy, but instead took the path of a dried apricot.

The next few nights you rent *Farrah's Wheel* instead, and Beau cracks inappropriate jokes with you, presuming you have a "thing" for the lead actress's curves. Little does he know you don't even know her name or the color of her eyes, much less the minutiae of her arguable ass. But those ears…those Gelfling ears poking through her perfect straight hair have haunted the corners of your most passionate dreams.

You fast forward directly to the end, but Barnabas Cross and his severed head are now nowhere to be found. You squint and it's possible you see his silhouette near the cypress tree, but you can't be sure. You feel like you have been robbed, as if all of the juicy curse words and violence have been filtered out for network television. Of course, this film contains none of those things. It is rated PG due to one scene that includes brief nudity.

Did that moment ever exist? Barnabas was trying to tell you something, wasn't he? Did you miss the message? Is it hidden in another film?

After a few days of fruitless searching, you decide to take a fresh approach.

You have never aspired to be a gravedigger, yet here you are at the Restwell Cemetery, precisely fifty miles from the comfort of your own home, at a time of night when most normal citizens are huddled in the fetal position awaiting the battle against their impending alarms. You are approaching Barnabas Cross's tombstone with a rusted shovel in hand.

It takes you a while to find it. On the stone, beneath the cotton cobwebs, the engraving reads:

A MAN SHALL ONLY BE NOTICED IF HE ALLOWS HIMSELF TO BE SEEN

You have set up a professional camera you borrowed from one of your aspiring filmmaker friends, and you already know you will forget to return it. You want to capture the moment of revelation, even though you already know you will be the only one to ever view its footage.

You have purchased a potion with a pentacle or a pentagram or some sort of starry symbol painted on the bottle. It is brown and sediment-ridden. You toss it back like a vodka shot. It tastes like week-old wheatgrass.

You pull a lock of hair from your pocket and lay it on the tombstone. It is equally brown and blonde, curly like a fried noodle. Kind of like Bailey's, you think. It's been a while, though, so it's difficult to say. A thick paste of blood has dried between the strands. It smells like salted fish.

You dig into the tough soil for what feels like hours, only pausing once when you hear the creak of a nearby gate. You are a chiseled statue. A handsome gargoyle. The exposed nerves in your teeth feel like they have been dipped in a bucket of dry ice. You wonder how long it would take for spiders to tickle at your toes and burrow between your bones if you continue to hold this position.

Your shovel makes a *THUNK,* then a *TINK* for good measure. You brush away the excess soil and lift the coffin's door. There's just one problem, and it's a substantial one:

The grave is empty.

As were the others.

This is either problematic or serendipitous.

The wind carries a heavy moan. Footsteps plod between the plots like tranquilized horses. A scent intrudes upon your nostrils, like limes left to mildew during a wet season. Shifting clicks of insect lust seep from every nearby crevice.

Your name is not Barnabas Cross, as you so hesitantly thought at one point. Of course not. Is that what you were expecting? That would make zero sense. Cross is another man from another life with another's intentions. You may want to *be* him on some level, but you are not *him.* You want to meet him, and you hope that moment has finally arrived. Of course it has. This was scripted from the very start.

Your name is not actually Shane, either.

Your name is...well, you can't recall that right now. There are so many other things on your mind. But it's not important. In this life, who you *are* does not mean nearly as much as who you will *become.* Who you will play in your next coveted role that no one will ever notice.

Shuffling and harsh dragging throughout all corners of the cemetery. A spirit's weight is heavier than its original flesh.

The extras have arrived right on time. You have offered industry standard pay and considerably cadaverous catering choices, all of which they have come to collect. One extra in particular looks familiar, as he well should. He leads the rest of the group like a purulent Pied Piper. You wonder if the camera's eye truly adds ten pounds. If one is as massive as Barnabas Cross, does it matter?

You open a glass vial filled with blood, paint, food coloring, something wet and red. You dab the liquid to your index finger and paint a cross from your hairline down the bridge of your nose, from one edge of your brow to the other.

You beg the wanderers to halt, to hold still, so the camera will capture them in all of their glory. Due to either a need to be near you or sheer obstinance, they ignore your command. You are the origin within their phantom circle.

You welcome their approach.

You have prepared well for your first leading role.

You have mastered the method.

You are dedicated to your craft.

"Adonis Addiction"
(original to this collection - set in the same universe as Stroup's novel
Secrets of the Weird)

adonis addiction

Jak Severin's mouth spread wide, a cavern leading to uncharted territories. His fingers fished inside, examining the precise stitching within, the tiny coarse hairs lining his gums and tongue—a tongue once capable of simultaneously exploring two distinct directions now no longer split down the middle. Satisfied with the healing's progress, Jak grinned to expose a brand new set of dental implants. The faux enamel gleamed bright enough to blind a man, but the placement of the teeth was set slightly askew, a deliberate choice so as not to appear *too* perfect.

Before falling slave to sutures, he'd had faux-feral teeth, filed to daggered perfection. Pure misery to have them removed, torn from their ligaments one by one, but the result had been worth it. The quality of Dr. Kurosawa's craft was remarkable. Not just professional accomplishment, but a true work of reconstructive art.

Jak turned to face Leila. His lover, her arms crossed tight.

"You're becoming a little too proud of yourself," she said. "It's not an attractive attribute."

"I think I'm finally getting close, Lei-Lei. I can almost pass."

"I prefer the old you."

"That makes one of us." He turned and kneeled before her, brushing his lips against her belly and vellicating her navel with his tongue. Their eyes formed an invisible bridge.

Said between moans and whimpers, "I'll never understand why you're so willing to rid yourself of such beautiful scarlet eyes. Jak."

His new contacts—merely a precaution. Simple, basic brown. No need to attract unnecessary questions or startle potential allies with abnormal hues. But he was starting to get used to them, to prefer them.

"Oh, please. These are only for the public, my special one. Kurosawa claims there's no way to transplant an entire eye without a brain transplant. *Yet*."

"Is that 'yet' yours or his?"

"I can remove them when I'm around you if you'd like."

Leila's gaze fell askew, severing the optic bridge.

"What's he doing with the bodies anyway?" she asked. "Did you ever find out?"

"Doesn't matter much anymore. What's worth the risk to him is worth triple to me. It's tough for a plastic surgeon to get paying gigs without keeping his hands well trained. And we're almost done with what's in store for me."

"Just please," she said, facing him once again, "whatever you do— don't get rid of this." Her fingers traced a curved scar that traveled from the middle of Jak's chest to his shoulder. A token of bravery earned protecting Leila during an assault by the Natural Born Devils before the lovers could leave Spokane voluntarily. The NBD had tracked them up the coast, all the long way from California, after they'd defected from the Eaters and their miserable leader who'd fallen prey to delusions of grandeur.

Like most men's scars, Jak's mark was tainted with nostalgia. The man who had attacked Jak and left him with this reminder, however, hadn't fared so well. A chunk of throat chewed, swallowed, eventually excreted. But the encounter had just given the NBD more fuel for their bigoted fire.

"Never," Jak said, his tone distant. "Of course not."

"Why go to all of this trouble, then? Why not just be proud of who you…who *we* are? Just because the rest of the world doesn't understand our spiritual choices doesn't give them the right to hunt us down. It doesn't mean we have to change our core or bow to someone else's beliefs."

The edges of Leila's fingernails came dangerously close to penetrating the scar tissue, then relaxed.

Jak respected his partner's fidelity to their former cause. The same level of loyalty she'd had for their love. But he also knew that the concept of Eating was in danger of reaching its expiration date. The time had come for a new chrysalis, one that would help him regain his humanity. If he could summon the strength to make the change.

"Is a leper proud of his lesions?" Jak said. "A eunuch of his impotence? Pride should be reserved for those who accomplish something of worth, not for those doomed to dwell in hiding."

"It doesn't need to be pride, then. Just contentment."

"Contentment is the death of desire, Leila. This change will be better for the both of us. You'll see once you start down the same path I have. Don't you want to stop living in fear? Don't you think it's long overdue?"

"And what about the feeling that they'll still know? That they'll see right through your façade. Don't act like that's ever going to change or go away. Jak, I've been afraid for so long I can't even remember a life before fear. Why stop now?"

"Oh, quit your fussing. I'll have a much easier time protecting you once I'm…complete." The way Jak had looked before, he'd never have garnered any sympathy for their cause. Not a chance. But soon he'd be able to walk and work amongst everyday people. And become like them as best he could. "Then we can finally move to living quarters far more secure than these. We're not safe here."

He thrust his arms up into the open space of their barely habitable studio apartment, as if showing it off to prospective new tenants. Roaches the size of rodents were late paying their sublet rent, the cracks in the walls begging to split into smiles and frowns.

Leila had decorated the room with strings of old chicken bones and hand woven dream catchers, while Jak had chosen random framed art acquired at garage sales around downtown Bellingham. Pollock knock-offs, abstract Rorschachs, a Velvet Christ. A botched version of humanity.

"We don't need something better or safer," Leila said. "We've lived in conditions far worse than this and treated it like a palace."

"There's nothing wrong with taking steps toward something that might help us blend."

"I don't believe there's a place on Earth willing to allow that."

Jak returned to his primping, engrossed in the mirror's flattery. "Besides," he said, "it doesn't matter that the rest of the world will never get to appreciate you. Your lovely looks have always been for these eyes only."

"Which eyes?" Her pout so pathetic now that Jak couldn't help but turn to her and embrace her. Her body squished against his like putty. "Which ones are really yours?"

"Lei-Lei…I see you with my heart. That is all that matters."

A nameless man sprawled in the courtyard, his innards draped like glistening red tinsel along the hedges. Whatcom Falls Park was deserted. Cruising open for business, operating during hours when most people were in the midst of banal dreams of work, death, unfulfilled fantasies. Tonight another slow night. Almost no one up for sale and zero stragglers. But Jak had always fancied himself a patient man. Patience brought payment.

Beyond the bushes, he'd propositioned a nervous gent, likely a closet case forsaking his wife and children for the night under the guise of "working late at the office." After some dull small talk and silent, lustful stares, the man briefly found fortune in caressing Jak's firm cullions before experiencing the slash of a straight razor at his throat. This swift act accomplished the kill, but just as the man's final throes failed him, Jak had also disemboweled him with a second, larger blade.

Now—Jak stirred his finger through the crimson soup gurgling in the man's torso. A therapeutic motion, the equivalent of squeezing a stress ball or chanting a sacred mantra. Plus, he rather enjoyed cleaning the mess he'd made. A fresh kill could be so…piquant. His restored tongue made it difficult to maneuver the offal into his mouth, and the dental implants prohibited proper chewing techniques, but—even though the beast would always lurk deep within the belly of the makeshift man— Jak knew he would adapt. Eventually.

With his untamed act, he'd surely committed heresy in the eyes of the Eaters. But what they could not see would not disturb their failed religion. And he believed each man who desired to change within would always struggle with the former self's attempts at judgment.

Why deprive myself? he thought. *I'm writhing in copper and roses. A delightful mixture. If only Leila were here to share. Perhaps I can bring her a souvenir.*

A stained white sneaker wedged in a bush. A crushed pair of specs balancing atop a bench. A knockoff watch still attached to the man's wrist.

Jak chose the watch.

Moonlight shimmering across a puddle of blood on the sidewalk. Jak caught his own reflection in the fresh ichor. The unfamiliarity of his drenched grin startled him. A savage sophisticate. Now with his full weight on top of the man, Jak slithered in his stew. He licked, lapped, swallowed.

Hmm. Looks like this old boy's getting some semblance of loving after all.

Jak paused his pleasures, dragged the kill to his car.

Nude atop a necropsy table, the chill of the steel matching his own cadaverous flesh, Jak tapped his perfectly manicured fingernails along the edge. The room smelled of stale mint and chlorine. A faint beeping cadence soothed in the background.

Dr. Kurosawa was clearly hesitant to speak. "Do you have your, er…payment?"

He slid a stethoscope across Jak's exposed chest. Tradition, habit, a formality. A way to allow the doctor to retain some sense of normalcy in the examination.

"In my trunk," Jak said. "What exactly have you been using these corpses for anyway?"

Kurosawa chuckled. He removed the stethoscope and came down from his stepstool, his true tiny height now exposed. Jak was the Chrysler Building to Kurosawa's single-story home.

"May I show you something?" the doctor asked. Before waiting for a reply, he scurried over to his desk and snatched something out of a drawer. He returned to Jak, presenting a small photo album to him. "I'd like you to take a look at some recent work an associate of mine performed."

Jak thumbed through the photos. Seamless surgical transformations that noticeably improved the further he delved into the album. Jak stopped and dwelled on one photo in particular, putting his finger on it for emphasis. Something familiar yet fresh about the woman. Fashion model cheekbones, overcast eyes, wet lips dipped deep in a strawberry's flesh.

"Ah, yes. Sasha," Kurosawa said. "She's a special one. Quite remarkable work."

Sasha. Can this really be the same Sasha I once knew? The most cunning of the Eaters?

"I can see why," Jak said, feigning aloofness. Disinterest to protect his own. Always vigilant. No telling who could be watching, listening. "She's as attractive as any other woman. Perhaps even more so, since she had to work so hard to achieve this new beauty."

"She lives in Seattle now. From what I understand, she's been acclimating well."

Jak placed a prodigious hand on the doctor's shoulder, trying to return his thoughts to his original sentiment despite the alluring distraction. "It's not just the quality of the work that matters, though. Most importantly…this surgeon…he empathizes. Who is he?"

"An old college chum. I can refer you to him. He has a practice near your old stomping grounds."

Jak nodded, withheld a gag. *Sweetville.* That cursed city. That shithole town. Too many debts to pay there, too many ghouls from his past prepared to gnaw at him.

Kurosawa held his head catawampus. "I have to say, though, I can't help but wonder why you've chosen to alter the beautiful anomaly that is the real you. I know I sound like one of those pitiful admirers, but—"

Jak laughed. "You're starting to sound too much like my Leila."

"I apologize, my friend. My place is not to question the cosmetological motives, but to bring comfort to the discomforted."

Jak nodded in polite agreement. His motives were simply a matter of self-preservation. The NBD had been gaining ground too quickly, too much public support for the eradication of what they deemed the "unseemly element." They weren't just a simple street gang anymore. They'd cleaned up their act, some even running for office now.

Kurosawa produced an insulin needle from a nearby tray. He passed it to Jak.

"I think this may be the solution to your most dire problem," the doctor said.

Jak peered into the tip of the needle, as if his eyes could extract the answer from it.

"It's a synthetic hormone," Kurosawa continued. "One daily subcutaneous injection into the stomach. At your weight, I'd recommend no more than one milligram per injection. Do this for fifteen days, then take another fifteen off. If the results show promise, I'll set you up with a higher dosage. Normally, I wouldn't even bother prescribing the first dosage, but you're somewhat of a unique case. The Gods of Genetics have been kind to you."

Jak stared at the doctor in disbelief. "Will this really work? Will it stop the craving?"

"Yes," Dr. Kurosawa replied. "In theory."

"What makes you think this is the trick?"

Kurosawa hesitated. Jak could see that the doctor was sorting out his secrets, determining which of them were safe enough to release.

"I've based my experiments on my colleague's notes regarding Sasha, and I've applied a placebo to the control group, but the dead can only tell so much. However, it's inconclusive at best. I need a—"

"You need a live specimen."

"Yes. The initial results may have been a fortunate fluke. I need to know for sure."

Jak hummed with delight, holding the insulin needle close to his chest like a delicate crucifix. He grinned, his mouth finally beginning to realize the charismatic potential of a human smile. He couldn't wait to go home and share the good news with Leila.

Jak had never been able to satisfy Leila by conventional means. Endless pleasure possibilities, and so few of them did the deed. Smother her in lukewarm oil, pick at the loosening scabs between her fingers after a kill, knead her torso's rolls like baker's dough. Jak hadn't experienced a comparable phenomenon with another woman in uncountable measures of time. For more years than he dared count, he and Leila had been near inseparable. Before she'd first wiggled into his life, before the Natural Born Devils had become an imminent threat to his very existence, Jak had travelled with General Chauncey's Secret Sideshow, billed as "Half-Man/Half-Monster." Venturing across forgotten cities of North America, in every town— almost without fail—there had been at least one woman willing to succumb to his salacity. Often he had taken two lovers in the same city, sometimes simultaneously. Other times the women had sought him out, though this was far more rare. Even though Jak had been blessed with an impressive set of genitalia, he was still considered just one of the freaks. Still, these women hadn't been desperate. Some could have bedded nearly any man they desired. They were thrill seekers, sexual deviants who had exhausted all toys, partners, and orifices. They wanted Jak's body as an experience they could dream about while twisted tight in their covers next to their unassuming husbands. And they would likely only admit the truth when in the eventual coffin, whispering to the worms that hollowed through them. Jak fucked them and forgot them all, moving on to the next town like a jaded rock star, the women mere tally marks in his sexual conquest.

Now he was sliding beneath fresh flannel sheets that smelled like baby powder, passionate nails raking across his back, nibbling at tender nipples that were in danger of being sucked until they were dry, chafed, and blackened.

Leila's claws raked across his chest, and then she stopped, sobbing. "Jak…what happened to your scar?"

"Laser treatment. It's coming along quite well, don't you think?" Jak's battle scar, once a crescent moon rich with history, symbolism, and undiscovered nooks now appeared to be no more than a severe welt.

"My sweet Jak. Is there anything left of you?"

"I'm not sure how to answer that."

Annoyed, Jak got up from the bed. He preened at his hair in the mirror, slicked his eyebrows down, admired his complete transformation. His skin was accepting the hormone at an unprecedented rate. So close to his desired result that he could taste the sweat of humanity on the tip of his tongue.

"Well," Leila said, "maybe your precious Dr. Kurosawa wouldn't have to worry about that if he wasn't performing illegal, unethical surgeries."

"Since when are we concerned with ethics?" Jak asked, turning to grab a clean shirt from the closet. He buttoned it and slid a frayed pea coat around his shoulders. In the coat's pocket—the watch he'd stolen from the corpse at Whatcom Falls Park. He'd never gifted it to Leila. And he had no desire to now.

"Are you going somewhere?" Leila asked.

"Yes. I'll be back late. Don't wait up."

"I can't take much more of this. I miss you. Being apart almost every night is ruining us."

"I know."

Jak exited the apartment. The room he left behind was cold. Empty. Lonely.

Jak stalked outside a dive bar, entranced by the gaudy neon lights. Once ready, he entered with a serpent's precision, eyes scanning the endless meat market. He yearned to bring Kurosawa the finest specimen his charm could secure.

Be positive, Jak. Confident. You're so close to completion. No one is out of your league anymore.

Jak planted himself at the bar, ordered a Moscow Mule. He subtly surveyed the crowd for hours in the size of minutes, just a lonely man lost in a bar measuring time by a different clock. Most of tonight's women were hypnotized by the allure of liquor purchased by other men and a pounding ruckus that some might have referred to as music. Jak was set to count his losses and head home to Leila, already preparing his apology, when he finally spotted his perfect target.

Short blonde hair chopped into an angled bob. Full pink pillow lips. Eyes like those of a sleepy puppy just separated from its master. Nervous hands boogieing across the bar as if playing a grand piano. Remnants of youthful flesh taking its final steps toward middle age. And oh, so alone.

Jak watched her as long as necessary to confirm her solitude. He caught her peeking in his direction, above the straw swimming in her watered down Mojito. He did not tear his stare away. Their eyes danced a flirty jig.

This is going to be easier than I thought.

The stool adjacent to hers became available. And so he approached her, introduced himself.

Her given name was Hope, but she insisted Jak call her by her nickname—"Less."

"All my friends call me that," she said, a giggle begging to escape her lips. "Get it? It's because of my crummy luck. Like, for instance—I went to culinary school, but I can barely toast a piece of bread without burning it. Funny, huh?"

"I don't think it's funny at all," Jak replied. "It's borderline cruel. Perhaps I'll call you Esperanza instead."

Her face shifted from kittenish to quizzical. "What does that mean?"

Jak chuckled, waved it off. "It doesn't matter. I do, however, believe it's an utter tragedy that the lowly men in this bar have proven they have absolutely no taste by passing up such a rare beauty."

He placed his hand upon hers, hovering between a threat and a caress.

She grinned. "I think you need to buy me another drink."

Soon they were fleeing the bar, gliding down Holly Street, drizzle needling their exposed faces. Jak couldn't decide if Less was adventurous, reckless, or somewhere in the blurring void between. She roped her arm around his, thanked him for walking her home even though it was only a few blocks away. He felt proud, without a hint of hubris. This was a milestone moment. Here he was, walking the streets without a care in his bones. This world of men almost within his grasp. He'd sampled the dream and desired a much larger slice.

The rain spit harder. Jak chose chivalry, removing his jacket and draping it around Less. She melted into it, into him.

They reached her apartment, and she invited him in.

Jak entered Less as a man, not a monster. She squealed with virgin delight. The heat of her slick walls fit his shaft like a winter glove, her orgasmic breath a bonfire's remnants.

As their bodies merged, a distinct sensation possessed him, one he had perhaps never consciously experienced before.

Warmth.

Any apologies Jak would have had to offer Leila upon returning home would have fallen upon severed ears. Lovely lobes that now lay in pieces on the floor.

Where her eye sockets should have been was instead a pale, clean meat canvas stretched across a stump that had once been a head. Other portions of her face were placed in unexpected crevices of her body, puzzle pieces that would never snap together. The curves and rolls of her torso resembled the excess clay of an unfinished sculpture.

The NBD had found them, tracked them down somehow. Again. And he hadn't been there to protect his promise to Leila.

Leila's mouth, unlike her other orifices, was still located where one might expect it to be. Frowning and pouting in Jak's direction. Judging him even in death. Jak pressed his finger against her lips, then leaned his face closer and licked inside, a final kiss.

He shed no tears, for it was far too early to claim that degree of humanity. Then he fled with only the clothes on his back.

A typically dreary afternoon in Seattle, but the weather was as wondrous as could be to Jak. The dark dew of the Northwest kept him well hidden. Even though he now had no reasonable need to remain within the shadows, the cloak of rainfall still offered him solace.

As did the pressure of Less's hand in his.

Time had passed between first, second, and third dates, but Less had soon professed her love to Jak. No fear, no pretension. She'd urged him to leave Bellingham with her soon after. She'd never wanted to stay anyway. Upon arriving in their new city, Jak quickly landed a security job at a shipyard. Less was not the type of woman that loved a man for his money. That much was certain.

"You're not like anyone else I've ever met," she'd said on the night her love had been revealed. "You're a special man."

He couldn't bring himself to return the endearment, though he knew he felt…something.

Is this love? The same as what I felt for Leila? Seems like I can barely remember that life.

"Do you wish all men were like me?"

"No," Less said. "You're one of a kind, and I wouldn't have it any other way."

"No one will ever have a reason to use your nickname again. You're my Hope. *Esperanza.* That has to count for something."

Jak had abandoned Leila. Her body and her soul. Regretful in many ways, but better to not retain any trace of the old life. A clean slate.

Now—Jak and Less were strolling through Pike Place Market, soaking in the scents of salmon and peaches, limbs locked like lifetime lovers, every step taken a memory in progress.

A woman caught Jak's eye, a few booths away. Not in a lascivious manner, but a curious one nevertheless. Less was engrossed in endless rainbows of produce, gabbing away with the vendors about lobster tail preparation and what fruits not to combine in a salad.

Besides, even if he did desire another woman, this mysterious one across the way was already with another man formidable enough to make even Jak wary of intrusion. She was an exotic beauty. Eyes the color of ripe plums, slightly elongated neck, a wispy body. He knew he had seen the woman before, but where?

It came to him in a rush.

Sasha. Yes. Of course.

Then, as if both of their names had been whispered through the bustling crowd, her eyes met his. She was beautiful, perfect. Human.

As was he, now.

An initial look of shock on her end, then quick and obvious recognition. Sasha offered a coy smile, a slight wave that her beau couldn't see, a wink that might have appeared as a nervous tic to any passersby. Her deliberate motions seemed to say to Jak, *"We've both made it, haven't we? We've arrived."* And his expression to her proclaimed, *"Isn't it wonderful?"*

"Good God, Jak—look at the size of this zucchini!" Less shook Jak out of his trance long enough for him to snicker and spit an obligatorily dirty joke. This was his life now. Comfortable. Normal. Jak was happy, save for the fact that he knew of no easy way to keep Less in his world forever. A part of him wanted to gnaw at Less some night when she slept soundly, make her want to be like him. The way he used to be, but still was in many ways and would ultimately forever be. Was he even capable of such power?

They turned to leave the market, to head to their shared home. Jak slid on his sunglasses as they stepped into the light. He snuck one last peek behind him into the market, scanning the human traffic for any trace of Sasha.

His search was to no avail. She was gone, blended, lost in the crowd.

"Cameron West's Nagging Sensation of Having an Unwanted Girlfriend"
(original to this collection)

cameron west's nagging sensation of having an unwanted girlfriend

On any normal night, in any suburban neighborhood, in any teen-age bedroom, ceilings are not typically known for growing teeth.

Cameron West was having an abnormal night.

Through his near-transparent sheet, he peeked up at the ceiling. Had the teeth been two-dimensional and printed in a textbook focused on dental anatomy, they might not have appeared so menacing. Small, overall free of plaque, and one of the molars had a tiny gold filling. Struggling to chew, the disembodied teeth dug canals in the plaster, dropping small bits of powder onto the bed in the process. They clicked together in a metronomic cadence. Cameron couldn't help but wonder if the teeth's motion meant they yearned to speak or to eat. This mouth wanted him. For sustenance, for sentiment—did it matter which at this point? Neither advance would be welcome. He also wasn't sure which would be worse.

How would he explain the damage to his mother this time? Couldn't blame it on rats like he had with last week's predicament. That old trick had already gone stale after two sets of groping fingers had clawed their way through a portion of one of the walls. And then they'd just bailed, clocked out before completing the job, leaving him with a mess and only a few half-awake hours to devise a semi-convincing lie.

Now—a tongue appeared between the teeth. Fleshy and wriggling, though not plump and pink like a healthy person's tongue. It was grey and caked in a thick white paste, as if it had fallen victim to chronic cottonmouth then attempted to cover the condition up with a layer of expired toothpaste. Next—a pair of lips pushed through the plaster. Beautifully shaped and androgynously pouty, but ravaged by chapping and cracking. They puckered and smooched as the tongue licked with determined desire, a mockery of lust. A film of perspiration seeped through Cameron's forehead, forming a damp veil. He couldn't fathom what it might be like to kiss these phantasmagoric lips. Applying balm with sandpaper seemed endlessly more appealing.

The shapes of hips, breasts, and legs pressed through the plaster as if the ceiling were made of chewing gum. A perfect pelvis gyrated. Thin, serpentine arms reached toward Cameron. Rulerlength fingers beckoned to him, begging for an eternal embrace. A full face pushed through, mannequin-still. Equally striking and startling. The tongue wormed out further, and it had grown much longer than it had any right to, with seemingly no intention of stopping. Under other paradoxical circumstances, in some dream logic-drenched pubescent fantasy that resulted in the need for a change of soiled sheets, this approach to arousal might have been encouraged, even expected. But this was not right in the slightest. Not for Cameron. There was one small problem.

Cameron didn't like girls.

"So you never saw its face?" Fully entranced by the tale he'd just been told, Lars Dietrich munched on a cheese and mayo sandwich, his voice raised to battle the school cafeteria's cacophony.

"Hmm?" Cameron was distracted, distant. He regretted not having a cup of coffee before school. His entire daily routine had been rattled from the previous night's events. He still hadn't caught up on sleep from that first visit a week ago.

"Don't think you're getting out of this convo that easy. The ghost thing in your dream, stupid. Was he cute at least? God, I hope so."

"Oh…well, I don't think that was what it was."

Cameron nibbled at a tater tot, only as a formality, only because acting as if he were hungry seemed like the sensible thing to do. The sane thing. He *was* still sane, though. Of course he was. Unless this was what it felt like when the final strands of stability snapped and spiraled into lunacy.

"What else could it've been?" Lars asked.

"Dunno. Definitely wasn't a dream, though. It really happened."

"Sure, Cam. And I'm having a scandalous tryst with Liam Hemsworth." Lars popped the tab of a soda, contorting his face into a tragic mask as the contents fizzed and spilled over. He did his best to suck the juices up before they escaped, lapping at it in such a way that Cameron couldn't help but think of what he'd seen last night, the tongue pushing through the ceiling.

Cameron shook the thought off, sipped from his juice carton. "It wasn't a guy, either," he said, his volume sinking.

"Ew." Lars pretended to spit up his well-chewed sandwich. "So this dream thing-that-might-or-might-not-be-a-ghost swings by and tries to make out with you or molest you or whatever, and it's a *girl*? Paging Dr. Freud. Your new patient is ready to see you."

"Come on…that's not fair. I mean, I kinda had a crush on Wendy Lucas in middle school, so it's not *that* weird."

"Yeah, and Wendy waxes her mustache now. What does that tell you?"

Cameron rolled his eyes.

"Besides," Lars continued, placing his hand across his cheek and puckering his lips, "who needs a bearded bitch to fawn over when you've got this utterly *gorgeous* face to gaze at every day?"

"Oh, whatever, Lars. Shut. Up."

Lars giggled, then lifted his sandwich to his mouth and snatched another bite. Cameron noticed something wedged in between the chunks of cheese and dripping mayo, something that should not have been there.

A tooth.

No. Not possible.

Before Lars could insert the remainder of his sandwich into his hungry mouth, Cameron leaned forward and smacked it out of his friend's hand. It fell to the ground.

A confused look washed over Lars's face. "Bitch, why you gotta go and ruin my lunch?"

Cameron hesitated before answering. "There was…something…in it."

"Oh no, it better not have been a bug. Geee-ross!"

"No, it wasn't that. It was…it was…"

Lars leaned over to pick up the ruined sandwich corner. Cameron clenched his ass cheeks together, expecting a shriek from Lars after being bitten. By a single tooth. A silly thought—not to mention the even more absurd notion that his Baby Huey-sized best friend would scream like a little girl. Wouldn't happen in this lifetime.

The sandwich was on the table now, and Lars opened it. Cameron grit his own teeth, only to discover that there was, in fact no tooth in the sandwich at all.

"Dammit, Ma," Lars said under his breath. "Drinking on the job again. That's the second time this week." He reached into the mess and pulled out a marshmallow. After studying it for a moment while scrunching up his face, he flicked it through an open window and into the nearby bushes.

Relief surged through Cameron. God, he needed to get some sleep tonight.

"What did you think it was?" Lars asked.

"Nothing. I'm just on edge today, I guess."

"What's on your mind, hon? Dr. Dietrich is listening. Just don't forget I charge by the hour."

"Um, there's something else I need to show you…something that'll prove what happened wasn't a dream."

"Oh, we're back to *that* again?"

Cameron paused, burning his reticent blue stare into Lars' reluctant browns. Unsure if he should share.

Lars affected a yawn. "The suspense is boring me."

"This…this was on my nightstand when I woke up." Cameron's hand quivered and passed a long, lined sticky note to Lars. The paper was adorned with printed purple flowers and baby bunnies. Written in handwriting so beautiful it could have been calligraphy was a recipe:

<u>Soup of the Gods</u>

3 cups pureed tomato

2 bouillon cubes

1 onion, thinly sliced

1 can organic garbanzo beans (must be organic)

1 bag frozen peas, thawed

1/3 cup virgin blood

2 cups coconut milk

2 ½ cups filtered water

1/4 t cumin

1/3 t sea salt

1. **Bring all ingredients to a fine boil, until a thick skin has formed at the top.**
2. **Chop the skin into equal triangles to later be dipped back into the soup.**
3. **Serve with chips, spinach dip, and chilled mango.**

"Okay," Lars said, "so your mom's on some wicked unorthodox new diet. Who are we to judge?"

Cameron backhanded Lars on the side of his arm, which had about as much impact as smacking a brick wall with a fish. "Come on, Lars. Give me a little credit. This isn't a joke. The ghost—the whatever-it-was—left this for me."

"So let me see if I follow this nonsense. This dream thing in your room…I mean this totally clueless girl-thing…aw, screw this—I'm too confused to even care anymore." Lars pulled out a second sandwich, this one with a small handful of potato chips wedged between the bread.

"Some friend you are. We'll see how you feel when this thing ends up killing me."

Lars pinched Cameron's cheek. "Don't think that's what it wants, sweetheart."

Cameron's arm dangled its dead weight alongside the bed. With sleep as his master, this was not a willful motion. But somewhere in that wicked void between dreaming and cognizance, his fingers tickled across something thick and moist, something that quivered, a jellyfish that had lost its way from sea to suburbia.

He awoke with a shriek, clutched his sweaty cushion as if it were a passionate paramour, chewing at the fabric to avoid releasing another embarrassing squeal. His toes were exposed, chilled little fleshsicles wiggling at the foot of the bed. He curled them tight and pulled them back under the security of the sheets. The duvet weighed down on him as if it were freshly poured concrete. He kept his breathing quiet and steady. No wind whistling through his window, no crickets in the midst of courtship and song. Seconds of silence preceded a sudden scuttling across the hardwood floor. Then—a puff of coconut breath wafted from below.

Cameron shook himself awake. He needed to remain alert, a soldier awaiting certain ambush. But from whom? From *what*? He wasn't sure he wanted to find out.

Though he couldn't see her, Cameron knew that she—that *it*—had returned. And was lurking somewhere in the room.

As if inspired by this latest intrusion, Cameron recalled a snippet from an obscure poem recited to him in his early youth, a verse passed down by ancient aunts, meant to keep naughty nephews in line. Its title—*Succubus Summer, Infinite Hunger*:

"A tongue, a touch, a taste of love/Wriggling both below n' above

Holds so tight with mealy arms/Seduces with such vicious charm
When th'clock strikes the darkest hour/The lover chooses whom to devour

By the time it ends this rhyme/You'll feel its brush of silky slime"

Chuckling at his own timidity, he shook away the shivers. But he could only fool himself for so long. Lame poem or not, it didn't prevent the surreality of certain recent developments from crashing head-on with actual reality. He wished he had drugs to blame, as that would have explained away the bizarre horror, but he'd never gone harder than his daily morning cup of heavily creamed coffee.

He tugged the chain to the lamp next to his bed—causing a minor bulb explosion that quickly reverted the room to near blackness. He tore the drawer from his nightstand and overturned it, spilling leftover hard candy and some pilfered pain pills that Lars had stashed there over a month ago, praying for a flashlight that wasn't there. Shadows even darker than the actual darkness in the room grew and stretched along the walls, smearing amidst persistent streaks of moonlight.

Even though it went against all laws of basic intelligence, he decided to check beneath the bed. Just to be sure. Hanging upside-down, his eyes hovering near the edge of the duvet cover, his hair in jagged bedhead formation. Squinting as he peeked below, knowing all too well that only half-seeing something didn't negate its existence.

Nothing. If darkness—or the absence of light—could be thought of as such. Maybe all of this really was just bullshit from a dream bleeding over into reality.

Satisfied, Cameron went in reverse until fully supine on the bed again, his breathing back to normal. He rolled onto his side, scissoring his legs until finding the perfect warm spot beneath the covers, returning to his favored fetal position.

Which would have been fine, save for the fact the other half of the bed began to creak behind him. And a spooning pressure tightened along his bare back. Then a leechlike prickle below the cotton sheets protected his chest. A wet, tender tickle ran down his jawline. Even worse were the suckling sounds, like a meat sculpture that had not fully formed, sinews that had yet to realize they were not sentient.

Cameron couldn't take the pressure anymore. He released a scream that would have made for a great audition. He hoped his mother would come save him and offer him the coveted role of Screaming Son #1.

But then he remembered that tonight was the night Mom worked the night shift.

A sweet feminine giggle stiffened the hairs in his ear. Either due to sheer fear or external, invisible force, Cameron couldn't move. He could only feel an ocean of phantasmal flesh washing against his back, clammy bare breasts gyrating in perfect rhythm, seductive scratches from unseen fingers. Nibbles from unseen teeth.

Worst of all, little Cameron was swelling down below. His groin throbbing. Defying all logic, betraying his orientation.

And then—a voice. Saccharine with a subtext of sinister. Five simple words:

"Hello, boyfriend. Let's get nasty."

"Oh. My. God," Lars said, his jaw drooping. "I can't believe she said that. This ghost whore has got some *nerve*. I think I kind of like her now."

"I told you already." Cameron said. "It's not a ghost."

"Well, call it a Hobbit from Hades for all I care, but one thing's clear—this little tramp's got one hell of a delusional crush."

A meatball soared through the cafeteria and landed on Cameron's plate, sending his peas soaring sideways. Cameron glanced in the direction the edible grenade had come from. Two tables over, some of the guys from the lacrosse team were snickering and high fiving. Greg Beach, the goalie, shouted over to Cameron and Lars. "Sorry, boys! Thought you liked balls!" The squealing from that table grew into a roar. Cameron wondered why the best looking boys were so often the cruelest.

Lars dropped his sandwich and spun around, ready to Hulk out. "Up yours, closet case! See you later underneath the bleachers, baby." He offered a faux-seductive smooch in Greg's direction. Greg launched to his feet, prepared to defend his precious masculinity, but Lars lunged from his seat without hesitation. The two devoted members of Greg's Goon Squad—Adam McKinley and Donnie Hutchins—stood behind their leader, their arms folded, their teeth bared. A fight was imminent. Cameron cowered, knowing he would be willing to help his friend if it came down to it, even though he would be about as useful as a gnat landing on Greg's neck.

Unlike Lars, Cameron was just a petite young man, probably be cursed to wear boys' sizes the rest of his life and never grow enough hair on his body to resemble anything manly. Many wicked words could have been formed into fists thrown at Lars—and they often were, but Lars had always been capable of pummeling the semantic stones into insignificant dust and wiping his hands clean. And Cameron had witnessed his friend hold his own in more than a few quarrels, never taking a beating from multiple assailants without getting a few solid haymakers in first.

The three jocks formed a semi-circle around Lars and Cameron's table. Other kids were starting to notice, forming a modest crowd. Cameron's eyes darted around, searching for safety. Outside, a few buildings away, he saw Vice Principal Stadtman, unaware of the trouble about to transpire on campus. The man was engrossed in conversation with another adult who—as far as Cameron knew—was not part of the faculty. A tall, skeletal freak of a man whose smile seemed painted on, his inhumanly white teeth gleaming in the mid-day sunshine.

A sneer forming on his face, Greg tousled Cameron's hair aggressively, though not very successfully, as excessive gel application ensured his hair remained a shiny, impenetrable helmet.

Hands now in fist mode, Lars said, "Touch my friend again, asshole, and I'll knock your teeth in and make you like it."

A few kids in the crowd oohed and aahed. Adam and Donnie turned and shot looks that quickly silenced them.

Greg removed his hand from Cameron's head and stepped toward Lars. "What's that, homo negro? Can't hear you from under all that lipstick."

Just before the strutting transformed into physical violence, the vice principal strolled into the cafeteria. The odd man Cameron had just seen him speaking to had apparently gone elsewhere. The boys returned to their seats before their scuffle had a chance to be noticed and broken up. Peace had been restored. Temporarily. The time would come to finish this, after school some other day in a park or back alley while on the way home. Greg and his Goons had promised as much.

Lars turned back to Cameron, his face pink with adrenaline.

"Thanks," Cameron said. "You didn't have to—"

"Don't mention it." Lars squeezed Cameron's shoulder. His hand lingered for a few seconds before he released his grip. "Anything for my favorite person ever."

Cameron smiled at the sentiment, thankful to have such a devoted friend. Despite their parallel romantic preferences, Cameron and Lars made quite the odd platonic pair. Cameron was pure preppie with a weakness for larping and Blue Note jazz. Lars had always been the more rebellious of the two. From hair that exploded with a colored extension or two (today's choice was a shock of blue) to intentionally androgynous attire, he harbored no shame about the cards he had been dealt.

"I swear," Lars said, "why do they always got to pull the race card? They only care about the black half. Assholes got not idea my mom's as eggshell as the rest of 'em."

Cameron shrugged, decided to return to their previous topic of conversation. "So she left another recipe."

Lars's eyes lit up. "Ooh, this is getting mega-juicy now. Must feel nice to have someone who wants to grope you *and* cook for you later. Your sex demon is so…domestic. I'd almost consider switching teams for that sort of attention. A beard and a personal chef in one? Tempt me, darling, I dare you."

Cameron shook his head and handed another lined sticky note to Lars, the words written in the same immaculate penmanship as before.

Cream of Custard Clusters

1 T HONEY MUSTARD

2 CUPS GLUTEN-FREE FLOUR

1 CUP WALNUTS, FINELY CHOPPED

1/3 CUP VIRGIN BLOOD

1 CUP ORGANIC BROWN SUGAR

1 ½ T EGG REPLACER **+2 T** WATER

1/2 CUP NON-HYDROGENATED CANOLA OIL

1 T COCOA POWDER

1. Preheat oven to 400 degrees.
2. Mix dry ingredients first, then slowly add all other items, mixing vigorously
3. Roll into tiny balls
4. Bake for 15-20 minutes
5. Serve with chocolate fondue or strawberries
6. Delicious with a glass of ginger limeade

"Well," Lars said, "there's that pesky virgin blood again, acting all innocent and demure around the other slutty ingredients."

"I know. That's exactly what I'm worried about."

"Honey, if losing your V-card is your main concern, you know it wouldn't be hard to get you some action. I know a guy who—"

"Oh, gee, thanks for reminding me how much of a loser I am, Lars."

"I aim to please."

Vice Principal Stadtman passed by the boys' table, smiling and nodding at Cameron. The two model students went silent, and Cameron returned a forced grin.

An eternity passed before the vice principal was out of earshot. When he felt it was safe to do so again, Cameron spoke. "Hey, can you come crash at my house Friday? My mom's going out of town to visit her sister for the weekend. We can just tell her we're working on a school project or whatever."

"Oh, that old trick again, huh? Sure, why not? Not like I've got a Valentine's date anyway."

"Thanks." Cameron had completely forgotten that Valentine's Day was this week. He hoped he hadn't inadvertently given the wrong impression. No. Of course not. This was *Lars*.

Lars threw his hands in the air, snapping his fingers. "Wait a sec. I just thought of something."

"What's that?"

"Holy *shit*. Why am I just now being graced with such brilliance?"

"*What?*"

"Do you think this thing in your bedroom is trying to turn you *straight*?"

Despite all of the signs pointing unmistakably toward Gay City, Mama West had never acknowledged her son's subtle attempts to come out. Denial—the most powerful of beasts. Cameron had resisted trying to get through to his mother in recent months, hoping she would deduce things from the sheer fact of his association with Lars, the blatantly obvious poster boy for alternative lifestyles. Their friendship had always been equal parts blessing and curse. Even though Cameron harbored no physical attraction toward Lars, he almost wished he did just so he could make a clear announcement to his mother. Just one fat smooch on his giant friend's lips in her presence and the secret would be blown wide open. If that didn't drill it into his mom's skull, nothing ever would. Problem was, the thought of kissing Lars irked him. It would have been like swapping spit with his brother.

Cameron and Lars always walked home after school together, and today was no different. Lars lived a good fifteen-minute walk in the opposite direction, but he claimed to enjoy the exercise. However, Cameron knew it was actually because of his mother's tendency to always have freshly prepared cake balls and homemade grape juice on hand.

The boys leaned against the kitchen island, chewing and drinking while Cameron's mother put away dishes.

"Oh, Cameron," his mom said, "I forgot to tell you a girl called for you this morning just after you left for school. On the landline. Does the name Juniper ring any bells?"

His mouth stuffed full of doughy treats, Cameron shook his head "no." He wondered why someone—especially a girl—would have been calling on that line, where she would have even tracked down the number. He was surprised the phone even still worked.

"Oh," his mother said, "well I suppose I could have gotten it wrong. She sounded sweet though."

"Maybe it was that girl who sits next to Cam in English," Lars said, winking with exaggerated glee. Cameron's face drained. His eyes formed into perfect surprised circles, burning toward Lars, wishing he could hurl every curse word known to man in his friend's direction. He only managed to mouth the word "stop."

"Sounds like someone's got a crush," Cameron's mother said, a prideful tone infiltrating her voice. "Why don't you invite her over sometime? I've got some new recipes I've been dying to try out."

The boys eyed each other, not sure whether to gasp or fall prey to laughter. "Sure Mom…I'll invite the girl whose name I don't even recognize over for a dinner date. Sounds like a real swell plan."

Lars gulped down the last of his grape juice. "Okay, gotta make like mascara and run. See ya tomorrow. Thanks for the snacks, second mom."

Cameron's mother beamed and waved goodbye.

The boys walked to the door together.

"Just one more night until our super duper gay sleepover," Lars said, beaming with glee.

"Yeah," Cameron said, "unless I get swallowed whole."

Lars placed both of his hands on Cameron's shoulders. "Oh, just let the poor thing suck you off. Lord knows you need the release. Just close your eyes and pretend it's Tom Hardy."

Cameron shook his head. Lars winked and skipped away.

Just as Cameron was about to close the door, he noticed something out of place. A car parked across the street. Canary yellow. He'd never seen it in the neighborhood before. And there was someone sitting in the driver's seat. He squinted, tried to get a good look. He was almost certain it was someone he recognized. And then the realization smacked him.

No mistaking it—the man he'd seen conversing with Vice Principal Stadtman.

The man with the endless smile.

If a song consisted of a steady beat, Lars Dietrich always figured out a way to dance to it. Today, as he pranced his way home from Cameron's, the tune stuck in his head was "Burning Up" by Madonna. The lyrics he'd committed to heart, and he sung them with his best belief that his voice was in key. Too focused on his vocal prowess, Lars did not notice the man quietly following behind him until said man was close enough that he could have bared his teeth and taken a bite.

The sound of a clearing throat startled Lars out of his song. He spun around, spreading his legs in a stance that begged for an altercation. Just say the wrong word, make the wrong move, and it's on.

He was met with an exaggerated smile that, while not completely unpleasant, seemed to be harboring something far more sinister behind it. Perhaps it had something to do with the fact that Lars didn't trust… well, practically anyone at all. But more likely it had something to do with the man's massive teeth. Thick as ice cubes popped straight from the tray, obnoxiously white, as if brushing and flossing were this man's religion.

"Can I help you?" Lars asked, loosening the tension in his calf muscles.

"As a matter of fact," the man replied, his smile never faltering, "I was hoping I could help *you*."

The man reached into his front coat pocket and whipped out a card, which he held out to Lars. Despite his natural instincts Lars took it, pinching it between his thumb and forefinger as if it were a snotty tissue.

Lars glanced at the card. It read:

LITTLE MISS CHRYSALIS

CONVERSION THERAPY

RUTHERFORD B. HAYVE

PROPRIETER

Lars eyed the man, then the card again. "What the hell is this?" he asked.

The peculiar man licked his thin lips. "An opportunity."

"Oh, you mean I should be begging you to spew some bullshit? Queen, you know just where you can shove this." Lars flicked the card back at the man, and it barely missed hitting him in the face, nicking his ear lobe. The man did not flinch. "And next time, I recommend coming up with a name that sounds a *little* less fake, *capiche*?"

The man seemed completely unfazed by the words being tossed his way, and the whole situation was becoming less and less fun for Lars by the second.

"I'll be speaking at an assembly at your school next Monday," the man said.

"Ask me if I give two squirts."

"I do hope you'll be there."

"Hmm…let me check my calendar. Oh. Wait. Whoops…that's the day I'll be conveniently calling in sick."

"Wouldn't you like to meet your new friend? Her name is Annabelle."

"No thanks. She sounds like a total bitch."

Rutherford, if that was in fact his name, held out his hand. His fingers were skeletal, his cuticles divine. "It's okay. You don't have to be afraid anymore. Not if you choose to come with me. To take this path."

Lars scrunched up his face. "Look. Here's the deal. I don't turn eighteen for another month. I could just scream for help and tell everyone you're a diddler trying to cop a feel. Kinda stupid of you to not come to my mom with this deprogramming crap in the first place. She might've actually drank your Kool-Aid. Well, only if you spiked it with vodka. But you know what? I'm in a reasonable mood. Just back off, baby, and I won't beat your ass purple."

The man clung devotedly to his stoicism. A true professional. He nodded, then kneeled and retrieved his business card from the gutter. "That's fine. I do understand. You won't be bothered any longer. Not by me." Without another word or even so much as an ironic wink, he brushed past Lars and power walked the remainder of the block. He soon turned a corner, at which point Lars could no longer see him. Nor did he care to.

Lars shrugged. Of all the times older men had hit on him, and there had been several, this had to have been the strangest and most creative approach.

Cameron had no idea who the hell the girl standing on his front porch was.

And he didn't want to invite her in.

She said her name was Juniper, which matched the name of the girl who had apparently called that morning, so that part checked out. But, as far as he knew, he'd never seen her before in his life. Still, she went on and on about the paper she was writing about *The Perks of Being a Wallflower* for Ms. Chaney's English class. How she wanted to get his opinion on her first draft. This was the problem, Cameron thought, about having zero interest in girls. They all tended to blur together. Sure, some of them were nice enough, but in a perfect world his time with the female gender would be as limited as possible. Lars had a couple of gal pals he hung out with from time to time—the "dedicated fag hags," he called them. But Cameron only had…Lars.

Cameron struggled to determine if Juniper could objectively be considered attractive, were he of that proclivity. Her sandy hair contained just enough curls to resemble the bow on a Christmas present. Blueberry eyes, strawberry lips. Fit enough to be a cheerleader, but almost too far-gone into full-blown Barbie-land to partake in anything so miserably physical. Her newborn flesh molded like perfect plastic, a parody of femininity, a trophy-in-the-making. He decided that, yes, she was quite pretty, but really what did he know?

He also couldn't help but notice that she had been subtly inching her way closer to him. Touching him whenever she thought he wasn't paying attention. Her tickles attacking even the sides of his body she couldn't realistically reach from where she stood.

"So Cameron," she said, a devious grin on her face, "when are you going to ask me to dinner and a movie, huh?" She brushed her fingers across his bare arm. The sensation was electric, just not necessarily in a good way.

"Oh, I…um…well, that is—"

"Yes, Cameron, don't be rude. Ask the poor girl on a date." His mom's voice startled him. He hadn't noticed she'd been lurking nearby. He'd assumed she was still in the kitchen preparing dinner.

Cameron didn't even realize until it was too late that Juniper had taken him by the hand. Mortification enveloped him. Who was this stranger, and why was she pestering him? Was she as clueless as his own mother?

Juniper smiled at him, a giant beam of sunshine. Near the back of her mouth, something gleamed. Something gold. A filling in one of her teeth.

And then it came to him. The truth. Or what he assumed to be so.

Her.

But it couldn't be her. Could it? The bizarre spirit that had been paying him unwelcome visits, accosting him in bed practically every night for weeks now, formed into a flesh fiend disguised as every mother and father's most desirable dream for their precious *straight* son.

What exactly was her game? Cameron still had not a clue. He couldn't wait to tell Lars about this new development at school tomorrow. Unless he didn't live that long. Now Juniper's armed was draped around Cameron's waist, and he wasn't sure when she'd had a chance to make the move. The affection was constricting, uncomfortable. Maybe tonight was the night he'd finally become the rodent to Juniper's python.

Cameron's mom observed the closeness between the two teens. Cameron had expected her to sweetly request that they maintain some distance between each other, like the proper June Cleaver she was. Instead she just smiled and said, "Well aren't you and your little girlfriend so cute together. I just adore young love."

"Mo-om."

Apparently satisfied with the developments, Juniper released her grip on Cameron. "Okay, I gotta get home and hit the books," she said. "Nice to finally meet you, Mrs. West."

"Same to you, darling. Stop by anytime."

Juniper winked. "Oh, I will. Definitely."

Cameron gulped. Juniper planted a big wet one on his cheek, got on her perfect pink bicycle, and rode off.

Placing her hand on Cameron's shoulder, his mother said, "What a catch you've got there, Cameron. She really is something."

Cameron shuddered, nodded. Yes, Juniper really was something. Some. Thing.

Each day, after school, Greg Beach, Adam McKinley, and Donnie Hutchins made it a point to hang out in the alley adjacent to Jimmy's Liquor. It gave them an image, an edge. They typically had little fortune in convincing passersby over the age of twenty-one to procure alcohol for them, and so smoking had become their game of choice. They bummed cigarettes, made freshly rolled spliffs, even did opium when they could get scrounge up the funds for it. Today they'd managed to score some changa and were passing some puffs around in their tight circle, each of them keeping a free eye on the entrance of the alley for concerned citizens or bored cops. One way in, one way out, nowhere to run were they to be caught.

After a long inhale, Greg turned to Donnie and said, "So did you finger Allie Myers yet or what?"

Donnie's eyes went sideways, all the answer the other boys needed.

"Fuckin' wuss," Adam said. Laughing, coughing. "Tina's already letting me do butt stuff."

"Aw, I don't know about that, man," Greg said. "That's just a couple steps away from going homo."

Adam jerked. "It is *not*. Not when it's with a chick. Jesus, Greg, you don't know what you're missing, dude."

"Oh, I ain't missing nothin'. I'm just no slave to one pussy. Gotta grow my wild oaks."

"What the fuck does *that* mean?" Donnie asked, the joint dangling from his lips.

Greg shook his head. "What are you, a gump? It means I'm boinking whoever I want, whenever I want. Ain't life grand?"

"Well, why didn't you just say—"

"Is that so?" A female voice echoed around them. All three boys whipped their heads in the direction of the sound. A girl about their age stood before them, at the alley's entrance. Petite but fit. Maybe a freshman cheerleader.

Donnie leaned over to Adam and whispered, "Does she go to our school?"

"Dunno," Adam said, "but she is fiiiiine."

Greg ignored the other boys, asked his own question, directed at the girl. "Who the hell are you?"

A wicked grin tugged at her lips, her beauty threatening to form into a weapon. "I'm Juniper."

"The fuck kind of name is that?" Adam said.

"It means 'Worst Nightmare' in Asshole Latin." She laughed, an unsettling cadence, a sprinkler working overtime. The mockery halted as abruptly as it had started, and her smile melted away.

The boys eyed each other, dumbfounded. No girl had ever dared to mouth off to them like this.

Juniper moved toward them, baby steps the entire way, only stopping when close enough for the boys to smell her. And she smelled wonderful. A blend of coconut and lime. She still looked pretty up close, but there was nothing cute about her. All mean, all lean. She meant business, and she'd come to close a deal.

"So I hear you losers have been harassing my boyfriend."

As if on cue, the boys all laughed. They understood. Of course this was a joke. And now they were in on it.

Greg leaned in toward Juniper. "Whoever your boyfriend is," he said, "ditch the chump. I'll be your new steady, how about that?"

She shook her head. Back and forth. Slower than slow motion. "My boyfriend is ten times the man of the three of you combined. And if you mess with him again, simple regret will be the least of your problems." The words sounded monotone, rehearsed.

"Okay, baby," Adam said. "What's the dickhead's name?"

"Cameron. Cameron West."

The boys' laughter returned, escalating to a collective roar. Donnie accidentally dropped the spliff and cursed at his own clumsiness. He picked it up and brushed it off, then stuck it back in his mouth. Five second rule.

"Sweetheart," Greg said, trying and failing to contain the mockery that shaped his smile, "you do know your boyfriend's a total fag, don't you?"

Juniper did not respond with words. Merely a stare. One that would make Medusa weep with mercy.

It was then that the situation became much, much worse.

The girl's face tore open, the split spreading from head to crotch, as if there had been a zipper keeping everything held together. The skin suit fell to the ground, discarded like a banana peel. From behind the flesh façade crawled something that none of the boys could clearly see, and it moved too quickly before their eyes had time to adjust. No longer a girl—or, at least, not one that could claim to be anything resembling human. A dripping, skeletal mess. Limbs that bent in ways they shouldn't have been allowed to. Teeth where they shouldn't be. A shimmer of gold deep in a growing black maw.

Donnie pissed himself, Adam chanted the name of his one true lord and savior over and over until it became one long word, and Greg stood still, his eyes widening to the point they were at risk of popping.

The creature moved with sinuous grace. Before Adam could react, she gripped his head with one taloned hand and shoved it backward, causing it to collide with the brick wall on the side of Jimmy's Liquor. A Vesuvius amount of blood erupted from his temple as he collapsed to the ground, out cold. She then turned to Donnie, who screamed as unseen claws created future scars just shy of his lower eyelid. Greg hadn't yet decided if he wanted to move, hadn't even turned to see his lackeys being brutalized. Just as he finally mustered the strength to use his voice, he felt powerful, uncomfortable pressure around his genitals.

She—no, *it*—stood just a few inches from him, clasping his crotch in a vice grip that she would not relinquish. Greg began to weep.

"Kneel," the monster said. Its voice was no longer that of a teenage girl's, instead like a denizen of the deepest hell.

Greg fell to his knees, pleading, and the creature kneeled with him, digging its claws in deeper.

She spoke again. "If you ever…*ever*…even so much as look in Cameron's direction again I will hunt you down and make sure I properly remove this pathetic meat that is so very important to you. And before you even have the chance to suffer the agony of your own castration, you will know precisely what it is like to perform fellatio on yourself. It will not be as pleasant as you have imagined in private."

A grin peeled across the creature's appalling face. Greg whimpered.

"Do you understand?" Her voice was a mighty bellow.

Greg nodded, and she released him. He fell forward, dizzy, forgetting to catch himself. His face smashed on the concrete, shattering his front teeth and splitting his lip.

Juniper scampered on all fours to the flesh costume she'd shed, stepped back into it and resealed. Within seconds she was picture perfect once again. She glared back at the boys. Adam still passed out, Donnie cowering in a corner. Greg in shock from all the blood pouring from his mouth.

She spat at them. "That'll teach you to mess with my special man."

"I mean, can you believe what happened to those dickheads?" Lars said, munching on the final crumbs in a bag of nacho cheese chips. "Not that they didn't deserve it, but wow."

Cameron's jaw dropped. "Lars. Geez, come on. That's just—"

"Honey, I stopped saving any sympathy for pointless hateful bullshit long ago. I sleep so much better at night now. Believe me, you'd benefit from letting a little of that go, too."

Cameron nodded. Lars wasn't wrong. Ever since they'd become friends, he'd always been able to see straight through to Cameron's damaged soul. Sometimes he even found a way to mend it.

"Besides," Lars continued, "better they're worrying about rival school bullshit or whatever earned them those bruises than focusing on us. Shit, they didn't even eat in the cafeteria today!"

Before Cameron could re-enter the conversation, Lars shifted gears, started rambling about some inane drama regarding their Humanities teacher flirting with one of the sophomore girls. Cameron pretended to listen, nodding with absent interest, but his thoughts had drifted elsewhere, dwelling on far more fearful possibilities. He knew exactly who had—*what* had—eviscerated Greg and his crew. Knew it in his gut. He wondered what had brought the violent spree on, and—more importantly—how much he might be at risk for a similar fate. Maybe he didn't have to worry at all. As far as he could tell, it seemed as if Juniper felt nothing but fondness for him.

He let her name sit atop his tongue. *Juniper.* There was something so attractive about the sound of it. Nearly epicene in its tone. He whispered the name in his mind, saving it for later thoughts, hoping it wouldn't haunt his sleep. Praying he would make it through the night long enough to be gifted with anything resembling slumber.

Hours passed. Awful television was consumed. On mute. The hard bop of Art Blakey and the Jazz Messengers' "Moanin'" played in the background. The final splashes of sun dipped away, and darkness wrapped its thick cloak around the house. The only light in the bedroom came from a dim lamp on the nightstand. Cameron and Lars both lay in the bed, facing opposite directions, each boy's feet level with the other's head. Their discussion shifted from video games to "Who Would You Rather?" to—eventually, as expected—Cameron's recent visitor. He'd managed to forget all about her, but now here she was again, wiggling her feminine ways in front of him without even having to be in the room. That he knew of.

"I don't think she's showing up tonight," Lars said. "That little tart must think I'm a threat."

"That's kind of the point."

"Too bad I can't just move in, right? I'd have to start charging your mom for security detail, though."

"She probably already owes you a few bucks in back pay for that."

Lars affected a devilish smirk, and Cameron noticed for a brief second that—once Lars outgrew his awkward phase—his friend was going to be breaking boys' hearts left and right.

"Would have been kinda cool to see it, though," Lars said. "Never had a special sex ghost of my very own, so I have to live vicariously through you."

"Jesus, Lars, how many times do I have to tell you that it's not a—I don't think you can actually *feel* a ghost touching you. It's gotta be something else. Like a…maybe like a…have you ever heard of a succubus?"

"Succ-u-*what*?" Lars raised an eyebrow. "Is that a request or an offer?"

"Oh, never mind. You're no help."

Cameron thought he heard soft scraping within the walls, a tapping at the window, steps atop the roof, creaks on the floorboards—all the classic sonic clichés of horror cinema. But the sounds soon faded. Just nature and his imagination teaming up to have some sadistic fun.

"Do you ever see yourself getting married?" Lars asked. "Maybe like adopting a kid or whatever?"

"Uh…random. I mean, *me* a dad? Flying cars'll exist by the time that happens. *If* it does."

"Oh, come on. You shouldn't think that way." Lars squeezed Cameron's leg, made eye contact. "You're amazing."

"No. I'm just me."

"Well, yeah…that's exactly what I'm talking about."

The boys broke their gaze. Lars examined his cuticles. Cameron thumbed the remote, flipping through channels like his life depended on it.

Before the awkward silence could form a cyst in Cameron's chest, Lars spoke. "Cam, I have a confession."

Cameron rolled his eyes. "Should I prepare the Sacrament of Penance?"

"No, come on. I'm serious."

Lars reached toward Cameron, found his hand and fit their fingers together. Nothing inherently odd about this action. The boys had often engaged in this harmless physical comfort when needed. The weirdness began when Lars started rubbing Cameron's thumb with his own. That was new. Not a terrible sensation, but an unexpected one.

"I've wanted to say this for a while," Lars said, "but it's so scary to even think about it. Right now I feel such a bond with you, though. But more than just, like, a protector. More than just a…a friend. Okay. So. This'll probably seem out of nowhere to you, but it's not. I think I'm starting to develop, you know…real feelings for you."

Cameron blew a raspberry and ripped his hand from the embrace. "All right, you can just quit it right there. I'm not in the mood for one of your stupid jokes."

Lars lunged up from the bed, his face more vulnerable than Cameron had ever thought possible. The fortress of fortitude had been demolished, the mask of strength ripped away, revealing a softer side the rest of the world would never see. And it was then that Cameron realized what Lars had said was no joke.

"I know this doesn't make sense," Lars said. "How could it? We're like opposite in almost every way. I get that. But it doesn't really matter. From the moment we met you've been so special to me. Things are different now, though. Deeper. At least for me they are. I think…I think I'm actually falling in lo—"

"Whoah there. Hold on." Cameron interrupted the sentence before Lars could finish, before the words crossed over into reality and could never revert back to fantasy. He licked his upper teeth beneath his lips, giving his face an apish appearance. All moisture suddenly evacuated his throat. "Lars, I mean, I can't think of anyone I'd rather spend my time with. Like, I love you, too. But not like…like that. I just—we're friends, you know? Best friends. Maybe you're confused. Maybe—"

"I want more."

"I…I need to pee." Cameron hopped off the bed and dashed out of the bedroom. He rushed down the hall to the bathroom, locking the door behind him. Sitting at the edge of the tub, he massaged his temples, trying to think of the best way to let Lars down easy. He wished he didn't have to, wished he could just return the romantic feelings, but they simply didn't exist. That was the fact of the matter. And there was no crystal ball to tell him whether they might emerge in the future. He needed to perform damage control in the present, find the balance that would salvage their friendship.

Lars's moans and wails bled through the walls, then moments later a concerning crash reverberated through the house. Past experience had proven that a Lars tantrum could result in rhinoceros-level destruction. Cameron waited until the ruckus in the bedroom stopped, until the sobbing subsided, before he decided it was time to go back and sort out both of their feelings. He hoped nothing too important had been broken.

But when Cameron returned to his room, he discovered something irreplaceable had, in fact, been broken beyond repair. Almost too surreal a sight to even react, and so he did not. He just observed, sucked in the chilling sight. Each image came to him as if directed by a camera in his eyes, in separate cuts and frames. Patterns of red across the wall, dripping down in jagged streams. A severed arm at his feet, the fingers still twitching like the legs of a dying beetle. A rib cage gaping wide in a sickening smile. A waist and legs, gushing deep, dark fluids all over the pillows and sheets. Severed genitals spat to the floor.

Lars. Poor, wonderful Lars, his head impaled on the bedpost, his body mutilated with ghastly glee, his special heart removed, never to beat again. His silver-filled tooth, ripped from his smile and left as a twisted peace offering.

Cameron should have screamed, should have shed a tear. But he wasn't granted the chance. His throat had been burglarized, his vocal cords the precious stolen jewels. Before he could turn and run out of the room, the door slammed behind him. Familiar giggling bounced off the walls, filled with flirtatious mirth. Something skittered at the far end of the room. It moved with predatory precision, slinking across the floor, leaving a thick snail trail behind it. The form was at Cameron's bed, a long, translucent arm reaching toward the remains of his friend, its fishlike sinews and veins visible and shifting. Then the whole body of the beast hunched up onto the bed in a primal position.

Jealous nymphs assumed many forms. All of them unpleasant, always.

One of Juniper's gooey arms moved its hair away from its face, pulled the coarse threads up into a ponytail, and kept it in place with a scrunchie. Its sensual lips expanded into a wide vacuum shape, its anteater tongue searching the sheets, lapping up fresh blood with relish. Cameron remained glued to his spot, though he shut his eyes, viewing the scene through a black jungle of eyelashes. Juniper lifted its head from its meal to look at him. A gorgeous mess of eyes, teeth, and tongue. Cameron's heart squeezed up into his head, throbbing, pulsing, vibrating. Ice tickled his toes.

Juniper slithered across the soggy bed toward Cameron. He remained stiff, still. The creature extended its dripping arm, further than logic allowed. It pointed at him, a bloodstained Valentine's Day card hanging limp, impaled on its curled claw. An image of a desperate pre-teen girl chasing a terrified boy, his cheeks stained with lipstick kisses. The text read:

I CHOOSE YOU! BE MINE 4-EVER!

Cameron swayed. For a split second he saw the ceiling as parallel to him.

Then he only saw blackness.

Though he'd been awake for quite some time, Lars still couldn't feel anything. Not a chilled breeze on his cheek, not an ache in the arches of his feet, not even a need to urinate. Zero. Zilch. Zed.

Life had taken a sharp left. Or maybe—Lars thought, as the memory of what had just happened to him in Cameron's bedroom came rushing back—maybe life had instead become the opposite of life. He'd never guessed what came after would have felt more or less like nothing at all.

Lars checked his shoulder blades, wiggled his fingers back as far as he could reach. No wings. He swatted above his head. No halo. This checked out. He'd never expected an unapologetic queer boy would be allowed admittance into Heaven—at least in any traditional sense of the term. And to be honest he wanted nothing to do with a self-professed paradise and a musty old God who wouldn't have pissed on Lars if he were begging for a golden shower.

But where he was—this didn't feel quite like Hell either. Which was something to rejoice, he supposed.

Though he couldn't feel his fabulous clothes clinging to him or check his positively glorious hair in a mirror, he knew he'd come to Cameron's house dressed to impress—a last ditch effort to get his best friend to notice him in another way. In *that* way. Worst. Fail. Ever. And no do-overs. His memory of what had actually happened was still a bit hazy but was starting to come back to him. And all he could focus on was a sudden sneak attack from that filthy ghost demon tramp. Sliced and diced him real nice, she had. Lars guessed that the gory result didn't carry over to the afterlife, and for that he was thankful. If he was going to have to spend eternity in some boring ass purgatory, at least he'd be looking fierce while doing so.

Time grew irrelevant. He walked for what may have been miles, yet his feet didn't feel a thing. He hoped it would at least benefit his figure. That and the fact that he didn't appear to have an appetite. He didn't think he'd enjoy getting used to that change. He walked and walked and only stopped because of a sudden tap on his shoulder, followed by a sharp, determined clearing of a throat behind him.

Lars half-pirouetted until he was face to face with a familiar visage. One that churned his stomach. Rutherford B. Hayve. His creepy grin once again taking up way too much space.

"Oh, great," Lars said. "You again."

"Hello, my boy."

Before Lars could spit back what surely would have been a witty retort, he shifted his gaze to the right. The man had brought an accomplice.

"There's someone I'd like you to meet," Rutherford said.

A girl. A mean look in her eye, but the good kind of mean. The I-take-no-shit-from-authority kind of mean. Greasy, unkempt hair. Eyeliner smeared in raccoon drag. She'd just finished smoking a clove cigarette and dropped it, stomping it dead with the heel of one of her combat boots.

"Hey," she said, a sneer curling on her face. "I'm Annabelle. Wanna hang?"

Lars eyed the flattened butt of her cigarette. "Um, can I bum one of those?"

Annabelle reached into the pocket of her bomber jacket and whipped out a pack of cigarettes. As she passed one to Lars, she bit her bottom lip and winked at him. When their fingers touched, Lars felt a strange sensation, one he couldn't put a label on. But he knew he didn't like it.

At least he didn't think he did.

Lars would never have run away, not without telling Cameron where he had gone. Such an action seemed out of character. And their trust had always been law. But it was how Cameron had rationalized the events that had occurred last month, what little bits his selective memory had shared with him. He'd awoken the following morning, drenched in a feverish sweat, a messy note taped to his mirror:

SORRY I HAD TO LEAVE, CAM. FORGET EVERYTHING I SAID LAST NIGHT. JUST PRETEND I WAS DRUNK OR SOME-THING. I DIDN'T MEAN IT. IT WAS STUPID. YOU CAN LET ME KNOW AT SCHOOL MONDAY HOW THINGS WENT WITH YOUR LAME DEPROGRAMMER GHOST. I NEED MY BEAUTY SLEEP. K CYA.

The words read like they'd come from Lars and the handwriting looked about right, though Cameron was no expert in penmanship.

Between the note and the fact that the pain pills in his drawer had gone missing, likely slipped into his grape juice in the midst of Lars's love confession, the whole mess more or less made sense. Still, there had been something *off* about the experience. His room should have looked like an abattoir. He should have been in police custody, under investigation for murder, no way to weasel his way out of it save for an insanity plea. But his room had been licked clean, more immaculate than ever before. Too clean. As if none of it had ever happened. Maybe it hadn't. Though the unmistakable sensation of terror lingered, and Cameron was certain it *had* transpired.

Drugs explained it. Without question. And he'd be mad at Lars for forcing the experiment when his friend knew very well how he felt about illicit substances. But he'd forgive Lars. He had to. He had no other friends to forgive.

One thing, however, still didn't sit well with Cameron. Lars had never been known to abandon anything he pursued, but maybe Cameron's rejection had been too much to handle. His friend had never made it home that night, never showed up to school that following Monday. And now it was as if he had never existed. No one spoke of him. Not at home, nor at school. He was just gone. To everyone but Cameron, it seemed as if it were a "good riddance to gay rubbish" situation, not worth the air it required to discuss the matter.

But Cameron would never accept that. He wanted Lars back, to be held, pressed against his bestie's enormous warm body. He would even be willing to give romance a try, risk ruining the friendship just to know Lars was alive and well. Deep down, though, Cameron suspected—no, *knew*—that wasn't the case. Not in the traditional sense, at least. The wicked, vivid dream of gore that now haunted him at every corner had been real, but there were no facts to prove it. Yet.

And, in the time since Lars had disappeared, there had been other changes in Cameron's life. Ones he had very little say in.

He stole one last look in the mirror and shuffled toward the living room. Geisha steps. Before he entered, he paused in the kitchen, a piece of paper catching his eye.

A recipe.

Much like the others, this one also included virgin blood in its ingredients. Except this time it had been in his mother's possession. Tuna Salad Surprise. She'd made that for Cameron's lunch just last week. The implications sent a shudder through him. He crumpled the paper and threw it, barely missing the trashcan.

In the living room, his mother sat cross-legged on the couch, speaking to a girl his age. He'd seen the girl before, met her several times, but each day it was as if he'd forgotten who she was and had to relearn. It didn't make sense, but lately nothing had been aligning with what he'd once associated with reality.

Both ladies turned their heads to him as he entered the room. The girl fluttered, her planet-sized eyes gleaming between butterfly eyelashes. And then he remembered.

"Hi, Cam," she said, wiggling her skinny fingers at him. Her voice laced with twisted sweetness.

"Hey, June." Nicknames were nice. Normal.

He locked eyes with his new girlfriend, and he was sure he saw it this time, hiding deep within those pools. The consumed essence of Lars. The soul of his missing friend. Or—perhaps more accurately—the knowledge of where such things currently resided.

Last night, Cameron had finally remembered the second verse to *Succubus Summer, Infinite Hunger*:

"Lustful hunger in her face/The shameful cringe at her embrace
With teeth she bites and chews and chews/Ignores the stigma of taboos
Hopeless souls she shall consume/Her ample bosom now their tomb
Such persistence cannot lose/It owns the hearts true love pursues"

And that told Cameron all he needed to know.

"I think this one's a keeper, kiddo," his mother said, her hopeful smile impossible to wipe from her face.

Cameron offered a flat-lipped expression in return. Mom took the hint.

Juniper looped her arm through Cameron's. "Ready to go, babe? Movie's starting soon. And I want popcorn and Jujubes."

"Sure. Can hardly wait."

Her body heated his with reptilian warmth, ready to uncoil and strike at any moment.

Perhaps passing would be easier. At least for now. Better to keep up the façade. If, in fact, that's what this truly was. Cameron tried to fool himself into thinking the situation could be worse, that maybe this was the real path he was supposed to take after all. A future wife, the shuddering thought of potential procreation, a straight, acceptable life. Juniper was beautiful and all of that, at least that's what everyone told him. He didn't have an opinion, really. Not one that held any weight. He just hoped that maybe, somewhere deep within, some remnant of Lars truly was still dwelling inside her, fighting to come out. And Cameron would find him, would suck his friend's soul free, release it from evil's grip.

Even if it meant kissing a girl.

ACKNOWLEDGEMENTS

TO ODDNESS, FOR BELIEVING IN THIS PROJECT.

TO MIKE DUBISCH, FOR THE ALWAYS STELLAR ILLUSTRATIONS.

TO ALL THE EDITORS WHO ORIGINALLY PUBLISHED SEVERAL OF THE STORIES IN THIS COLLECTION.

TO BRIAN ASMAN, FOR THE GENEROUS FOREWORD—YOU TRULY "GET" ME.

TO VALERIE, FOR BEING THE BLOOD THAT FLOWS THROUGH MY HEART.

AND TO YOU, THE READER, WHETHER THIS IS YOUR FIRST EXPERIENCE WITH MY DARK AND STRANGE FICTION OR YOU'VE JOINED THE PARTY FOR THE LAST COUPLE BOOKS, I OFFER MY UNDYING GRATITUDE. THIS IS FOR YOU AS MUCH AS IT IS FOR ME.

CHAD STROUP

IN ADDITION TO AUTHORING THE STORIES FOUND IN THIS COLLECTION, CHAD STROUP IS ALSO THE CREATOR OF SUCH NOVELS AS SECRETS OF THE WEIRD (GREY MATTER PRESS) AND SEXY LEPER (BIZARRO PULP PRESS). WHEN NOT WRITING, HE IS ALSO THE VOCALIST FOR THE BAND ICEPIELD AND A FIERCE DRAG QUEEN BY THE NAME OF JENN X. NO, HE DOESN'T SLEEP MUCH. STROUP RECEIVED HIS MFA IN FICTION FROM SAN DIEGO STATE UNIVERSITY. FOLLOW HIM ON INSTAGRAM OR TWITTER @ CHADXSTROUP.

MIKE DUBISCH

THIS GRAPHIC NOVELIST AND ILLUSTRATOR HAS BEEN CRE-ATING AND PUBLISHING COMICS AND ART SINCE THE 1980'S. DUBISCH HAS CARVED OUT A UNIQUE PLACE FOR HIMSELF IN THE WORLD OF ART AND COMICS, CREATING WORKS OF HOR-ROR, SCIENCE-FICTION, SURREALISM, AND YA ADVENTURE USING ALL BUT LOST TRADITIONAL TECHNIQUES. BORN IN CALIFORNIA, USA, THE ARTIST HAS TRAVELED THE WORLD AND LIVED IN FIVE COUNTRIES. DUBISCH HAS BEEN AN IN-STRUCTOR AT THE ACADEMY OF ART UNIVERSITY SINCE 2012, AND IS MARRIED TO CHILDREN' S BOOK ILLUSTRATOR AND SCULPTOR CAROLYN WATSON DUBISCH WITH WHOM HE HAS THREE DAUGHTERS.